WYOMING

**Center Point
Large Print**

**This Large Print Book carries the
Seal of Approval of N.A.V.H.**

WYOMING

WILLIAM MACLEOD RAINE

CENTER POINT PUBLISHING
THORNDIKE, MAINE

This Center Point Large Print edition
is published in the year 2006 by arrangement with
Golden West Literary Agency.

Copyright © 1908 by William MacLeod Raine.
Copyright © renewed 1936 by William MacLeod Raine.

All rights reserved.

The text of this Large Print edition is unabridged. In other
aspects, this book may vary from the original edition. Printed in
Thailand. Set in 16-point Times New Roman type.

ISBN 1-58547-839-3

Library of Congress Cataloging-in-Publication Data

Raine, William MacLeod, 1871-1954.
 Wyoming / William MacLeod Raine. -- Center Point large print ed.
 p. cm.
 ISBN 1-58547-839-3 (lib. bdg. : alk. paper)
 1. Wyoming--Fiction. 2. Large type books. I. Title.

 PS3535.A385W96 2006
 813'.52--dc22

2006011105

To My Father,
WILLIAM RAINE,
A Man Foursquare,
This Tale is Dedicated with Love and Respect.

CONTENTS

CONTENTS

CHAPTER I

A DESERT MEETING

An automobile shot out from a gash in the hills and slipped swiftly down to the butte. Here it came to a halt on the white, dusty road, while its occupant gazed with eager, unsated eyes on the great panorama that stretched before her. The earth rolled in waves like a mighty sea to the distant horizon line. From a wonderful blue sky poured down upon the land a bath of sunbeat. The air was like wine, pure and strong, and above the desert swam the rare, untempered light of Wyoming. Surely here was a peace primeval, a silence unbroken since the birth of creation.

It was all new to her, and wonderfully exhilarating. The infinite roll of plain, the distant shining mountains, the multitudinous voices of the desert drowned in a sunlit sea of space—they were all details of the situation that ministered to a large serenity.

And while she breathed deeply the satisfaction of it, an exploding rifle echo shattered the stillness. With excited sputtering came the prompt answer of a fusillade. She was new to the West; but some instinct stronger than reason told the girl that here was no playful puncher shooting up the scenery to ventilate his exuberance. Her imagination conceived something more deadly; a sinister picture of men pumping lead in a grim, close-lipped silence; a lusty plainsman, with murder in his heart, crumpling into a lifeless heap, while the thin smoke-spiral curled from his hot rifle.

So the girl imagined the scene as she ran swiftly forward through the pines to the edge of the butte bluff whence she might look down upon the coulee that nestled against it. Nor had she greatly erred, for her first sweeping glance showed her the thing she had dreaded.

In a semicircle, well back from the foot of the butte, half a dozen men crouched in the cover of the sagebrush and a scattered group of cottonwoods. They were perhaps fifty yards apart, and the attention of all of them was focused on a spot directly beneath her. Even as she looked, in that first swift moment of apprehension, a spurt of smoke came from one of the rifles and was flung back from the forked pine at the bottom of the mesa. She saw him then, kneeling behind his insufficient shelter, a trapped man making his last stand.

From where she stood the girl distinguished him very clearly, and under the field-glasses that she turned on him the details leaped to life. Tall, strong, slender, with the lean, clean build of a greyhound, he seemed as wary and alert as a panther. The broad, soft hat, the scarlet handkerchief loosely knotted about his throat, the gray shirt, spurs and overalls, proclaimed him a stockman, just as his dead horse at the entrance to the coulee told of an accidental meeting in the desert and a hurried run for cover.

That he had no chance was quite plain, but no plainer than the cool vigilance with which he proposed to make them pay. Even in the matter of defense he was worse off than they were, but he knew how to make the most of what he had; knew how to avail himself of every inch of sagebrush that helped to render him indistinct to their eyes.

One of the attackers, eager for a clearer shot, exposed himself a trifle too far in taking aim. Without any loss of time in sighting, swift as a lightning-flash, the rifle behind the forked pine spoke. That the bullet reached its mark she saw with a gasp of dismay. For the man suddenly huddled down and rolled over on his side.

His comrades appeared to take warning by this example. The men at both ends of the crescent fell back, and for a minute the girl's heart leaped with the hope that they were about to abandon the siege. Apparently the man in the scarlet kerchief had no such expectation. He deserted his position behind the pine and ran back, crouching low in the brush, to another little clump of trees closer to the bluff. The reason for this was at first not apparent to her, but she understood presently when the men who had fallen back behind the rolling hillocks appeared again well in to the edge of the bluff. Only by his timely retreat had the man saved himself from being outflanked.

It was very plain that the attackers meant to take their time to finish him in perfect safety. He was surrounded on every side by a cordon of rifles, except where the bare face of the butte hung down behind him. To attempt to scale it would have been to expose himself as a mark for every gun to certain death.

It was now that she heard the man who seemed to be

directing the attack call out to another on his right. She was too far to make out the words, but their effect was clear to her. He pointed to the brow of the butte above, and a puncher in white woolen chaps dropped back out of range and swung to the saddle upon one of the ponies bunched in the rear. He cantered round in a wide circle and made for the butte. His purpose was obviously to catch their victim in the unprotected rear, and fire down upon him from above.

The young woman shouted a warning, but her voice failed to carry. For a moment she stood with her hands pressed together in despair, then turned and swiftly scudded to her machine. She sprang in, swept forward, reached the rim of the mesa, and plunged down. Never before had she attempted so precarious a descent in such wild haste. The car fairly leaped into space, and after it struck swayed dizzily as it shot down. The girl hung on, her face white and set, the pulse in her temple beating wildly. She could do nothing, as the machine rocked down, but hope against many chances that instant destruction might be averted.

Utterly beyond her control, the motor-car thundered down, reached the foot of the butte, and swept over a little hill in its wild flight. She rushed by a mounted horseman in the thousandth part of a second. She was still speeding at a tremendous velocity, but a second hill reduced this somewhat. She had not yet recovered control of the machine, but, though her eyes instinctively followed the white road that flashed past, she again had photographed on her brain the scene of the turbid tragedy in which she was intervening.

At the foot of the butte the road circled and dipped into the coulee. She braced herself for the shock, but, though the wheels skidded till her heart was in her throat, the automobile, hanging on the balance of disaster, swept round in safety.

Her horn screamed an instant warning to the trapped man. She could not see him, and for an instant her heart sank with the fear that they had killed him. But she saw then that they were still firing, and she continued her honking invitation as the car leaped forward into the zone of spitting bullets.

By this time she was recovering control of the motor, and she dared not let her attention wander, but out of the corner of her eye she appreciated the situation. Temporarily, out of sheer amaze at this apparition from the blue, the guns ceased their sniping. She became aware that a light curly head, crouched low in the sagebrush, was moving rapidly to meet her at right angles, and in doing so was approaching directly the line of fire. She could see him dodging to and fro as he moved forward, for the rifles were again barking.

She was within two hundred yards of him, still going rapidly, but not with the same headlong rush as before, when the curly head disappeared in the sagebrush. It was up again presently, but she could see that the man came limping, and so uncertainly that twice he pitched forward to the ground. Incautiously one of his assailants ran forward with a shout the second time his head went down. Crack! The unerring rifle rang out, and the impetuous one dropped in his tracks.

As she approached, the young woman slowed without stopping, and as the car swept past Curly Head flung himself in headlong. He picked himself up from her feet, crept past her to the seat beyond, and almost instantly whipped his rifle to his shoulder in prompt defiance of the fire that was now converged on them.

Yet in a few moments the sound died away, for a voice midway in the crescent had shouted an amazed discovery:

"By God, it's a woman!"

The car skimmed forward over the uneven ground toward the end of the semicircle, and passed within fifty yards of the second man from the end, the one she had picked out as the leader of the party. He was a black, swarthy fellow in plain leather chaps and blue shirt. As they passed he took a long, steady aim.

"Duck!" shouted the man beside her, and dragged her down on the seat so that his body covered hers.

A puff of wind fanned the girl's cheek.

"Near thing," her companion said coolly. He looked back at the swarthy man and laughed softly. "Some day you'll mebbe wish you had sent your pills straighter, Mr. Judd Morgan."

Yet a few wheel-turns and they had dipped forward out of range among the great land waves that seemed to stretch before them forever. The unexpected had happened, and she had achieved a rescue in the face of the impossible.

"Hurt badly?" the girl inquired briefly, her dark-blue

eyes meeting his as frankly as those of a boy.

"No need for an undertaker. I reckon I'll survive, ma'am."

"Where are you hit?"

"I just got a telegram from my ankle saying there was a cargo of lead arrived there unexpected," he drawled easily.

"Hurts a good deal, doesn't it?"

"No more than is needful to keep my memory jogged up. It's a sort of a forget-me-not souvenir. For a good boy; compliments of Mr. Jim Henson," he explained.

Her dark glance swept him searchingly. She disapproved the assurance of his manner even while the youth in her applauded his reckless sufficiency. His gay courage held her unconsenting admiration even while she resented it. He was a trifle too much at his ease for one who had just been snatched from dire peril. Yet even in his insouciance there was something engaging; something almost of distinction.

"What was the trouble?"

Mirth bubbled in his gray eyes. "I gathered, ma'am, that they wanted to collect my scalp."

"Do what?" she frowned.

"Bump me off—send me across the divide."

"Oh, I know that. But why?"

He seemed to reproach himself. "Now how could I be so neglectful? I clean forgot to ask."

"That's ridiculous," was her sharp verdict.

"Yes, ma'am, plumb ridiculous. My only excuse is that they began scattering lead so sudden I didn't have time to ask many 'Whyfors.' I reckon we'll just have to call it a Wyoming difference of opinion," he concluded pleasantly.

"Which means, I suppose, that you are not going to tell me."

"I got so much else to tell y'u that's a heap more important," he laughed. "Y'u see, I'm enjoyin' my first automobile ride. It was ce'tainly thoughtful of y'u to ask me to go riding with y'u, Miss Messiter."

"So you know my name. May I ask how?" was her astonished question.

He gave the low laugh that always seemed to suggest a private source of amusement of his own. "I suspicioned that might be your name when I saw y'u come a-sailin' down from heaven to gather me up like Enoch."

"Why?"

"Well, ma'am, I happened to drift in to Gimlet Butte two or three days ago, and while I was up at the depot looking for some freight a train sashaid in and side tracked a flat car. There was an automobile on that car addressed to Miss Helen Messiter. Now, automobiles are awful seldom in this country. I don't seem to remember having seen one before."

"I see. You're quite a Sherlock Holmes. Do you know anything more about me?"

"I know y'u have just fallen heir to the Lazy D. They say y'u are a schoolmarm, but I don't believe it."

"Well, I am." Then, "Why don't you believe it?" she added.

He surveyed her with his smile audacious, let his amused eyes wander down from the mobile face with the wild-rose bloom to the slim young figure so long and supple, then serenely met her frown.

"Y'u don't look it."

"No? Are you the owner of a composite photograph of the teachers of the country?"

He enjoyed again his private mirth. "I should like right well to have the pictures of some of them."

She glanced at him sharply, but he was gazing so innocently at the purple Shoshones in the distance that she could not give him the snub she thought he needed.

"You are right. My name is Helen Messiter," she said, by way of stimulating a counter fund of information. For, though she was a young woman not much given to curiosity, she was aware of an interest in this spare, broad-shouldered youth who was such an incarnation of bronzed vigor.

"Glad to meet y'u, Miss Messiter," he responded, and offered his firm brown hand in Western fashion.

But she observed resentfully that he did not mention his own name. It was impossible to suppose that he knew no better, and she was driven to conclude that he was silent of set purpose. Very well! If he did not want to introduce himself she was not going to urge it upon him. In a businesslike manner she gave her attention to eating up the dusty miles.

"Yes, ma'am. I reckon I never was more glad to death to meet a lady than I was to meet up with y'u," he continued, cheerfully. "Y'u sure looked good to me as y'u come a-foggin' down the road. I fair had been yearnin' for company, but was some discouraged for fear the invitation had miscarried." He broke off his sardonic raillery and let his level gaze possess her for a long moment. "Miss Messiter, I'm ce'tainly under an obligation to y'u I can't repay. Y'u saved my life," he finished gravely.

"Nonsense."

"Fact."

"It isn't a personal matter at all," she assured him, with a touch of impatient hauteur.

"It's a heap personal to me."

In spite of her healthy young resentment she laughed at the way in which he drawled this out, and with a swift sweep her boyish eyes took in again his compelling devil-may-care charm. She was a tenderfoot, but intuition as well as experience taught her that he was unusual enough to be one of ten thousand. No young Greek god's head could have risen more superbly above the brick-tanned column of the neck than this close-cropped curly one. Gray eyes, deep and unwavering and masterful, looked out of a face as brown as Wyoming. He was got up with no thought of effect, but the tigerish litheness, the picturesque competency of him, spake louder than costuming.

"Aren't you really hurt worse than you pretend? I'm sure your ankle ought to be attended to as soon as possible."

"Don't tell me you're a lady doctor, ma'am," he burlesqued his alarm.

"Can you tell me where the nearest ranch house is?" she asked, ignoring his diversion.

"The Lazy D is the nearest, I reckon."

"Which direction?"

"North by east, ma'am."

"Then I'll take the most direct road to it."

"In that case I'll thank y'u for my ride and get out here."

"But—why?"

He waved a jaunty hand toward the recent battlefield. "The Lazy D lies right back of that hill. I expect, mebbe, those wolves might howl again if we went back."

"Where, then, shall I take you?"

"I hate to trouble y'u to go out of your way."

"I dare say, but I'm going just the same," she told him, dryly.

"If you're right determined—" He interrupted himself to point to the south. "Do y'u see that camel-back peak over there?"

"The one with the sunshine on its lower edge?"

"That's it, Miss Messiter. They call those two humps the Antelope Peaks. If y'u can drop me somewhere near there I think I'll manage all right."

"I'm not going to leave you till we reach a house," she informed him promptly. "You're not fit to walk fifty yards."

"That's right kind of y'u, but I could not think of asking so much. My friends will find me if y'u leave me where I can work a heliograph."

"Or your enemies," she cut in.

"I hope not. I'd not likely have the luck to get another invitation right then to go riding with a friendly young lady."

She gave him direct, cool, black-blue eyes that met and searched his. "I'm not at all sure she *is* friendly. I shall want to find out the cause of the trouble you have just had before I make up my mind as to that."

"I judge people by their actions. Y'u didn't wait to find out before bringing the ambulance into action," he laughed.

"I see you do not mean to tell me."

"You're quite a lawyer, ma'am," he evaded.

"I find you a very slippery witness, then."

"Ask anything y'u like and I'll tell you."

"Very well. Who were those men, and why were they trying to kill you?"

"They turned their wolf loose on me because I shot up one of them yesterday."

"Dear me! Is it your business to go around shooting people? That's three I happen to know that you have shot. How many more?"

"No more, ma'am—not recently."

"Well, three is quite enough—recently," she mimicked. "You seem to me a good deal of a desperado."

"Yes, ma'am."

"Don't say 'Yes, ma'am,' like that, as if it didn't matter in the least whether you are or not," she ordered.

"No, ma'am."

"Oh!" She broke off with a gesture of impatience at

20

his burlesque of obedience. "You know what I mean—that you ought to deny it; ought to be furious at me for suggesting it."

"Ought I?"

"Of course you ought."

"There's a heap of ways I ain't up to specifications," he admitted, cheerfully.

"And who are they—the men that were attacking you?"

There was a gleam of irrepressible humor in the bold eyes. "Your cow-punchers, ma'am."

"My cow-punchers?"

"They ce'tainly belong to the Lazy D outfit."

"And you say that you shot one of my men yesterday?" He could see her getting ready for a declaration of war.

"Down by Willow Creek— Yes, ma'am," he answered, comfortably.

"And why, may I ask?" she flamed.

"That's a long story, Miss Messiter. It wouldn't be square for me to get my version in before your boys. Y'u ask them." He permitted himself a genial smile, somewhat ironic. "I shouldn't wonder but what they'll give me a gilt-edged testimonial as an unhanged horse thief."

"Isn't there such a thing as law in Wyoming?" the girl demanded.

"Lots of it. Y'u can buy just as good law right here as in Kalamazoo."

"I wish I knew where to find it."

21

"Like to put me in the calaboose?"

"In the penitentiary. Yes, sir!" A moment later the question that was in her thoughts leaped hotly from her lips. "Who are you, sir, that dare to commit murder and boast of it?"

She had flicked him on the raw at last. Something that was near to pain rested for a second in his eyes. "Murder is a hard name, ma'am. And I didn't say he was daid, or any of the three," came his gentle answer.

"You *meant* to kill them, anyhow."

"Did I?" There was the ghost of a sad smile about his eyes.

"The way you act a person might think you one of Ned Bannister's men," she told him, scornfully.

"I expect you're right."

She repented her a little at a charge so unjust. "If you are not ashamed of your name why are you so loath to part with it?"

"Y'u didn't ask me my name," he said, a dark flush sweeping his face.

"I ask it now."

Like the light from a snuffed candle the boyish recklessness had gone out of his face. His jaws were set like a vise and he looked hard as hammered steel.

"My name is Bannister," he said, coldly.

"Ned Bannister, the outlaw," she let slip, and was aware of a strange sinking of the heart.

It seemed to her that something sinister came to the surface in his handsome face. "I reckon we might as well let it go at that," he returned, with bitter briefness.

CHAPTER II

THE KING OF THE BIG HORN COUNTRY

Two months before this time Helen Messiter had been serenely teaching a second grade at Kalamazoo, Michigan, notwithstanding the earnest efforts of several youths of that city to induce her to retire to domesticity. "What's the use of being a schoolmarm?" had been the burden of their plaint. "Any spinster can teach kids *C-a-t,* Cat, but only one in several thousand can be the prettiest bride in Kalamazoo." None of them, however, had been able to drive the point sufficiently home, and it is probable that she would have continued to devote herself to Young America if an uncle she had never seen had not died without a will and left her a ranch in Wyoming yclept the Lazy D.

When her lawyer proposed to put the ranch on the market Miss Helen had a word to say.

"I think not. I'll go out and see it first, anyhow," she said.

"But really, my dear young lady, it isn't at all necessary. Fact is, I've already had an offer of a hundred thousand dollars for it. Now, I should judge that a fair price—"

"Very likely," his client interrupted, quietly. "But, you see, I don't care to sell."

"Then what in the world are you going to do with it?"

"Run it."

23

"But, my dear Miss Messiter, it isn't an automobile or any other kind of toy. You must remember that it takes a business head and a great deal of experience to make such an investment pay. I really think—"

"My school ends on the fourteenth of June. I'll get a substitute for the last two months. I shall start for Wyoming on the eighteenth of April."

The man of law gasped, explained the difficulties again carefully as to a child, found that he was wasting his breath, and wisely gave it up.

Miss Messiter had started on the eighteenth of April, as she had announced. When she reached Gimlet Butte, the nearest railroad point to the Lazy D, she found a group of curious, weather-beaten individuals gathered round a machine foreign to their experience. It was on a flat car, and the general opinion ran the gamut from a newfangled sewing machine to a thresher. Into this guessing contest came its owner with so brisk and businesslike an energy that inside of two hours she was testing it up and down the wide street of Gimlet Butte, to the wonder and delight of an audience to which each one of the eleven saloons of the city had contributed its admiring quota.

Meanwhile the young woman attended strictly to business. She had disappeared for half an hour with a suitcase into the Elk House; and when she returned in a short-skirted corduroy suit, leggings and wide-brimmed gray Stetson hat, all Gimlet Butte took an absorbing interest in the details of this delightful adventure that had happened to the town. The population was out *en masse* to watch her slip down the road on a trial trip.

Presently "Soapy" Sothern, drifting in on his buckskin from the Hoodoo Peak country, where for private reasons of his own he had been for the past month a sojourner, reported that he had seen the prettiest sight in the State climbing under a gasoline bronc with a monkey-wrench in her hand. Where? Right over the hill on the edge of town. The immediate stampede for the cow ponies was averted by a warning chug-chug that sounded down the road, followed by the appearance of a flashing whir that made the ponies dance on their hind legs.

"The gasoline bronc lady sure makes a hit with me," announced "Texas," gravely. "I allow I'll rustle a job with the Lazy D outfit."

"She ce'tainly rides herd on that machine like a champeen," admitted Soapy. "I reckon I'll drift over to the Lazy D with you to look after yore remains, Tex, when the lightning hits you."

Miss Messiter swung the automobile round in a swift circle, came to an abrupt halt in front of the hotel, and alighted without delay. As she passed in through the half score of admirers she had won, her dark eyes swept smilingly over assembled Cattleland. She had already met most of them at the launching of the machine from the flat car, and had directed their perspiring energies as they labored to follow her orders. Now she nodded a recognition with a little ripple of gay laughter.

"I'm delighted to be able to contribute to the entertainment of Gimlet Butte," she said, as she swept in. For this young woman was possessed of Western adaptation. It gave her no conscientious qualms to exchange conversation fraternal with these genial savages.

The Elk House did not rejoice in a private dining room, and competition strenuous ensued as to who should have the pleasure of sitting beside the guest of honor. To avoid ill feeling, the matter was determined by a game of freeze-out, in which Texas and a mature gentleman named, from his complexion, "Beet" Collins, were the lucky victors. Texas immediately repaired to the general store, where he purchased a new scarlet bandanna for the occasion; also a cake of soap with which to rout the alkali dust that had filtered into every pore of his hands and face from a long ride across the desert.

Came supper and Texas simultaneously, the cowpuncher's face scrubbed to an apple shine. At the last moment Collins defaulted, his nerve completely gone. Since, however, he was a thrifty soul, he sold his place to Soapy for ten dollars, and proceeded to invest the proceeds in an immediate drunk.

During the first ten minutes of supper Miss Messiter did not appear, and the two guardians who flanked her chair solicitously were the object of much badinage.

"She got one glimpse of that red haid of Tex and the pore lady's took to the sage," explained Yorky.

"And him scrubbed so shiny fust time since Christmas befo' the big blizzard," sighed Doc Rogers.

"Shucks! She ain't scared of no sawed-off, hammered-down runt like Tex. No, siree! Miss Messiter's on the absent list 'cause she's afraid she cayn't resist the blandishments of Soapy. Did yo' ever hear about Soapy and that Caspar hash slinger?"

"Forget it, Slim," advised Soapy, promptly. He had been engaged in lofty and oblivious conversation with Texas, but he did not intend to allow reminiscences to get under way just now.

At this opportune juncture arrived the mistress of the "gasoline bronc," neatly clad in a simple white lawn with blue trimmings. She looked like a gleam of sunshine in her fresh, sweet youth; and not even in her own school room had she ever found herself the focus of a cleaner, more unstinted admiration. For the outdoors West takes off its hat reverently to women worthy of respect, especially when they are young and friendly.

Helen Messiter had come to Wyoming because the call of adventure, the desire for experience outside of rutted convention, were stirring her warm-blooded youth. She had seen enough of life lived in a parlor, and when there came knocking at her door a chance to know the big, untamed outdoors at first hand she had at once embraced it like a lover. She was eager for her new life, and she set out skillfully to make these men tell her what she wanted to know. To them, of course, it was an old story, and whatever of romance it held was unconscious. But since she wanted to talk of the West they were more than ready to please her.

So she listened, and drew them out with adroit questions when it was necessary. She made them talk of life on the open range, of rustlers and those who lived outside the law in the upper Shoshone country, of the deadly war waging between the cattle and sheep industries.

"Are there any sheep near the Lazy D ranch?" she asked, intensely interested in Soapy's tale of how cattle and sheep could no more be got to mix than oil and water.

For an instant nobody answered her question; then Soapy replied, with what seemed elaborate carelessness:

"Ned Bannister runs a bunch of about twelve thousand not more'n fifteen or twenty miles from your place."

"And you say they are spoiling the range?"

"They're ce'tainly spoiling it for cows."

"But can't something be done? If my cows were there first I don't see what right he has to bring his sheep there," the girl frowned.

The assembled company attended strictly to supper. The girl, surprised at the stillness, looked round. "Well?"

"Now you're shouting, ma'am! That's what we say," enthused Texas, spurring to the rescue.

"It doesn't much matter what you say. What do you do?" asked Helen, impatiently. "Do you lie down and let Mr. Bannister and his kind drive their sheep over you?"

"Do we, Soapy?" grinned Texas. Yet it seemed to her his smile was not quite carefree.

28

"I'm not a cowman myself," explained Soapy to the girl. "Nor do I run sheep. I—"

"Tell Miss Messiter what yore business is, Soapy," advised Yorky from the end of the table, with a mouthful of biscuit swelling his cheeks.

Soapy crushed the irrepressible Yorky with a look, but that young man hit back smilingly.

"Soapy, he sells soap, ma'am. He's a sorter city salesman, I reckon."

"I should never have guessed it. Mr. Sothern does not *look* like a salesman," said the girl, with a glance at his shrewd, hard, expressionless face.

"Yes, ma'am, he's a first-class seller of soap, is Mr. Sothern," chuckled the cow-puncher, kicking his friends gayly under the table.

You can see I never sold *him* any, Miss Messiter," came back Soapy, sorrowfully.

All this was Greek to the young lady from Kalamazoo. How was she to know that Mr. Sothern had vended his soap in small cubes on street corners, and that he wrapped bank notes of various denominations in the bars, which same were retailed to eager customers for the small sum of fifty cents, after a guarantee that the soap was good? His customers rarely patronized him twice; and frequently they used bad language because the soap wrapping was not as valuable as they had expected. This was manifestly unfair, for Mr. Sothern, who made no claims to philanthropy, often warned them that the soap should be bought on its merits, and not with an eye single to the premium that might or might not accompany the package.

"I started to tell you, ma'am, when that infant interrupted, that the cowmen don't aim to quit business yet a while. They've drawn a dead-line, Miss Messiter."

"A dead-line?"

"Yes, ma'am, beyond which no sheep herder is to run his bunch."

"And if he does?" the girl asked, open eyed.

"He don't do it twict, ma'am. Why don't you pass the fritters to Miss Messiter, Slim?"

"And about this Bannister— Who is he?"

Her innocent question seemed to ring a bell for silence; seemed to carry with it some hidden portent that stopped idle conversation as a striking clock that marks the hour of an execution. The smile that had been gay grew grim, and men forgot the subject of their light, casual talk. It was Sothern that answered her, and she observed that his voice was grave, his face studiously without expression.

"Mr. Bannister, ma'am, is a sheepman."

"So I understood, but—" Her eyes traveled swiftly round the table, and appraised the sudden sense of responsibility that had fallen on these reckless, careless frontiersmen. "I am wondering what else he is. Really, he seems to be the bogey man of Gimlet Butte."

There was another instant silence, and again it was Soapy that lifted it. "I expaict you'll like Wyoming, Miss Messiter; leastways I hope you will. There's a right smart of country here." His gaze went out of the open door to the vast sea of space that swam in the fine

30

sunset light. "Yes, most folks that ain't plumb spoilt with city ways likes it."

"Sure she'll like it. Y'u want to get a good, easy-riding hawss, Miss Messiter," advised Slim.

"And a rifle," added Texas, promptly.

It occurred to her that they were all working together to drift the conversation back to a safe topic. She followed the lead given her, but she made up her mind to know what it was about her neighbor, Mr. Bannister, the sheep herder, that needed to be handled with such wariness and circumspection of speech.

Her chance came half an hour later, when she stood talking to the landlady on the hotel porch in the mellow twilight that seemed to rest on the land like a moonlit aura. For the moment they were alone.

"What is it about this man Bannister that makes men afraid to speak of him?" she demanded, with swift impulse.

Her landlady's startled eyes went alertly round to see that they were alone. "Hush, child! You mustn't speak of him like that," warned the older woman.

"Why mustn't I? That's what I want to know."

"Is isn't healthy."

"What do you mean?"

Again that anxious look flashed round in the dusk. "The Bannister outfit is the worst in the land. Ned Bannister is king of the whole Big Horn country and beyond that to the Tetons."

"And you mean to tell me that everybody is afraid of him—that men like Mr. Sothern dare not say their soul is their own?" the newcomer asked, contemptuously.

"Not so loud, child. He has spies everywhere. That's the trouble. You don't know who is in with him. He's got the whole region terrified."

"Is he so bad?"

"He is a devil. Last year he and his hell riders swept down on Topaz and killed two bartenders just to see them kick, Ned Bannister said. Folks allow they knew too much."

"But the law—the Government? Haven't you a sheriff and officers?"

"Bannister has. He elects the sheriff in this county."

"Aren't there more honest people here than villains?"

"Ten times as many, but the trouble is that the honest folks can't trust each other. You see, if one of them made a mistake and confided in the wrong man—well, some fine day he would go riding herd and would not turn up at night. Next week, or next month, maybe, one of his partners might find a pile of bones in an arroyo."

"Have you ever seen this Bannister?"

"You *must* speak lower when you talk of him, Miss Messiter," the woman insisted. "Yes, I saw him once; at least I think I did. Mighty few folks know for sure that they have seen him. He is a mystery, and he travels under many names and disguises."

"When was it you think you saw him?"

"Two years ago at Ayr. The bank was looted that night and robbed of thirty thousand dollars. They roused the cashier from his bed and made him give the combination. He didn't want to, and Ned Bannister"—her voice

32

sank to a tremulous whisper—" put red-hot running-irons between his fingers till he weakened. It was a moonlight night—much such a night as this—and after it was done I peeped through the blind of my room and saw them ride away. He rode in front of them and sang like an angel—did it out of daredeviltry to mock the people of the town that hadn't nerve enough to shoot him. You see, he knew that nobody would dare hurt him 'count of the revenge of his men."

"What was he like?" the mistress of the Lazy D asked, strangely awed at this recital of transcendent villainy.

"'Course he was masked, and I didn't see his face. But I'd know him anywhere. He's a long, slim fellow, built like a mountain lion. You couldn't look at him and ever forget him. He's one of these graceful, easy men that go so fur with fool women; one of the kind that half shuts his dark, devil eyes and masters them without seeming to try."

"So he's a woman killer, too, is he? Any more outstanding inconsistencies in this versatile Jesse James?"

"He's plumb crazy about music, they say. Has a piano and plays Grigg and Chopping, and all that classical kind of music. He went clear down to Denver last year to hear Mrs. Shoeman sing."

Helen smiled, guessing at Schumann-Heink as the singer in question, and Grieg and Chopin as the composers named. Her interest was incredibly aroused. She had expected the West and its products to exhilarate her, but she had not looked to find so finished a Mephisto

33

among its vaunted "bad men." He was probably over-
rated; considered a wonder because his accomplish-
ments outstepped those of the range. But Helen Messiter had quite determined on one thing. She was going
to meet this redoubtable villain and make up her mind
for herself. Already, before she had been in Wyoming
six hours, this emancipated young woman had decided
on that.

CHAPTER III

AN INVITATION GIVEN AND ACCEPTED

And already she had met him. Not only met him,
but saved him from the just vengeance about to
fall upon him. She had not yet seen her own ranch,
had not spoken to a single one of her employees, for it
had been a part of her plan to drop in unexpected and
examine the situation before her foreman had a chance
to put his best foot forward. So she had started alone
from Gimlet Butte that morning in her machine, and
had come almost in sight of the Lazy D ranch houses
when the battle in the coulee invited her to take a
hand.

She had acted on generous impulse, and the unforeseen result had been to save this desperado from justice.
But the worst of it was that she could not find it in her
heart to regret it. Granted that he was a villain, double-
dyed and beyond hope, yet he was the home of such
courage, such virility, that her unconsenting admiration

went out in spite of herself. He was, at any rate, a *man,* square-jawed, resolute, implacable. In the sinuous trail of his life might lie arson, robbery, murder, but he still held to that dynamic spark of self-respect that is akin to the divine. Nor was it possible to believe that those unblinking gray eyes, with the capability of a latent sadness of despair in them, expressed a soul entirely without nobility. He had a certain gallant ease, a certain attractive candor, that did not consist with villainy unadulterated.

It was characteristic even of her impulsiveness that Helen Messiter curbed the swift condemnation that leaped to her lips when she knew that the man sitting beside her was the notorious bandit of the Shoshone fastnesses. She was not in the least afraid. A sure instinct told her he was not the kind of a man of whom a woman need have fear so long as her own anchor held fast. In good time she meant to let him have her unvarnished opinion of him, but she did not mean it to be an unconsidered one. Wherefore she drove the machine forward toward the camel-backed peak he had indicated, her eyes straight before her, a frown corrugating her forehead.

For him, having made his dramatic announcement, he seemed content for the present with silence. He leaned back in the car and appreciated her with a coolness that just missed impudence. Certainly her appearance proclaimed her very much worth while. To dwell on the long lines of her supple young body, the exquisite throat and chin curve, was a pleasure with a thrill to it. As a physical creation, a mere innocent young animal, he thought her perfect; attuned to a fine harmony of grace and color. But it was the animating vitality of her, the lightness of motion, the fire and sparkle of expression that gave her the captivating charm she possessed.

They were two miles nearer the camel-backed peak before he broke the silence.

"Beats a bronco for getting over the ground. Think I'll have to get one," he mused aloud.

"With the money you took from the Ayr bank?" she flashed.

"I might drive off some of your cows and sell them," he countered, promptly. "About how much will they hold me up for a machine like this?"

"This is only a runabout. You can get one for twelve or fourteen hundred dollars of anybody's money."

"Of yours?" he laughed.

"I haven't that much with me. If you'll come over and hold up the ranch perhaps we might raise it among us," she jeered.

His mirth was genuine. "But right now I couldn't get more than how much off y'u?"

"Sixty-three dollars is all I have with me, and I couldn't give you more—*not even if you put red-hot irons between my fingers*." She gave it to him straight, her blue eyes fixed steadily on him.

Yet she was not prepared for the effect of her words. The last thing she had expected was to see the blood wash out of his bronzed face, to see his sensitive nostrils twitch with pain. He made her feel as if she had insulted him, as if she had been needlessly cruel. And because of it she hardened her heart. Why should she spare him the mention of it? He had not hesitated at the shameless deed itself. Why should she shrink before that wounded look that leaped to his fine eyes in that flash of time before he hardened them to steel?

"You did it—didn't you?" she demanded.

"That's what they say." His gaze met hers defiantly.

"And it is true, isn't it?"

"Oh, anything is true of a man that herds sheep," he returned, bitterly.

"If that is true it would not be possible for you to understand how much I despise you."

"Thank you," he retorted, ironically.

"I don't understand at all. I don't see how you can be the man they say you are. Before I met you it was easy to understand. But somehow—I don't know—you don't *look* like a villain." She found herself strangely voicing the deep hope of her heart. It was surely impossible to look at him and believe him guilty of the things of which he was accused. And yet he offered no denial, suggested no defense.

Her troubled eyes went over his thin, sunbaked face with its touch of bitterness, and she did not find it possible to dismiss the subject without giving him a chance to *set* himself right. "You can't be as bad as they say. You are not, are you?" she asked, naively.

"What do y'u think?" he responded, coolly.

She flushed angrily at what she accepted as his insolence. "A man of any decency would have jumped at the chance to explain."

"But if there is nothing to explain?"

"You are then guilty."

Their eyes met, and neither of them quailed.

"If I pleaded not guilty would y'u believe me?"

She hesitated. "I don't know. How could I when it is known by everybody? And yet—"

He smiled. "Why should I trouble y'u, then, with explanations? I reckon we'll let it go at guilty."

"Is that all you can say for yourself?"

He seemed to hang in doubt an instant, then shook his head and refused the opening.

"I expect if we changed the subject I could say a good deal for y'u," he drawled. "I never saw anything pluckier than the way y'u flew down from the mesa and conducted the cutting-out expedition. Y'u sure drilled through your punchers like a streak of lightning."

"I didn't know who you were," she explained, proudly.

"Would it have made any difference if y'u had?"

Again the angry flush touched her cheeks. "Not a bit. I would have saved you in order to have you properly hanged later," she cut back promptly.

He shook his head gayly. "I'm ce'tainly going to disappoint y'u some. Your enterprising punchers may collect me yet, but not alive, I reckon."

"I'll give them strict orders to bring you in alive."

"Did you ever want the moon when y'u was a little kid?" he asked.

"We'll see, Mr. Outlaw Bannister."

He laughed softly, in the quiet, indolent fashion that would have been pleasant if it had not been at her. "It's right kind of you to take so much interest in me. I'd most be willing to oblige by letting your boys rope me to renew this acquaintance, ma'am." Then, "I get out here, Miss Messiter," he added.

She stopped on the instant. Plainly she could not get rid of him too soon. "Haven't you forgot one thing?" she asked, ironically.

"Yes, ma'am. To thank you proper for what y'u did for me." He limped gingerly down from the car and stood with his hand on one of the tires. "I have been trying to think how to say it right; but I guess I'll have to give it up. All is, that if I ever get a chance to even the score—"

She waved his thanks aside impatiently. "I didn't mean that. You have forgotten to take my purse."

His gravity was broken on the instant, and his laughter was certainly delightfully fresh. "I clean forgot, but I expect I'll drop over to the ranch for it some day."

"We'll try to make you welcome, Mr. Bannister."

"Don't put yourself out at all. I'll take potluck when I come."

"How many of you may we expect?" she asked, defiantly.

"Oh, I allow to come alone."

"You'll very likely forget."

"No, ma'am, I don't know so many ladies that I'm liable to such an oversight."

"I have heard a different story. But if you do remember to come, and will let us know when you expect to honor the Lazy D, I'll have messengers sent to meet you."

He perfectly understood her to mean leaden ones; and the humorous gleam in his eye sparkled in appreciation of her spirit. "I don't want all that fuss made over me. I reckon I'll drop in unexpected," he said.

She nodded curtly. "Good-bye. Hope your ankle won't trouble you very much."

"Thank y'u, ma'am. I reckon it won't. Good-bye, Miss Messiter."

Out of the tail of her eye she saw him bowing like an Italian opera singer, as impudently insouciant, as gracefully graceless as any stage villain in her memory. Once again she saw him, when her machine swept round a curve and she could look back without seeming to do so, limping across through the sage brush toward a little hillock near the road. And as she looked the bare, curly head was inclined toward her in another low, mocking bow. He was certainly the gallantest vagabond unhanged.

CHAPTER IV

AT THE LAZY D RANCH

H elen Messiter was a young woman very much alive, which implies that she was given to emotions; and as her machine skimmed over the ground to

40

the Lazy D she had them to spare. For from the first this young man had taken her eye, and it had come upon her with a distinct shock that he was the notorious scoundrel who was terrorizing the countryside. She told herself almost passionately that she would never have believed it if he had not said so himself. She knew quite well that the coldness that had clutched her heart when he gave his name had had nothing to do with fear. There had been chagrin, disappointment, but nothing in the least like the terror she might have expected. The simple truth was that he had seemed so much a man that it had hurt her to find him also a wild beast.

Deep in her heart she resented the conviction forced upon her. Reckless he undoubtedly was, at odds with the law surely, but it was hard to admit that attractive personality to be the mask of fiendish cruelty and sinister malice. And yet—the facts spoke for themselves. He had not even attempted a denial. Still there was a mystery about him, else how was it possible for two so distinct personalities to dwell together in the same body.

She hated him with all her lusty young will; not only for what he was, but also for what she had been disappointed in not finding him after her first instinctive liking. Yet it was with an odd little thrill that she ran down again into the coulee where her prosaic life had found its first real adventure. He might be all they said, but nothing could wipe out the facts that she had offered her life to save his, and that he had lent her his

41

body as a living shield for one exhilarating moment of danger.

As she reached the hill summit beyond the coulee, Helen Messiter was aware that a rider in ungainly chaps of white wool was rapidly approaching. He dipped down into the next depression without seeing her; and when they came face to face at the top of the rise the result was instantaneous. His pony did an animated two-step not on the program. It took one glance at the diabolical machine, and went up on its hind legs, preliminary to giving an elaborate exhibition of pitching. The rider indulged in vivid profanity and plied his quirt vigorously. But the bronco, with the fear of this unknown evil on its soul, varied its bucking so effectively that the puncher astride its hurricane deck was forced, in the language of his kind, to "take the dust."

His red head sailed through the air and landed in the white sand at the girl's feet. For a moment he sat in the road and gazed with chagrin after the vanishing heels of his mount. Then his wrathful eyes came round to the owner of the machine that had caused the eruption. His mouth had opened to give adequate expression to his feelings, when he discovered anew the forgotten fact that he was dealing with a woman. His jaw hung open for an instant in amaze; and when he remembered the unedited vocabulary he had turned loose on the world a flood of purple swept his tanned face.

She wanted to laugh, but wisely refrained. "I'm very sorry," was what she said.

He stared in silence as he slowly picked himself from

42

the ground. His red hair rose like the quills of a porcupine above a face that had the appearance of being unfinished. Neither nose nor mouth nor chin seemed to be quite definite enough.

She choked down her gayety and offered renewed apologies.

"I was going for a doc," he explained, by way of opening his share of the conversation.

"Then perhaps you had better jump in with me and ride back to the Lazy D. I suppose that's where you came from?"

He scratched his vivid head helplessly. "Yes, ma'am."

"Then jump in."

"I was going to Bear Creek, ma'am," he added, dubiously.

"How far is it?"

"'Bout twenty-five miles, and then some."

"You don't expect to walk, do you?"

"No; I allowed—"

"I'll take you back to the ranch, where you can get another horse."

"I reckon, ma'am, I'd ruther walk."

"Nonsense! Why?"

"I ain't used to them gas wagons."

"It's quite safe. There is nothing to be afraid of."

Reluctantly he got in beside her, as happy as a calf in a branding pen.

"Are you the lady that sashaid off with Ned Bannister?" he asked presently, after he had had time to smother successively some of his fear, wonder and

43

delight at their smooth, swift progress.

"Yes. Why?"

"The boys allow you hadn't oughter have done it." Then, to place the responsibility properly on shoulders broader than his own, he added: "That's what Judd says."

"And who is Judd?"

"Judd, he's the foreman of the Lazy D."

Below them appeared the corrals and houses of a ranch nestling in a little valley flanked by hills.

"This yere's the Lazy D," announced the youth, with pride, and in the spirit of friendliness suggested a caution. "Judd, he's some peppery. You wanter smooth him down some, seeing as he's riled up today."

A flicker of steel came into the blue eyes. "Indeed! Well, here we are."

"If it ain't Reddy, *and* the lady with the flying machine," murmured a freckled youth named McWilliams, emerging from the bunkhouse with a pan of water which had been used to bathe the wound of one of the punctured combatants.

"What's that?" snapped a voice from within; and immediately its owner appeared in the doorway and bored with narrowed black eyes the young woman in the machine.

"Who are you?" he demanded, brusquely.

"Your target," she answered, quietly. "Would you like to take another shot at me?"

The freckled lad broke out into a gurgle of laughter, at which the black, swarthy man beside him wheeled round in a rage. "What you cacklin' at, Mac?" he demanded, in a low voice.

"Oh, the things I notice," returned that youth jauntily, meeting the other's anger without the flicker of an eyelid.

"It ain't healthy to be so noticin'," insinuated the other.

"Y'u don't say," came the prompt, sarcastic retort. "If you're such a darned good judge of health, y'u better be attending to some of your patients." He jerked a casual thumb over his shoulder toward the bunks on which lay the wounded men.

"I shouldn't wonder but what there might be another patient for me to attend to," snarled the foreman.

"That so? Well, turn your wolf loose when y'u get to feelin' real devilish," jeered the undismayed one, strolling forward to assist Miss Messiter to alight.

The mistress of the Lazy D had been aware of the byplay, but she had caught neither the words nor their import. She took the offered brown hand smilingly, for here again she looked into the frank eyes of the West, unafraid and steady. She judged him not more than twenty-two, but the school where he had learned of life had held open and strenuous session every day since he could remember.

"Glad to meet y'u, ma'am," he assured her, in the current phrase of the semi-arid lands.

"I'm sure I am glad to meet *you*," she answered, heartily. "Can you tell me where is the foreman of the Lazy D?"

45

He introduced with a smile the swarthy man in the doorway. "This is him, ma'am—Mr. Judd Morgan."

Now it happened that Mr. Judd Morgan was simmering with suppressed spleen.

"All I've got to say is that you had no business mixing up in that shootin' affair back there. Perhaps you don't know that the man you saved is Ned Bannister, the outlaw," was his surly greeting.

"Oh, *yes,* I know that."

"Then what d'ye mean— Who are you, anyway?" His insolent eyes coasted malevolently over her.

"Helen Messiter is my name."

It was ludicrous to see the change that came over the man. He had been prepared to bully her; and with a word she had pricked the bubble of his arrogance. He swallowed his anger and got a mechanical smile in working order.

"Glad to see you here, Miss Messiter," he said, his sinister gaze attempting to meet hers frankly. "I been looking for you every day."

"But y'u managed to surprise him, after all, ma'am," chuckled Mac.

"Where's yo' hawss, Reddy?" inquired a tall young man, who had appeared silently in the doorway of the bunkhouse.

Reddy pinked violently. "I had an accident, Denver," he explained. "This lady yere, she—"

"Scooped y'u right off yore hawss. Y'u *don't* say," sympathized Mac so breathlessly that even Reddy joined in the chorus of laughter that went up at his expense.

The young woman thought to make it easy for him, and suggested an explanation.

"His horse isn't used to automobiles, and so when it met this one—"

"I got off," interposed Reddy hastily, displaying a complexion like a boiled beet.

"He got off," Mac explained gravely to the increasing audience.

Denver nodded with an imperturbable face. "He got off."

Mac introduced Miss Messiter to such of her employees as were on hand. "Shake hands with Miss Messiter, Missou," was the formula, the name alone varying to suit the embarrassed gentlemen in leathers. Each of them in turn presented a huge hand, in which her little one disappeared for the time, and was sawed up and down in the air like a pump-handle. Yet if she was amused she did not show it; and her pleasure at meeting the simple, elemental products of the plains outweighed a great deal her sense of the ludicrous.

"How are your patients getting along?" she presently asked of her foreman.

"I reckon all right. I sent Reddy for a doc, but—"

"He got off," murmured Mac pensively.

"I'll go rope another hawss," put in the man who had got off.

"Get a jump on you, then. Miss Messiter, would you like to look over the place?"

"Not now. I want to see the men that were hurt. Per-

47

haps I can help them. Once I took a few weeks in nursing."

"Bully for you, ma'am," whooped Mac. "I've a notion those boys are sufferin' for a woman to put the diamond-hitch on them bandages."

"Bring that suit-case in," she commanded Denver, in the gentlest voice he had ever heard, after she had made a hasty inspection of the first wounded man.

From the suit-case she took a little leather medicine-case, the kind that can be bought already prepared for use. It held among other things a roll of medicated cotton, some antiseptic tablets, and a little steel instrument for probing.

"Some warm water, please; and have some boiling on the range," were her next commands.

Mac flew to execute them.

It was a pleasure to see her work, so deftly the skillful hands accomplished what her brain told them. In admiring awe the punchers stood awkwardly around while she washed and dressed the hurts. Two of the bullets had gone through the fleshy part of the arm and left clean wounds. In the case of the third man she had to probe for the lead, but fortunately found it with little difficulty. Meanwhile she soothed the victim with gentle womanly sympathy.

"I know it hurts a good deal. Just a minute and I'll be through."

His hands clutched tightly the edges of his bunk. "That's all right, doc. You attend to roping that pill and I'll endure the grief."

48

A long sigh of relief went up from the assembled cowboys when she drew the bullet out. The sinewy hands fastened on the wooden bunk relaxed suddenly.

" 'Frisco's daid," gasped the cook, who bore the title of Wun Hop for no reason except that he was an Irishman in a place formerly held by a Chinese.

"He has only fainted," she said quietly, and continued with the antispetic dressing.

When it was all over, the big, tanned men gathered at the entrance to the calf corral and expanded in admiration of their new boss.

"She's a pure for fair. She grades up any old way yuh take her to the best corn-fed article on the market," pronounced Denver, with enthusiasm.

"I got to ride the boundary," sighed Missou. "I kinder hate to go right now."

"Here, too," acquiesced another. "I got a round-up on Wind Creek to cut out them two-year-olds. If 'twas my say-so, I'd order Mac on that job."

"Right kind of y'u. Seems to me"—Mac's sarcastic eye trailed around to include all those who had been singing her praises—"the new queen of this hacienda won't have no trouble at all picking a prince consort when she gets round to it. Here's Wun Hop, not what y'u might call anxious, but ce'tainly willing. Then Denver's some in the turtle-dove business, according to that hash-slinger in Cheyenne. Missou might be induced to accept if it was offered him proper; and I allow Jim ain't turned the color of Redtop's hair jest for instance. I don't want to leave out 'Frisco and the

49

other boys carrying Bannister's pills—"

"Nor McWilliams. I'd admire to include him," murmured Denver.

That sunburned, nonchalant youth laughed musically. "Sure thing. I'd hate to be left out. The only difference is—"

"Well?"

His roving eye circled blandly round. "I stand about one show in a million. Y'u roughnecks are dead ones already."

With which cold comfort he sauntered away to join Miss Messiter and the foreman, who now appeared together at the door of the ranchhouse, prepared to make a tour of the buildings and the immediate corrals.

"Isn't there a woman on the place?" she was asking Morgan.

"No'm, there ain't. Henderson's daughter would come and stay with y'u a while I reckon."

"Please send for her at once, then, and ask her to come today."

"All right. I'll send one of the boys right away."

"Hew did y'u leave 'Frisco, ma'am?" asked Mac, by way of including himself easily.

"He's resting quietly. Unless blood-poisoning sets in they ought all to do well."

"It's right lucky for them y'u happened along. This is the hawss corral, ma'am," explained the young man just as Morgan opened his thin lips to tell her.

Judd contrived to get rid of him promptly. "Slap on a

saddle, Mac, and run up the remuda so Miss Messiter can see the hawsses for herself," he ordered.

"Mebbe she'd rather ride down and look at the bunch," suggested the capable McWilliams.

As it chanced, she did prefer to ride down the pasture and look over the place from on horseback. She was in love with her ranch already. Its spacious distances, the thousands of cattle and the horses, these picturesque retainers who served her even to the shedding of an enemy's blood; they all struck an answering echo in her gallant young heart that nothing in Kalamazoo had been able to stir. She bubbled over with enthusiasm, the while Morgan covertly sneered and McWilliams warmed to the untamed youth in her.

"What about this man Bannister?" she flung out suddenly, after they had cantered back to the house when the remuda had been inspected.

Her abrupt question brought again the short, tense silence she had become used to expect.

"He runs sheep about twenty or thirty miles southwest of here," explained McWilliams, in a carefully casual tone.

"So everybody tells me, but it seems to me he spills a good deal of lead on my men," she answered impatiently. "What's the trouble?"

"Last week he crossed the dead-line with a bunch of five thousand sheep."

"Who draws this dead-line?"

"The cattlemen got together and drew it. Your uncle was one of those that marked it off, ma'am."

"And Bannister crossed it?"

"Yes, ma'am. Yesterday 'Frisco come on him and one of his herders with a big bunch of them less than fifteen miles from here. He didn't know it was Bannister, and took a pot-shot at him. 'Course Bannister came back at him, and he got 'Frisco in the laig."

"Didn't know it was Bannister? What difference would that make?" she said impatiently.

Mac laughed. "What difference *would* it make, Judd?"

Morgan scowled, and the young man answered his own question. "We don't any of us go out of our way more'n a mile to cross Bannister's trail," he drawled.

"Do you wear this for an ornament? Are you upholstered with hardware to catch the eyes of some girl?" she asked, touching with the end of her whip the revolver in the holster strapped to his chaps.

His serene, gay smile flashed at her. "Are y'u ordering me to go out and get Ned Bannister's scalp?"

"No, I am not," she explained promptly. "What I am trying to discover is why you all seem to be afraid of one man. He is only a man, isn't he?"

A veil of ice seemed to fall over the boyish face and leave it chiseled marble. His unspeaking eyes rested on the swarthy foreman as he answered:

"I don't know what he is, ma'am. He may be one man, or he may be a hundred. What's more, I ain't particularly suffering to find out. Fact is, I haven't lost any Bannisters."

The girl became aware that her foreman was looking

52

at her with a wary silent vigilance sinister in its intensity.

"In short, you're like the rest of the people in this section. You're afraid."

"Now y'u're shoutin', Miss Messiter. I sure am when it comes to shootin' off my mouth about Bannister."

"And you, Mr. Morgan?"

It struck her that the young puncher waited with a curious interest for the answer of the foreman.

"Did it look like I was afraid this mawnin', ma'am?" he asked, with narrowed eyes.

"No, you all seemed brave enough then—when you had him eight to one."

"I wasn't there," hastily put in McWilliams. "I don't go gunning for my man without giving him a show."

"I do," retorted Morgan cruelly. "I'd go if we was fifty to one. We'd 'a' got him, too, if it hadn't been for Miss Messiter. 'Twas a chance we ain't likely to get again for a year."

"It wasn't your fault you didn't kill him, Mr. Morgan," she said, looking hard at him. "You may be interested to know that your last shot missed him only about six inches, and me about four."

"I didn't know who you were," he sullenly defended.

"I see. You only shoot at women when you don't know who they are." She turned her back on him pointedly and addressed herself to McWilliams. "You can tell the men working on this ranch that I won't have any more such attacks on this man Bannister. I don't care what or who he is. I don't propose to have him murdered by my employees. Let the law take him and hang him. Do you hear?"

"I ce'tainly do, and the boys will get the word straight," he replied.

"I take it since yuh are *giving* your orders through Mac, yuh don't need me any longer for your foreman," bullied Morgan.

"You take it right, sir," came her crisp reply. "McWilliams will be my foreman from today."

The man's face, malignant and wolfish, suddenly lost its mask. That she would so promptly call his bluff was the last thing he had expected. "That's all right. I reckon yuh think yuh know your own business, but I'll put it to yuh straight. Long as yuh live you'll be sorry for this."

And with that he wheeled away.

She turned to her new foreman and found him less radiant than she could have desired. "I'm right sorry y'u did that. I'm afraid y'u'll make trouble for yourself," he said quietly.

"Why?"

"I don't know myself just why." He hesitated before adding: "They say him and Bannister is thicker than they'd ought to be. It's a cinch that he's in cahoots somehow with that Shoshone bunch of bad men."

"But—why, that's ridiculous. Only this morning he was trying to kill Bannister himself."

"That's what I don't just savvy. There's a whole lot about that business I don't get next to, I guess Bannister is at the head of them. Everybody seems agreed about that. But the whole thing is a tangle of contradiction to me. I've milled it over a heap in my mind, too."

"What are some of the contradictions?"

"Well, here's one right off the bat, as we used to say back in the States. Bannister is a great musician, they claim; fine singer, and all that. Now I happen to know he can't sing any more than a bellowing yearling."

"How do you know?" she asked, her eyes shining with interest.

"Because I heard him try it. 'Twas one day last summer when I was out cutting trail of a bunch of strays down by Dead Cow Creek. The day was hot, and I lay down behind a cottonwood and dropped off to sleep. When I awakened it didn't take me longer'n an hour to discover what had woke me. Somebody on the other side of the creek was trying to sing. It was ce'tainly the limit. Pretty soon he come out of the brush, and I seen it was Bannister."

"You're sure it was Bannister?"

"If seeing is believing, I'm sure."

"And was his singing really so bad?"

"I'd hate ever to hear worse."

"Was he singing when you saw him?"

"No, he'd just quit. He caught sight of my pony grazing, and hunted cover real prompt."

"Then it might have been another man singing in the thicket."

"It might, but it wasn't. Y'u see, I'd followed him through the bush by his song, and he showed up the moment I expected him."

"Still there might have been another man there singing."

"One chance in a million," he conceded.

A sudden hope flamed up like tow in her heart. Perhaps, after all, Ned Bannister was not the leader of the outlaws. Perhaps somebody else was masquerading in his name, using Bannister's unpopularity as a shield to cover his iniquities. Still, this was an unlikely hypothesis, she had to admit. For why should he allow his good name to be dragged in the dust without any effort to save it? On a sudden impulse the girl confided her doubt to McWilliams.

"You don't suppose there can be any mistake, do you? Somehow I can't think him as bad as they say. He looks awfully reckless, but one feels one could trust his face."

"Same here," agreed the new foreman. "First off when I saw him my think was, 'I'd like to have that man backing my play when I'm sitting in the game with Old Man Hard Luck reaching out for my blue chips.'"

"You don't think faces lie, do you?"

"I've seen them that did, but, gen'rally speaking, tongues are a heap likelier to get tangled with the truth. But I reckon there ain't any doubt about Bannister. He's known over all this Western country."

The young woman sighed. "I'm afraid you're right."

CHAPTER V

THE DANCE AT FRASER'S

H eard tell yet of the dance over to Fraser's?"
He was a young man of a brick red countenance and he wore loosely round his neck the best polka dot silk handkerchief that could be bought in Gimlet Butte, also such gala attire as was usually reserved only for events of importance. Sitting his horse carelessly in the plainsman's indolent fashion, he asked his question of McWilliams in front of the Lazy D bunkhouse.

"Nope. When does the shindig come off?"

"Friday night. Big thing. Y'u want to be there. All y'u lads."

"Mebbe some of us will ride over."

He of the polka dot kerchief did not appear quite satisfied. His glance wandered toward the house, as it had been doing occasionally since the moment of his arrival.

"Y'u bet this dance is ace high, Mac. Fancy costumes and masks. Y'u can rent the costumes over to Slauson's for three per. Texas, he's going to call the dances. Music from Gimlet Butte. Y'u want to get it tucked away in your thinker that this dance ain't on the order of culls. No, sirree, it's cornfed."

"Glad to hear of it. I'll cipher out somehow to be there, Slim."

Slim's glance took in the ranchhouse again. He had

ridden twenty-three miles out of his way to catch a glimpse of the newly arrived mistress of the Lazy D, the report of whose good looks and adventures had traveled hand in hand through many cañons even to the heart of the Tetons. It had been on Skunk Creek that he had heard of her three days before, and now he had come to verify the tongue of rumor, to see her quite casually, of course, and do his own appraising. It began to look as if he were going to have to ride off without a glimpse of her.

He nodded toward the house, turning a shade more purple than his native choleric hue. "Y'u want to bring your boss with y'u, Mac. We been hearing a right smart lot about her and the boys would admire to have her present. It's going to be strictly according to Hoyle—no rough-house plays go, y'understand."

"I'll speak to her about it." Mac's deep amusement did not reach the surface. He was quite well aware that Slim was playing for time and that he was too bashful to plump out the desire that was in him. "Great the way cows are jumpin', ain't it?"

"Sure. Well, I'll be movin' along to Slauson's. I just drapped in on my way. Thought mebbe y'u hadn't heard tell of the dance."

"Much obliged. Was it for old man Slauson y'u dug up all them togs, Slim? He'll ce'tainly admire to see y'u in that silk tablecloth y'u got round your neck."

Slim's purple deepened again. "Y'u go to grass, Mac. I don't aim to ask y'u to be my valley yet awhile."

"C'rect. I was just wondering do all the Triangle Bar

58

boys ride the range so handsome?"

"Don't y'u worry about the Triangle Bar boys," advised the embarrassed Slim, gathering up his bridle reins.

With one more reluctant glance in the direction of the house he rode away. When he reached the corral he looked back again. His gaze showed him the boyish foreman doubled up with laughter; also the sweep of a white skirt descending from the piazza.

"Now, ain't that hoodooed luck?" the aggrieved rider of the Triangle Bar outfit demanded of himself "I made my getaway about three shakes too soon, by gum!"

Her foreman was in the throes of mirth when Helen Messiter reached him.

"Include me in the joke," she suggested.

"Oh, I was just thinkin'," he explained inadequately.

"Does it always take you that way?"

"About these boys that drop in so frequent on business these days. Funny how fond they're getting of the Lazy D. There was that stock detective happened in yesterday to show how anxious he was about your cows. Then the two Willow Creek riders that wanted a job punching for y'u, not to mention the Shoshone miner and the storekeeper from Gimlet Butte and Soapy Sothern and—"

"Still I don't quite see the joke."

"It ain't any joke with them. Serious business, ma'am."

"What happened to start you on this line?"

"The lad riding down the road on that piebald pinto.

He come twenty miles out of his way, plumb dressed for a wedding, all to give me an invite to a dance at Fraser's. Y'u would call that real thoughtful of him, I expect."

She gayly sparkled. "A real ranch dance—the kind you have been telling me about. Are Ida and I invited?"

"Invited? Slim hinted at a lynching if I came without y'u."

She laughed softly, merry eyes flashing swiftly at him. "How gallant you Westerners are, even though you do turn it into burlesque."

His young laugh echoed hers. "Burlesque nothing. My life wouldn't be worth a thing if I went alone. Honest, I wouldn't dare."

"Since the ranch can't afford to lose its foreman Ida and I will go along," she promised. "That is, if it is considered proper here."

"Proper. Good gracious, ma'am! Every lady for thirty miles round will be there, from six months old to eighty odd years. It wouldn't be *proper* to stay at home."

The foreman drove her to Fraser's in a surrey, with Ida Henderson and one of the Lazy D punchers on the back seat. The drive was over twenty-five miles, but in that silent starry night every mile was a delight. Part of the way led through a beautiful cañon, along the rocky mountain road of which the young man guided the rig with unerring skill. Beyond the gorge the country debouched into a grassy park that fell away from their feet for miles. It was in this basin that the Fraser ranch lay.

The strains of the fiddle and the thumping of feet could be heard as they drove up. Already the rooms seemed to be pretty well filled, as Helen noticed when they entered. Three sets were on the floor for a quadrille and the house shook with the energy of the dancers. On benches against the walls were seated the spectators, and on one of them stood Texas calling the dance.

"Alemane left. Right hand t'yer pardner and grand right and left. Ev-v-rybody swing," chanted the caller.

A dozen rough young fellows were clustered near the front door, apparently afraid to venture farther lest their escape be cut off. Through these McWilliams pushed a way for his charges, the cowboys falling back respectfully at once when they discovered the presence of Miss Messiter.

In the bedroom where she left her wraps the mistress of the Lazy D found a dozen or more infants and several of their mothers. In the kitchen were still other women and babies, some of the former very old and of the latter very young. A few of the babies were asleep, but most of them were still very much alive to this scene of unwonted hilarity in their young lives.

As soon as she emerged into the general publicity of the dancing room her foreman pounced upon Helen and led her to a place in the head set that was making up. The floor was rough, the music jerky and uncertain, the quadrilling an exhibition of joyous and awkward abandon; but its picturesque lack of convention appealed to the girl from Michigan. It rather startled her to be swung so vigorously, but a glance about the room

61

showed that these humorous-eyed Westerners were merely living up to the duty of the hour as they understood it.

At the close of the quadrille Helen found herself being introduced to "Mr. Robins," alias Slim, who drew one of his feet back in an embarrassed bow.

"I enjoy to meet y'u, ma'am," he assured her, and supplemented this with a request for the next dance, after which he fell into silence that was painful in its intensity.

Nearly all the dances were squares, as few of those present understood the intricacies of the waltz and two-step. Hence it happened that the proficient McWilliams secured three round dances with his mistress.

It was during the lunch of sandwiches, cake and coffee that Helen perceived an addition to the company. The affair had been advertised a costume ball, but most of those present had construed this very liberally. She herself, to be sure, had come as Mary Queen of Scots, Mac was arrayed in the scarlet tunic and tight-fitting breeches of the Northwest Mounted Police, and perhaps eight or ten others had made some attempt at representing some one other than they were. She now saw another, apparently a new arrival, standing in the doorway negligently. A glance told her that he was made up for a road agent and that his revolvers and mask were a part of the necessary costuming.

Slowly his gaze circled the room and came round to her. His eyes were hard as diamonds and as flashing, so that the impact of their meeting looks seemed to shock her physically. He was a tall man, swarthy of hue, and he carried himself with a light ease that looked silken strong. Something in the bearing was familiar, yet not quite familiar either. It seemed to suggest a resemblance to somebody she knew. And in the next thought she knew that the somebody was Ned Bannister.

The man spoke to Fraser, just then passing with a cup of coffee, and Helen saw the two men approach. The stranger was coming to be formally introduced.

"Shake hands with Mr. Holloway, Miss Messiter. He's from up in the hill country and he rode to our frolic. Y'u've got three guesses to figure out what he's made up as."

"One will be quite enough, I think," she answered coldly.

Fraser departed on his destination with the coffee and the newcomer sat down on the bench beside her.

"One's enough, is it?" he drawled smilingly.

"Quite, but I'm surprised so few came in costume. Why didn't you? But I suppose you had your reasons."

"Didn't I? I'm supposed to be a bad man from the hills."

She swept him casually with an indifferent glance. "And isn't that what you are in real life?"

His sharp scrutiny chiseled into her. "What's that?"

"You won't mind if I forget and call you Mr. Bannister instead of Mr. Holloway?"

She thought his counterfeit astonishment perfect.

"So I'm Ned Bannister, am I?"

Their eyes clashed.

"Aren't you?"

She felt sure of it, and yet there was a lurking doubt. For there was in his manner something indescribably more sinister than she had felt in him on that occasion when she had saved his life. Then a debonair recklessness had been the outstanding note, but now there was something ribald and wicked in him.

"Since y'u put it as a question, common politeness demands an answer. Ned Bannister is my name."

"You are the terror of this country?"

"I shan't be a terror to y'u, ma'am, if I can help it," he smiled.

"But you are the man they call the king?"

"I have that honor."

"Honor?"

At the sharp scorn of her accent he laughed.

"Do you mean that you are proud of your villainy?" she demanded.

"Y'u've ce'tainly got the teacher habit of asking questions," he replied with a laugh that was a sneer.

A shadow fell across them and a voice said quietly, "She didn't wait to ask any when she saved your life down in the coulee back of the Lazy D."

The shadow was Jim McWilliams's, and its owner looked down at the man beside the girl with steady, hostile eyes.

"Is this your put in, sir?" the other flashed back.

"Yes, seh, it is. The boys don't quite like seeing your hardware so prominent at a social gathering. In this community guns don't come into the house at a ranch

64

dance. I'm a committee to mention the subject and to collect your thirty-eights if y'u agree with us."

"And if I don't agree with y'u?"

"There's all outdoors ready to receive y'u, seh. It would be a pity to stay in the one spot where your welcome's wore thin."

"Still I may choose to stay."

"Ce'tainly, but if y'u decide that way y'u better step out on the porch and talk it over with us where there ain't ladies present."

"Isn't this a costume dance? What's the matter with my guns? I'm an outlaw, ain't I?"

"I don't know whether y'u are or not, seh. If y'u say y'u are we're ready to take your word. The guns have to be shucked if y'u stay here. They might go off accidental and scare the ladies."

The man rose blackly. "I'll remember this. If y'u knew who y'u were getting so gay with—"

I can guess, Mr. Holloway, the kind of an outfit y'u freight with, and I expect I could put a handle to another name for you."

"By God, if y'u dare to say—"

"I don't dare, especially among so many ladies," came McWilliams's jaunty answer.

The eyes of the two men gripped, after which Holloway swung on his heel and swaggered defiantly out of the house.

Presently there came the sound of a pony's feet galloping down the road. It had not yet died away when Texas announced that the supper intermission was over.

"Pardners for a quadrille. Ladies' choice." The dance was on again full swing. The fiddlers were tuning up and couples gathering for a quadrille. Denver came to claim Miss Messiter for a partner. Apparently even the existence of the vanished Holloway was forgotten. But Helen remembered it, and pondered over the affair long after daylight had come and brought with it an end to the festivities.

CHAPTER VI

A PARTY CALL

T he mistress of the Lazy D, just through with her morning visit to the hospital in the bunkhouse, stopped to read the gaudy poster tacked to the wall. It was embellished with the drawing of a placid rider astride the embodiment of fury incarnate, under which was the legend: "Stick to Your Saddle."

BIG FOURTH OF JULY CELEBRATION
AT GIMLET BUTTE.

ROPING AND BRONCO BUSTING CONTESTS
FOR THE CHAMPIONSHIP OF THE WORLD
AND BIG PRIZES,

Including $1,000 for the Best Rider and the Same for Best Roper. Cow Pony Races, Ladies' Races and Ladies' Riding Contest, Fireworks,

EVERYBODY COME AND TURN YOUR WOLF LOOSE.

A sudden thud of pounding hoofs, a snatch of rag-time, and her foreman swept up in a cloud of white dust. His pony came from a gallop to an instant halt, and simultaneously Mac landed beside her, one hand holding the wide-brimmed hat he had snatched off in his descent, the other hitched by a casual thumb to the belt of his chaps.

She laughed. "You really did it very well."

Mac blushed. He was still young enough to take pride in his picturesque regalia, to prefer the dramatic way of doing a commonplace thing. But, though he liked this girl's trick of laughing at him with a perfectly grave face out of those dark, long-lashed eyes, he would have liked it better if sometimes they had given back the applause he thought his little tricks merited.

"Sho! That's foolishness," he deprecated.

"I suppose they got you to sit for this picture;" and she indicated the poster with a wave of her hand.

"That ain't a real picture," he explained, and when she smiled added, "as of cou'se y'u know. No hawss ever pitched that way—and the saddle ain't right. Fact is, it's all wrong."

"How did it come here? It wasn't here last night."

I reckon Denver brought it from Slauson's. He was ridin' that country yesterday, and as the boys was out of smokin' he come home that way."

"I supose you'll all go?"

"I reckon."

"And you'll ride?"

"I aim to sit in."

"At the roping, too?"

"No, m'm. I ain't so much with the rope. it takes a Mexican to snake a rope."

"Then I'll be able to borrow only a thousand dollars from you to help buy that bunch of young cows we were speaking about," she mocked.

"Only a thousand," he grinned. "And it ain't a cinch I'll win. There are three or four straight-up riders on this range. A fellow come from the Hole-in-the-Wall and won out last year."

"And where were you?"

"Oh, I took second prize," he explained, with obvious indifference.

"Well, you had better get first this year. We'll have to show them the Lazy D hasn't gone to sleep."

"Sure thing," he agreed.

"Has that buyer from Cheyenne turned up yet?" she asked, reverting to business.

"Not yet. Do y'u want I should make the cut soon as he comes?"

"Don't you think his price is a little low—twenty dollars from brand up?"

"It's a scrub bunch. We want to get rid of them, anyway. But you're the doctor," he concluded slangily.

She thought a moment. "We'll let him have them, but

don't make the cut till I come back. I'm going to ride over to the Twin Buttes."

His admiring eyes followed her as she went toward the pony that was waiting saddled with the rein thrown to the ground. She carried her slim, lithe figure with a grace, a lightness, that few women could have rivaled. When she had swung to the saddle, she half-turned in her seat to call an order to the foreman.

"I think, Mac, you had better run up those horses from Eagle Creek. Have Denver and Missou look after them."

"Sure, ma'am," he said aloud; and to himself: "She's ce'tainly a thoroughbred. Does everything well she tackles. I never saw anything like it. I'm a Chink if she doesn't run this ranch like she had been at it fohty years. Same thing with her gasoline bronc. That pinto, too. He's got a bad eye for fair, but she makes him eat out of her hand. I reckon the pinto is like the rest of us— clean mashed." He put his arms on the corral fence and grew introspective. "Blamed if I know what it is about her. 'Course she's a winner on looks, but that ain't it alone. I guess it's on account of her being such a game little gentleman. When she turns that smile loose on a fellow—well, there's sure sunshine in the air. And game—why, Ned Bannister ain't gamer himself."

Mr. McWilliams had climbed lazily to the top board of the fence. He was an energetic youth, but he liked to do his thinking at his ease. Now, as his gaze still followed its lodestar, he suddenly slipped from his seat and ran forward, pulling the revolver from its scabbard as he ran. Into his eyes had crept a tense alertness, the shining watchfulness of the tiger ready for its spring.

The cause of the change in the foreman of the Lazy D was a simple one, and on its face innocent enough. It was merely that a stranger had swung in casually at the gate of the short stable lane, and was due to meet Miss Messiter in about ten seconds. So far good enough. A dozen travelers dropped in every day, but this particular one happened to be Ned Bannister.

From the stable door a shot rang out. Bannister ducked and shouted genially: "Try again."

But Helen Messiter whirled her pony as on a half-dollar, and charged down on the stable.

"Who fired that shot?" she demanded, her eyes blazing.

The horse-wrangler showed embarrassment. He had found time only to lean the rifle against the wall.

"I reckon I did, ma'am. Y'u see—"

"Did you get my orders about this feud?" she interrupted crisply.

"Yes, ma'am, but—"

"Then you may call for your time. When I give my men orders I expect them to obey."

"I wouldn't 'a' shot if I'd knowed y'u was so near him. Y'u was behind that summer kitchen," he explained lamely.

"You only expect to obey orders when I'm in sight. Is that it?" she asked hotly, and without waiting for an answer delivered her ultimatum. "Well, I won't have it.

70

I run this ranch as long as I am its owner. Do you understand?"

"Yes, ma'am. I hadn't ought to have did it, but when I seen Bannister it come over me I owed him a pill for the one he sent me last week down in the coulee. So I up and grabbed the rifle and let him have it."

"Then you may up and grab your trunk for Medicine Hill. Shorty will drive you tomorrow."

When she returned to her unexpected guest, Helen found him in conversation with McWilliams. The latter's gun had found again its holster, but his brown, graceful hand hovered close to its butt.

"Seems like a long time since the Lazy D has been honored by a visit from Mr. Bannister," he was saying, with gentle irony.

"That's right. So I have come to make up for lost time," came Bannister's quiet retort.

Miss Messiter did not know much about Wyoming human nature in the raw, but she had learned enough to be sure that the soft courtesy of these two youths covered a stark courage that might leap to life any moment. Wherefore she interposed.

"We'll be pleased to show you over the place, Mr. Bannister. As it happens, we are close to the hospital. Shall we begin there?"

Her cool, silken defiance earned a smile from the visitor. "All your cases doing well, ma'am?"

"It's very kind of you to ask. I suppose you take an interest because they are *your* cases, too, in a way of speaking?"

"Mine? Indeed!"

"Yes. If it were not for you I'm afraid our hospital would be empty."

"It must be right pleasant to be nursed by Miss Messiter. I reckon the boys are grateful to me for scattering my lead so promiscuous."

"I heard one say he would like to lam your haid tenderly," murmured McWilliams.

"With a two-by-four, I suppose," laughed Bannister.

"Shouldn't wonder. But, looking y'u over casual, it occurs to me he might get sick of his job befo' he turned y'u loose," McWilliams admitted, with a glance of admiration at the clean power showing in the other's supple lines.

Nor could either the foreman or his mistress deny the tribute of their respect to the bravado of this scamp who sat so jauntily his seat regardless of what the next moment might bring forth. Three wounded men were about the place, all presumably quite willing to get a clean shot at him in the open. One of them had taken his chance already, and missed. Their visitor had no warrant for knowing that a second might not any instant try his luck with better success. Yet he looked every inch the man on horseback, no whit disturbed, not the least conscious of any danger. Tall, spare, broad shouldered, this berry-brown young man, crowned with close-cropped curls, sat at the gates of the enemy very much at his insolent ease.

"I came over to pay my party call," he explained.

"It really wasn't necessary. A run in the machine is

72

not a formal function."

"Maybe not in Kalamazoo."

"I thought perhaps you had come to get my purse and the sixty-three dollars," she derided.

"No, ma'am; nor yet to get that bunch of cows I was going to rustle from you to buy an auto. I came to ask you to go riding with me."

The audacity of it took her breath. Of all the outrageous things she had ever heard, this was the cream. An acknowledged outlaw, engaged in feud with her retainers over that deadly question of the run of the range, he had sauntered over to the ranch where lived a dozen of his enemies, three of them still scarred with his bullets, merely to ask her to go riding with him. The magnificence of his bravado almost obliterated its impudence. Of course she would not think of going. The idea! But her eyes glowed with appreciation of his courage, not the less because the consciousness of it was so conspicuously absent from his manner.

"I think not, Mr. Bannister"—and her face almost imperceptibly stiffened. "I don't go riding with strangers, nor with men who shoot my boys. And I'll give you a piece of advice, sir. That is, to burn the wind back to your home. Otherwise I won't answer for your life. My punchers don't love you, and I don't know how long I can keep them from you. You're not wanted here any more than you were at the dance the other evening."

McWilliams nodded. "That's right. Y'u better roll your trail, seh; and if y'u take my advice, you'll throw gravel lively. I seen two of the boys cutting acrost that pasture five minutes ago. They looked as if they might be haided to cut y'u off, and I allow it may be their night to howl. Miss Messiter don't want to be responsible for y'u getting lead poisoning."

"Indeed!" Their visitor looked politely interested. "This solicitude for me is very touching. I observe that both of you are care fully blocking me from the bunkhouse in order to prevent another practice-shot. If I can't persuade you to join me in a ride, Miss Messiter, I reckon I'll go while I'm still unpunctured." He bowed, and gathered the reins for departure.

"One moment! Mr. McWilliams and I are going with you," the girl announced.

"Changed your mind? Think you'll take a little *pasear,* after all?"

"I don't want to be responsible for your killing. We'll see you safe off the place," she answered curtly.

The foreman fell in on one side of Bannister, his mistress on the other. They rode in close formation, to lessen the chance of an ambuscade. Bannister alone chatted at his debonair ease, ignoring the responsibility they felt for his safety.

"I got my ride, after all," he presently chuckled. "To be sure, I wasn't expecting Mr. McWilliams to chaperon us. But that's an added pleasure."

"Would it be an added pleasure to get bumped off to kingdom come?" drawled the foreman, giving a reluctant admiration to his aplomb.

"Thinking of those willing boys of yours again, are

74

you?" laughed Bannister. "They're ce'tainly a heap prevalent with their hardware, but their hunting don't seem to bring home any meat."

"By the way, how *is* your ankle, Mr. Bannister? I forgot to ask." This shot from the young woman.

He enjoyed it with internal mirth. "They did happen on the target that time," he admitted. "Oh, it's getting along fine, but I aim to do most of my walking on horseback for a while."

They swept past the first dangerous grove of cottonwoods in safety, and rounded the boundary fence corner.

"They're in that bunch of pines over there," said the foreman, after a single sweep of his eyes in that direction.

"Yes, I see they are. You oughtn't to let your boys wear red bandannas when they go gunning, Miss Messiter. It's an awful careless habit."

Helen herself could see no sign of life in the group of pines, but she knew their keen, trained eyes had found what hers could not. Riding with one or another of her cowboys, she had often noticed how infallibly they could read the country for miles around. A scattered patch on a distant hillside, though it might be a half-hour's ride from them, told them a great deal more than seemed possible. To her the dark spots sifted on that slope meant scrub underbrush, if there was any meaning at all in them. But her riders could tell not only whether they were alive, but could differentiate between sheep and cattle. Indeed, McWilliams could nearly always tell whether they were *her* cattle or not. He was unable to explain to her how he did it. By a sort of instinct, she supposed.

The pines were negotiated in safety, and on the part of the men with a carelessness she could not understand. For after they had passed there was a spot between her shoulder-blades that seemed to tingle in expectation of a possible bullet boring its way through. But she would have died rather than let them know how she felt.

Perhaps Bannister understood, however, for he remarked casually: "I wouldn't be ambling past so leisurely if I was riding alone. It makes a heap of difference who your company is, too. Those punchers wouldn't take a chance at me now for a million dollars."

"No, they're some haidstrong, but they ain't plumb locoed," agreed Mac.

Fifteen minutes later Helen drew up at the line corner. "We'll part company here, Mr. Bannister. I don't think there is any more danger from my men."

"Before we part there is something I want to say. I hold that a man has as much right to run sheep on these hills as cows. It's government land, and neither one of us owns it. It's bound to be a case of the survival of the fittest. If sheep are hardier and more adapted to the country, then cows have got to *vamos*. That's nature, as it looks to me. The buffalo and the antelope have gone, and I guess cows have got to take their turn."

Her scornful eyes burned him. "You came to tell me

76

that, did you? Well, I don't believe a word of it. I'll not yield my rights without a fight. You may depend on that."

"Here, too," nodded her foreman. "I'm with my boss clear down the line. And as soon as she lets lets me turn loose my six-gun, you'll hear it pop, seh."

"I have not a doubt of it, Mr. McWilliams," returned the sheepman blithely. "In the meantime I was going to say that though most of my interests are in sheep instead of cattle—"

"I thought most of your interests were in other people's property," interrupted the young woman.

"It goes into sheep ultimately," he smiled. "Now, what I am trying to get at is this: I'm in debt to you a heap, Miss Messiter, and since I'm not all yellow cur, I intend to play fair with you. I have ordered my sheep back across the dead-line. You can have this range to yourself for your cattle. The fight's off so far as we personally are concerned."

A hint of deeper color touched her cheeks. Her manner had been cavalier at best; for the most part frankly hostile; and all the time the man was on an errand of good-will. Certainly he had scored at her expense, and she was ashamed of herself.

"Y'u mean that you're going to respect the dead-line?" asked Mac in surprise.

"I didn't say quite that," explained the sheepman. "What I said was that I meant to keep on my side of it so far as the Lazy D cattle are concerned. I'll let your range alone."

"But y'u mean to cross it down below where the Bar Double-E cows run?"

Bannister's gay smile touched the sardonic face. "Do you invite the public to examine your hand when you sit into a game of poker, Mr. McWilliams?"

"You're dead right. It's none of my business what y'u do so long as y'u keep off our range," admitted the foreman. "And next time the conversation happens on Mr. Bannister, I'll put in my little say-so that he ain't all black."

"That's very good of you, sir," was the other's ironical retort.

The girl's gauntleted hand offered itself impulsively. "We can't be friends under existing circumstances, Mr. Bannister. But that does not alter the fact that I owe you an apology. You came as a peace envoy, and one of my men shot at you. Of course, he did not understand the reason why you came, but that does not matter. I did not know your reason myself, and I know I have been very inhospitable."

"Are you shaking hands with Ned Bannister the sheepman or Ned Bannister the outlaw?" asked the owner of that name, with a queer little smile that seemed to mock himself.

"With Ned Bannister the gentleman. If there is another side to him I don't know it personally."

He flushed underneath the tan, but very plainly with pleasure. "Your opinions are right contrary to Hoyle, ma'am. Aren't you aware that a sheepman is the lowest thing that walks? Ask Mr. McWilliams."

"I have known stockmen of that opinion, but—"

The foreman's sentence was never finished. From a clump of bushes a hundred yards away came the crack of a rifle. A bullet sang past, cutting a line that left on one side of it Bannister, on the other Miss Messiter and her foreman. Instantly the two men slid from their horses on the farther side, dragged down the young woman behind the cover of the broncos, and arranged the three ponies so as to give her the greatest protection available. Somehow the weapons that garnished them had leaped to their hands before their feet touched the ground.

"That coyote isn't one of our men. I'll back that opinion high," said McWilliams promptly.

"Who is he?" the girl whispered.

"That's what we're going to find out pretty soon," returned Bannister grimly. "Chances are it's me he is trying to gather. Now, I'm going to make a break for that cottonwood. When I go, you better run up a white handkerchief and move back from the firing-line. Turn Buck loose when you leave. He'll stay around and come when I whistle."

He made a run for it, zigzagging through the sage-brush so swiftly as to offer the least certain mark possible for a sharpshooter. Yet twice the rifle spoke before he reached the cottonwood.

Meanwhile Mac had fastened the handkerchief of his mistress on the end of a switch he had picked up and was edging out of range. His tense, narrowed gaze never left the bush-clump from which the shots were

79

being pumped, and he was careful during their retreat to remain on the danger side of the road, in order to cover Helen.

"I guess Bannister's right. He don't want us, whoever he is."

And even as he murmured it, the wind of a bullet lifted his hat from his head. He picked it up and examined it. The course of the bullet was marked by a hole in the wide brim, and two more in the side and crown.

"He ce'tainly ventilated it proper. I reckon, ma'am, we'll make a run for it. Lie low on the pinto's neck, with your haid on the off side. That's right. Let him out."

A mile and a half farther up the road Mac reined in, and made the Indian peace-sign. Two dejected figures came over the hill and resolved themselves into punchers of the Lazy D. Each of them trailed a rifle by his side.

"You're a fine pair of ring-tailed snorters, ain't y'u?" jeered the foreman. "Got to get gay and go projectin' round on the shoot after y'u got your ordehs to stay hitched. Anything to say for yo'selves?"

If they had it was said very silently.

"Now, Miss Messiter is going to pass it up this time, but from now on y'u don't go off on any private massacrees while y'u punch at the Lazy D. Git that? This hyer is the last call for supper in the dining-cah. If y'u miss it, y'u'll feed at some other chuckhouse." Suddenly the drawl of his sarcasm vanished. His voice carried the ring of peremptory command. "Jim, y'u go

80

back to the ranch with Miss Messiter, *and keep your eyes open.* Missou, I need y'u. We're going back. I reckon y'u better hang on to the stirrup, for we got to travel some. *Adios, señorita!*"

He was off at a slow lope on the road he had just come, the other man running beside the horse. Presently he stopped, as if the arrangement were not satisfactory; and the second man swung behind him on the pony. Later, when she turned in her saddle, she saw that they had left the road and were cutting across the plain, as if to take the sharpshooter in the rear.

Her troubled thoughts stayed with her even after she had reached the ranch. She was nervously excited, keyed up to a high pitch; for she knew that out on the desert, within a mile or two of her, men were stalking each other with life or death in the balance as the price of vigilance, skill and an unflawed steel nerve. While she herself had been in danger, she had been mistress of her fear. But now she could do nothing but wait, after ordering out such reinforcements as she could recruit without delay; and the inaction told upon her swift, impulsive temperament. Once, twice, the wind brought to her a faint sound.

She had been pacing the porch, but she stopped, white as a sheet. Behind those faint explosions might lie a sinister tragedy. Her mind projected itself into a score of imaginary possibilities. She listened, breathless in her tensity, but no further echo of that battlefield reached her. The sun still shone warmly on brown Wyoming. She looked down into a rolling plain that blurred in the distance from knobs and flat spaces into a single stretch that included a thousand rises and depressions. That roll of country teemed with life, but the steady, inexorable sun beat down on what seemed a shining, primeval waste of space. Yet somewhere in that space the tragedy was being determined—unless it had been already enacted.

She wanted to scream. The very stillness mocked her. So, too, did the clicking windmill, with its monotonous regularity. Her pony still stood saddled in the yard. She knew that her place was at home, and she fought down a dozen times the tremendous impulse to mount and fly to the field of combat.

She looked at her watch. How slowly the minutes dragged! It could not be only five minutes since she had looked last time. Again she fell to pacing the long west porch, and interrupted herself a dozen times to stop and listen.

"I can bear it no longer," she told herself at last, and in another moment was in the saddle plying her pinto with the quirt.

But before she reached the first cottonwoods she saw them coming. Her glasses swept the distant group, and with a shiver she made out the dreadful truth. They were coming slowly, carrying something between them. The girl did not need to be told that the object they were bringing home was their dead or wounded.

A figure on horseback detached itself from the huddle of men and galloped towards her. He was coming to break the news. But who was the victim? Bannister or

McWilliams she felt sure, by reason of the sinking heart in her; and then it came home that she would be hard hit if it were either.

The approaching rider began to take distinct form through her glasses. As he pounded forward she recognized him. It was the man nicknamed Denver. The wind was blowing strongly from her to him, and while he was still a hundred yards away she hurled her question.

His answer was lost in the wind sweep, but one word of it she caught. That word was "Mac."

CHAPTER VII

THE MAN FROM THE SHOSHONE FASTNESSES

Though the sharpshooter's rifle cracked twice during his run for the cottonwood, the sheepman reached the tree in safety . He could dodge through the brush as elusively as any man in Wyoming. It was a trick he had learned on the whitewashed football gridiron. For in his buried past this man had been the noted half-back of a famous college, and one of his specialties had been running the ball back after a catch through a broken field of opponents. The lesson that experience had then thumped into him had since saved his life on more than one occasion.

Having reached the tree, Bannister took immediate advantage of the lie of the ground to snake forward unobserved for another hundred feet. There was a dip from the foot of the tree, down which he rolled into the sage below. He wormed his way through the thick scrub brush to the edge of a dry creek, into the bed of which he slid. Then swiftly, his body bent beneath the level of the bank, he ran forward in the sand. He moved noiselessly, eyes and ears alert to aid him, and climbed the bank at a point where a live oak grew.

Warily he peeped out from behind its trunk and swept the plain for his foe. Nothing was to be seen of him. Slowly and patiently his eyes again went over the semicircle before him, for where death may lurk behind every foot of vegetation, every bump or hillock, the plainsman leaves as little as may be to chance. No faintest movement could escape the sheepman's eyes, no least stir fail to apprise his ears. Yet for many minutes he waited in vain, and the delay told him that he had to do with a trained hunter rather than a mere reckless cow-puncher. For somewhere in the rough country before him his enemy lay motionless, every faculty alive to the least hint of his presence.

It was the whirring flight of a startled dove that told Bannister the whereabouts of his foe. Two hundred yards from him the bird rose, and the direction it took showed that the man must have been trailing forward from the opposite quarter. The sheepman slipped back into the dry creek bed, retraced his steps for about a stone-throw, and again crawled up the bank.

For a long time he lay face down in the grass, his gaze riveted to the spot where he knew his opponent to be hidden. A faint rustle not born of the wind stirred the sage. Still Bannister waited. A less experienced plainsman would have blazed away and exposed his own position. But not this young man with the steel-wire nerves. Silent as the coming of dusk, no breaking twig or displaced brush betrayed his self-contained presence.

Something in the clump he watched wriggled forward and showed indistinctly through an opening in the underscrub. He whipped his rifle into position and fired twice. The huddled brown mass lurched forward and disappeared.

"Wonder if I got him? Seems to me I couldn't have missed clean," thought Bannister.

Silence as before, vast and unbroken.

A scramble of running feet tearing a path through the brush, a crouching body showing darkly for an eye-flash, and then the pounding of a horse's retreating feet.

Bannister leaped up, ran lightly across the intervening space, and with his repeater took a potshot at the galloping horseman.

"Missed!" he muttered, and at once gave a sharp whistle that brought his pony to him on the trot. He vaulted to the saddle and gave chase. It was rough going, but nothing in reason can stop a cow-pony. As sure footed as a mountain goat, as good a climber almost as a cat, Buck followed the flying horseman over perilous rock rims and across deep-cut creek beds. Panther-like he climbed up the steep creek sides without hesitation, for the round-up had taught him never to falter at stiff going so long as his rider put him at it.

It was while he was clambering out of the sheer sides of a wash that Bannister made a discovery. The man he pursued was wounded. Something in the manner of the fellow's riding had suggested this to him, but a drop of blood splashed on a stone that happened to meet his eye made the surmise a certainty.

He was gaining now—not fast, almost imperceptibly, but none the less surely. He could see the man looking over his shoulder, once, twice, and then again, with that hurried, fearful glance that measures the approach of retribution. Barring accidents, the man was his.

But the unforeseen happened. Buck stepped in the hole of a prairie dog and went down. Over his head flew the rider like a stone from a catapult.

How long Ned Bannister lay unconscious he never knew. But when he came to himself it was none too soon. He sat up dizzily and passed his hand over his head. Something had happened, What was it? Oh, yes, he had been thrown from his horse. A wave of recollection passed over, him, and his mind was clear once more. Presently he got to his feet and moved rather uncertainly toward Buck, for the horse was grazing quietly a few yards from him.

But half way to the pony he stopped. Voices, approaching by way of the bed of Dry Creek, drifted to him.

"He must 'a' turned and gone back. Mebbe he guessed we was there."

And a voice that Bannister knew, one that had a strangely penetrant, cruel ring of power through the drawl, made answer: "Judd said before he fainted he was sure the man was Ned Bannister. I'd ce'tainly like to meet up with my beloved cousin right now and even up a few old scores. By God, I'd make him sick before I finished with him!"

"I'll bet y'u would, Cap," returned the other, admiringly. "Think we'd better deploy here and beat up the scenery a few as we go?"

There are times when the mind works like lightning, flashes its messages on the wings of an electric current. For Bannister this was one of them. The whole situation lighted for him plainly as if it had been explained for an hour. His cousin had been out with a band of his cutthroats on some errand, and while returning to the fastnesses of the Shoshone Mountains had stopped to noon at a cow spring three or four miles from the Lazy D. Judd Morgan, whom he knew to be a lieutenant of the notorious bandit, had ridden toward the ranch in the hope of getting an opportunity to vent his anger against its mistress or some of her men. While pursuing the renegade Bannister had stumbled into a hornet's nest, and was in imminent danger of being stung to death. Even now the last speaker was scrambling up the bank toward him.

The sheepman had to choose between leaving his rifle and immediate flight. The latter was such a forlorn hope that he gave up Buck for the moment, and ran back to the place where his repeating Winchester had fallen. Without stopping he scooped the rifle up as he passed. In his day he had been a famous sprinter, and he scudded now for dear life. It was no longer a question of secrecy. The sound of men breaking their hurried way through the heavy brush of the creek bank came crisply to him. A voice behind shouted a warning, and from not a hundred yards in front of him came an answering shout. Hemmed in from the fore and the rear, he swung off at a right angle. An open stretch lay before him, but he had to take his desperate chance without cover. Anything was better than to be trapped like a wild beast driven by the beaters to the guns.

Across the bare, brown mesa he plunged; and before he had taken a dozen steps the first rifle had located its prey and was sniping at him. He had perhaps a hundred yards to cover ere the mesa fell away into a hollow, where he might find temporary protection in the scrub pines. And now a second marksman joined himself to the first. But he was going fast, already had covered half the distance, and it is no easy thing to bring down a live, dodging target.

Again the first gun spoke, and scored another miss, whereat a mocking, devilish laugh rang out in the sunshine.

"Y'u boys splash a heap of useless lead around the horizon. I reckon Cousin Ned's my meat. Y'u see, I get him in the flapper without spoiling him complete." And at the word he flung the rifle to his shoulder and fired with no apparent aim.

The running man doubled up like a cottontail, but found his feet again in an instant, though one arm hung limp by his side. He was within a dozen feet of the hilldrop and momentary safety.

"Shall I take him, Cap?" cried one of the men.

"No; he's mine." The rifle smoked once more and again the runner went down. But this time he plunged headlong down the slope and out of sight.

The outlaw chief turned on his heel. "I reckon he'll not run any more today. Bring him into camp and we'll take him along with us," he said carelessly, and walked away to his horse in the creek bed.

Two of the men started forward, but they stopped half way, as if rooted to the ground. For a galloping horseman suddenly drew up at the very point for which they were starting. He leaped to the ground and warned them back with his rifle. While he covered them a second man rode up and lifted Bannister to his saddle.

"Ready, Mac," he gave the word, and both horses disappeared with their riders over the brow of the hill. When the surprised desperadoes recovered themselves and reached that point the rescuers had disappeared in the heavy brush.

The alarm was at once given, and their captain, cursing them in a raucous bellow for their blunder, ordered immediate pursuit. It was some little time before the trail of the fugitives was picked up, but once discovered they were overhauled rapidly.

"We're not going to get out without swapping lead," McWilliams admitted anxiously. "I wisht y'u wasn't hampered with that load, but I reckon I'll have to try to stand them off alone."

"We bucked into a slice of luck when I happened on

his bronc mavericking around alone. Hadn't been for that we could never have made it," said Missou, who never crossed a bridge until he came to it.

"We haven't made it yet, old hoss, not by a long mile, and two more on top o' that. They're beginning to pump lead already. Huh! Got to drop your pills closer'n that 'fore y'u worry me."

"I believe he's daid, anyway," said Missou presently, peering down into the white face of the unconscious man.

"Got to hang onto the remains, anyhow, for Miss Helen. Those coyotes are too much of the wolf breed to leave him with them."

"Looks like they're gittin' the aim some better," equably remarked the other a minute later, when a spurt of sand flew up in front of him.

"They're ce'tainly crowding us. I expaict I better send them a 'How-de-do?' so as to discourage them a few." He took as careful aim as he could on the galloping horse, but his bullet went wide.

"They're gaining like sixty. It's my offhand opinion we better stop at that bunch of trees and argue some with them. No use buck-jumpin' along to burn the wind while they drill streaks of light through us."

"All right. Take the trees. Y'u'll be able to get into the game some then."

They debouched from the road to the little grove and slipped from their horses.

"Deader'n hell," murmured Missou, as he lifted the limp body from his horse. "But I guess we'll pack what's left back to the little lady at the Lazy D."

The leader of the pursuers halted his men just out of range and came forward alone, holding his right hand up in the usual signal of peace. In appearance he was not unlike Ned Bannister. There was the same long, slim, tiger build, with the flowing muscles rippling easily beneath the loose shirt; the same effect of power and dominance, the same clean, springy stride. The pose of the head, too, even the sweep of salient jaw, bore a marked resemblance. But similarity ceased at the expression. For instead of frankness there lurked here that hint of the devil of strong passion uncontrolled. He was the victim of his own moods, and in the space of an hour one might, perhaps, read in that face cold cunning, cruel malignity, leering ribaldry, as well as the hard-bitten virtues of unflinching courage and implacable purpose.

"I reckon you're near enough," suggested Mac, when the man had approached to within a hundred feet of the tree clump.

"*Y'u're* drawing the dead-line," the other acknowledged, indolently. "It won't take ten words to tell y'u what I want and mean to have. I'm giving y'u two minutes to hand me over the body of Ned Bannister. If y'u don't see it that way I'll come and make a lead mine of your whole outfit."

"Y'u can't come too quick, seh. We're here a-shootin', and don't y'u forget it," was McWilliams's prompt answer.

The sinister face of the man from the Shoshones darkened. "Y'u've signed your own death warrants," he let out through set teeth, and at the word swung on his heel.

"The ball's about to open. Pardners for a waltz. Have a dust-cutter, Mac, before she grows warm."

The puncher handed over his flask, and the other held it before his eye and appraised the contents in approved fashion. "Don't mind if I do. Here's how!"

"How!" echoed Missou, in turn, and tipped up the bottle till the liquor gurgled down his baked throat.

"He's fanning out his men so as to get us both at the front and back door. Lucky there ain't but four of them."

"I guess we better lie back to back," proposed Missou. "If our luck's good I reckon they're going to have a gay time rushing this fort."

A few desultory shots had already been dropped among the cottonwoods, and returned by the defendants when Missou let out a yell of triumph.

"Glory Hallelujah! Here comes the boys splittin' down the road hell-for-leather. That lopsided, ring-tailed snorter of a hawss-thief is gathering his wolves for a hike back to the tall timber. Feed me a cigareet, Mac. I plumb want to celebrate."

It was as the cow-puncher had said. Down the road a cloud of dust was sweeping toward them, in the centre of which they made out three hard-riding cowboys from the ranch. Farther back, in the distance, was another dust whirl. The outlaw chief's hard, vigilant gaze swept over the reinforcements, and decided instantly that the game had gone against him for the present. He whistled shrilly twice, and began a slow retreat toward the hills. The miscreants flung a few defiant shots at the advancing cowmen, and disappeared, swallowed up in the earth swells.

The homeward march was a slow one, for Bannister had begun to show signs of consciousness, and it was necessary to carry him with extreme care. While they were still a mile from the ranch-house the pinto and its rider could be seen loping toward them.

"Ride forward, Denver, and tell Miss Helen we're coming. Better have her get everything fixed to doctor him soon as we get there. Give him the best show in the world, and he'll still be sailing awful close to the divide. I'll bet a hundred plunks he'll cash in, anyway."

"Done!"

The voice came faintly from the improvised litter. Mac turned with a start, for he had not known that Bannister was awake to his surroundings. The man appeared the picture of helplessness, all the lusty power and vigor stricken out of him; but his indomitable spirit still triumphed over the physical collapse, for as the foreman looked a faint smile touched the ashen lips. It seemed to say: "Still in the ring, old man."

CHAPTER VIII

IN THE LAZY D HOSPITAL

Helen's first swift glance showed that the wounded man was Bannister. She turned in crisp command to her foreman.

"Have him taken to my room and put to bed there. We have no time to prepare another. And send one of the boys on your best horse for a doctor."

They carried the limp figure in with rough tenderness and laid him in the bed. McWilliams unbuckled the belt and drew off the chaps; then, with the help of Denver, undressed the wounded man and covered him with quilts. So Helen found him when she came in to attend his wounds, bringing with her such things as she needed for her task. Mrs. Winslow, the housekeeper, assisted her, and the foreman stayed to help, but it was on the mistress of the ranch that the responsibility of saving him fell. Missou was already galloping to Bear Creek for a doctor, but the girl knew that the battle must be fought and the issue decided before he could arrive.

He had fallen again into insensibility and she rinsed and dressed his wounds, working with the quiet impersonal certainty of touch that did not betray the inner turmoil of her soul. But McWilliams, his eyes following her every motion and alert to anticipate her needs, saw that the color had washed from her face and that she was controlling herself only to meet the demands of the occasion.

As she was finishing, the sheepman opened his eyes and looked at her.

"You are not to speak or ask questions. You have been wounded and we are going to take care of you," she ordered.

"That's right good of y'u. I ce'tainly feel mighty trifling." His wide eyes traveled round till they fell on the foreman. "Y'u see I came back to help fill your hospital. Am I there now? Where am I?" His gaze returned to Helen with the sudden irritation of the irresponsible sick.

"You are at the Lazy D, in my room. You are not to worry about anything. Everything's all right."

He took her at her word and his eyes closed; but presently he began to mutter unconnected words and phrases. When his lids lifted again there was a wilder look in his eyes, and she knew that delirium was beginning. At intervals it lasted for long; indeed, until the doctor came next morning in the small hours. He talked of many things Helen Messiter did not understand, of incidents in his past life, some of them jerky with the excitement of a tense moment, others apparently snatches of talk with relatives. It was like the babbling of a child, irrelevant and yet often insistent. He would in one breath give orders connected with the lambing of his sheep, in the next break into football talk, calling out signals and imploring his men to hold them or to break through and get the ball. Once he broke into curses, but his very oaths seemed to come from a clean heart and missed the vulgarity they might have had. Again his talk rambled inconsequently over his youth, and he would urge himself or someone else of the same name to better life.

"Ned, Ned, remember your mother," he would beseech. "She asked me to look after you. Don't go wrong." Or else it would be, "Don't disgrace the general, Ned. You'll break his heart if you blacken the old name." To this theme he recurred repeatedly, and she noticed that when he imagined himself in the East his language was correct and his intonation cultured, though still with a suggestion of a Southern softness.

But when he spoke of her his speech lapsed into the familiar drawl of Cattleland. "I ain't such a sweep as y'u think, girl. Some day I'll sure tell y'u all about it, and how I have loved y'u ever since y'u scooped me up in your car. You're the gamest little lady! To see y'u come a-sailin' down after me, so steady and businesslike, not turning a hair when the bullets hummed— I sure do love y'u, Helen." And then he fell upon her first name and called her by it a hundred times softly to himself.

This happened when she was alone with him, just before the doctor came. She heard it with starry eyes and with a heart that flushed for joy a warmer color into her cheeks. Brushing back the short curls, she kissed his damp forehead. It was in the thick of the battle, before he had weathered that point where the issues of life and death pressed closely, and even in the midst of her great fears it brought her comfort. She was to think often of it later, and always the memory was to be music in her heart. Even when she denied her love for him, assured herself it was impossible she could care for so shameful a villain, even then it was a sweet torture to allow herself the luxury of recalling his broken delirious phrases. At the very worst he could not be as bad as they said; some instinct told her this was impossible. His fearless devil-may-care smile, his jaunty, gallant bearing, these pleaded against the evidence for him. And yet was it conceivable that a man of spirit, a gentleman by training at least, would let himself lie under the odium of such a charge if he were not guilty? Her tangled thoughts fought this profitless conflict for days. Nor could she dismiss it from her mind. Even after he began to mend she was still on the rack. For in some snatch of good talk, when the fine quality of the man seemed to glow in his face, poignant remembrance would stab her with recollection of the difference between what he was and what he seemed to be.

One of the things that had been a continual surprise to Helen was the short time required by these deep-chested and clean-blooded Westerners to recover from apparently serious wounds. It was scarce more than two weeks since Bannister had filled the bunkhouse with wounded men, and already two of them were back at work and the third almost fit for service. For perhaps three days the sheepman's life hung in the balance, after which his splendid constitution and his outdoor life began to tell. The thermometer showed that the fever had slipped down a notch, and he was now sleeping wholesomely a good part of his time. Altogether, unless for some unseen contingency, the doctor prophesied that the sheepman was going to upset the probabilities and get well.

"Which merely shows, ma'am, what is possible when you give a sound man twenty-four hours a day in our hills for a few years," he added. "Thanks to your nursing he's going to shave through by the narrowest margin possible. I told him today that he owed his life to you, Miss Messiter."

"I don't think you need have told him that, Doctor," returned that young woman, not a little vexed at him, "especially since you have just been telling me that he owes it to Wyoming air and his own soundness of con-stitution."

When she returned to the sickroom to give her patient his medicine he wanted to tell her what the doctor had said, but she cut him off ruthlessly and told him not to talk.

"Mayn't I even say 'Thank you?'" he wanted to know.

"No; you talk far too much as it is."

He smiled. "All right. Y'u sit there in that chair, where I can see y'u doing that fancywork and I'll not say a word. It'll keep, all right, what I want to say."

"I notice you keep talking," she told him, dryly.

"Yes, ma'am. Y'u had better have let me say what I wanted to, but I'll be good now."

He fell asleep watching her, and when he awoke she

was still sitting there, though it was beginning to grow dark. He spoke before she knew he was awake.

"I'm going to get well, the doctor thinks."

"Yes, he told me," she answered.

"Did he tell y'u it was your nursing saved me?"

"Please don't think about that."

"What am I to think about? I owe y'u a heap, and it keeps piling up. I reckon y'u do it all because it's your Christian duty?" he demanded.

"It is my duty, isn't it?"

"I didn't say it wasn't, though I expaict Bighorn County will forget to give y'u a unanimous vote of thanks for doing it. I asked if y'u did it because it was your duty?"

"The reason doesn't matter so that I do it," she answered, steadily.

"Reasons matter some, too, though they ain't as important as actions out in this country. Back in Boston they figure more, and since y'u used to go to school back there y'u hadn't ought to throw down your professor of ethics."

"Don't you think you have talked enough for the present?" she smiled, and added: "If I make you talk whenever I sit beside you I shall have to stay away."

"That's where y'u've ce'tainly got the drop on me, ma'am. I'm a clam till y'u give the word."

Before a week he was able to sit up in a chair for an hour or two, and soon after could limp into the living room with the aid of a walking stick and his hostess. Under the tan he still wore an interesting pallor, but there could be no question that he was on the road to health.

"A man doesn't know what he's missing until he gets shot up and is brought to the Lazy D hospital, so as to let Miss Messiter exercise her Christian duty on him," he drawled, cheerfully, observing the sudden glow on her cheek brought by the reference to his unanswered question.

He made the lounge in the big sunny window his headquarters. From it he could look out on some of the ranch activities when she was not with him, could watch the line riders as they passed to and fro and command a view of one of the corrals. There was always, too, the turquoise sky, out of which poured a flood of light on the roll of hilltops. Sometimes he read to himself, but he was still easily tired, and preferred usually to rest. More often she read aloud to him while he lay back with his leveled eyes gravely on her till the gentle, cool abstraction she affected was disturbed and her perplexed lashes rose to reproach the intensity of his gaze.

She was of those women who have the heaven-born faculty of making home of such fortuitous elements as are to their hands. Except her piano and such knick-knacks as she had brought in a single trunk she had had to depend upon the resources of the establishment to which she had come, but it is wonderful how much can be done with some Navajo rugs, a bearskin, a few bits of Indian pottery and woven baskets and a judicious arrangement of scenic photographs. In a few days she would have her pictures from Kalamazoo, pending which her touch had transformed the big living room from a cheerless barn into a spot that was a comfort to the eye and heart. To the wounded man who lay there slowly renewing the blood he had lost the room was the apotheosis of home, less, perhaps, by reason of what it was in itself than because it was the setting for her presence—for her grave, sympathetic eyes, the sound of her clear voice, the light grace of her motion. He rejoiced in the delightful intimacy the circumstances made necessary. To hear snatches of joyous song and gay laughter even from a distance, to watch her as she came in and out on her daily tasks, to contest her opinions of books and life and see how eagerly she defended them; he wondered himself at the strength of the appeal these simple things made to him. Already he was dreading the day when he must mount his horse and ride back into the turbulent life from which she had for a time snatched him.

"I'll hate to go back to sheepherding," he told her one day at lunch, looking at her across a snow-white tablecloth upon which were a service of shining silver, fragile china teacups and plates stamped Limoges.

He was at the moment buttering a delicious French roll and she was daintily pouring tea from an old family heirloom. The contrast between this and the dust and the grease of a midday meal at the end of a "chuck wagon" lent accent to his smiling lamentation.

"A lot of sheepherding *you* do," she derided.

"A shepherd has to look after his sheep, y'u know."

"You herd sheep just about as much as I punch cows."

"I have to herd my herders, anyhow, and that keeps me on the move."

"I'm glad there isn't going to be any more trouble between you and the Lazy D. And that reminds me of another thing. I've often wondered who those men could have been that attacked you the day you were hurt."

She had asked the question almost carelessly, without any thought that this might be something he wished to conceal, but she recognized her mistake by the wariness that filmed his eyes instantly.

"Room there for a right interesting guessing contest," he replied.

"*You* wouldn't need to guess," she charged, on swift impulse.

"Meaning that I know?"

"You do know. You can't deny that you know."

"Well, say that I know?"

"Aren't you going to tell?"

He shook his head. "Not just yet. I've got private reasons for keeping it quiet a while."

"I'm sure they are creditable to you," came her swift ironic retort.

"Sure," he agreed, whimsically. "I must live up to the professional standard. Honor among thieves, y'u know."

CHAPTER IX

MISS DARLING ARRIVES

Miss Messiter clung to civilization enough, at least, to prefer that her chambermaid should be a woman rather than a Chinese. It did not suit her preconceived idea of the proper thing that Lee Ming should sweep floors, dust bric-a-brac, and make the beds. To see him slosh-sloshing around in his felt slippers made her homesick for Kalamazoo. There were other reasons why the proprieties would be better served by having another woman about the place; reasons that had to do with the chaperon system that even in the uncombed West makes its claims upon unmarried young women of respectability. She had with her for the present fourteen-year-old Ida Henderson, but this arrangement was merely temporary.

Wherefore on the morning after her arrival Helen had sent two letters back to "the States." One of these had been to Mrs. Winslow, a widow of fifty-five, inviting her to come out on a business basis as housekeeper of the Lazy D. The buxom widow had loved Helen since she had been a toddling baby, and her reply was immediate and enthusiastic. Eight days later she had reported in person. The second letter bore the affectionate address of Nora Darling, Detroit, Michigan. This also in time bore fruit at the ranch in a manner worthy of special mention.

It was the fourth day after Ned Bannister had been carried back to the Lazy D that Helen Messiter came out to the porch of the house with a letter in her hand. She found her foreman sitting on the steps waiting for her, but he got up as soon as he heard the fall of her light footsteps behind him.

"You sent for me, ma'am?" he asked, hat in hand.

"Yes; I want you to drive into Gimlet Butte and bring back a person whom you'll find at the Elk House waiting for you. I had rather you would go yourself, because I know you're reliable."

"Thank you, ma'am. How will I know him?"

"It's a woman—a spinster. She's coming to help Mrs. Winslow. Inquire for Miss Darling. She isn't used to jolting two days in a rig, but I know you will be careful of her."

"I'll surely be as careful of the old lady as if she was my own mother."

The mistress of the ranch smothered a desire to laugh. "I'm sure you will. At her age she may need a good deal of care. Be certain you take rugs enough."

"I'll take care of her the best I know how. I expect she's likely rheumatic, but I'll wrop her up till she looks like a Cheyenne squaw when a tourist is trying to get a free shoot at her with a camera."

"Please do. I want her to get a good impression of Wyoming so that she will stay. I don't know about the rheumatism, but you might ask her."

There were pinpoints of merriment behind the guileless innocence of her eyes, but they came to the surface only after the foreman had departed.

McWilliams ordered a team of young horses hitched, and presently set out on his two days' journey to Gimlet Butte. He reached that town in good season, left the team at a corral and walked back to the Elk House. The white dust of the plains was heavy on him, from the bandanna that loosely embraced the brown throat above the flannel shirt to the encrusted boots, but through it the good humor of his tanned face smiled fraternally on a young woman he passed at the entrance to the hotel. Her gay smile met his cordially, and she was still in his mind while he ran his eye down the register in search of the name he wanted. There it was—Miss Nora Darling, Detroit, Michigan—in the neatest of little round letters, under date of the previous day's arrivals.

"Is Miss Darling in?" asked McWilliams of the half-grown son of the landlady who served in lieu of clerk and porter.

"Nope! Went out a little while ago. Said to tell anybody to wait that asked for her."

Mac nodded, relieved to find that duty had postponed itself long enough for him to pursue the friendly smile that had not been wasted on him a few seconds before. He strolled out to the porch and decided at once that he needed a cigar more than anything else on earth. He was helped to a realization of his need by seeing the owner of the smile disappear in an adjoining drug store.

She was beginning on a nut sundae when the puncher drifted in. She continued to devote even her eyes to its consumption, while the foreman opened a casual con-

105

versation with the drug clerk and lit his cigar.

"How are things coming in Gimlet Butte?" he asked, by way of prolonging his stay rather than out of desire for information.

Yes, she certainly had the longest, softest lashes he had ever seen, and the ripest of cherry lips, behind the smiling depths of which sparkled two rows of tiny pearls. He wished she would look at *him* and smile again. There wasn't any use trying to melt a sundae with it, anyhow.

"Sure, it's a good year on the range and the price of cows jumping," he heard his sub-conscious self make answer to the patronizing inquiries of him of the "boiled" shirt.

Funny how pretty hair of that color was, especially when there was so much of it. You might call it a sort of coppery gold where the little curls escaped in tendrils and ran wild. A fellow—"

"Yes, I reckon most of the boys will drop around to the Fourth of July celebration. Got to cut loose once in a while, y'u know."

A shy glance shot him and set him a-tingle with a queer delight. Gracious, what pretty dark, velvety lashes she had!

She was rising already, and as she paid for her ice cream that innocent gaze smote him again with the brightest of Irish eyes conceivable. It lingered for just a ponderable sunlit moment on him. She had smiled once more.

After a decent interval Mac pursued his *petite*

charmer to the hotel. She was seated on the porch reading a magazine, and was absorbedly unconscious of him when he passed. For a few awkward moments he hung around the office, then returned to the porch and took the chair most distant from her. He had sat there a long ten minutes before she let her hands and the magazine fall into her lap and demurely gave him his chance.

"Can you tell me how far it is to the Lazy D ranch?"

"Seventy-two miles as the crow flies, ma'am."

"Thank you."

The conversation threatened to die before it was well born. Desperately McWilliams tried to think of something to say to keep it alive without being too bold.

"If y'u were thinking of traveling out that way I could give y'u a lift. I just came in to get another lady—an old lady that has just come to this country."

"Thank you, but I'm expecting a conveyance to meet me here. You didn't happen to pass one on the way, I suppose?"

"No, I didn't. What ranch were y'u going to, ma'am?"

"Miss Messiter's—the Lazy D."

A suspicion began to penetrate the foreman's brain. "Y'u ain't Miss Darling?"

"What makes you so sure I'm not?" she asked, tilting her dimpled chin toward him aggressively.

"Y'u're too young," he protested, helplessly.

"I'm no younger than you are," came her quick, indignant retort.

Thus boldly accused of his youth, the foreman blushed. "I didn't mean that. Miss Messiter said she was an old lady—"

"You needn't tell fibs about it. She couldn't have said anything of the kind. Who are *you,* anyhow?" the girl demanded, with spirit.

"I'm the foreman of the Lazy D, come to get Miss Darling. My name is McWilliams—Jim McWilliams."

"I don't need your first name, Mr. McWilliams," she assured him, sweetly. "And will you please tell me why you have kept me waiting here more than thirty hours?"

"Miss Messiter didn't get your letter in time. Y'u see, we don't get mail every day at the Lazy D," he explained, the while he hopefully wondered just when she was going to need his last name.

"I don't see why you don't go after your mail every day at least, especially when Miss Messiter was expecting me. To leave me waiting here thirty hours— I'll not stand it. When does the next train leave for Detroit?" she asked, imperiously.

The situation seemed to call for diplomacy, and Jim McWilliams moved to a nearer chair. "I'm right sorry it happened, ma'am, and I'll bet Miss Messiter is, too. Y'u see, we been awful busy one way and 'nother, and I plumb neglected to send one of the boys to the post office."

"Why didn't one of them walk over after supper?" she demanded, severely.

He curbed the smile that was twitching at his facial muscles.

"Well, o' course it ain't so far—only forty-three miles—still—"

"Forty-three miles to the post office?"

"Yes, ma'am, only forty-three. If you'll excuse me this time—"

"Is it really forty-three?"

He saw that her sudden smile had brought out the dimples in the oval face and that her petulance had been swept away by his astounding information.

"Forty-three, sure as shootin', except twict a week when it comes to Slauson's, and that's only twenty miles," he assured her. "Used to be seventy-two, but the Government got busy with its rural free delivery, and now we get it right at our doors.

"You must have big doors," she laughed.

All out o' doors," he punned. "Y'u see, our house is under our hat, and like as not that's twenty miles from the ranchhouse when night falls."

"Dear me!" She swept his graceful figure sarcastically. "And, of course, twenty miles from a brush, too."

He laughed with deep delight at her thrust, for the warm youth in him did not ask for pointed wit on the part of a young woman so attractive and with a manner so delightfully provoking.

"I expaict I have gathered up some scenery on the journey. I'll go brush it off and get ready for supper. I'd admire to sit beside y'u and pass the butter and the hash if y'u don't object. Y'u see, I don't often meet up with ladies, and I'd ought to improve my table manners when I get a chanct with one so much older than I am and o' course so much more experienced."

"I see you don't intend to pass any honey with the hash," she flashed, with a glimpse of the pearls.

"*Didn't* y'u say y'u was older than me? I believe I've plumb forgot how old y'u said y'u was, Miss Darling."

"Your memory's such a sieve it wouldn't be worth while telling you. After you've been to school a while longer maybe I'll try you again."

"Some ladies like 'em young," he suggested, amiably.

"But full grown," she amended.

"Do y'u judge by my looks or my ways?" he inquired, anxiously.

"By both."

"That's right strange," he mused aloud. "For judging by some of your ways you're the spinster Miss Messiter was telling me about, but judging by your looks y'u're only the prettiest and sassiest twenty-year-old in Wyoming."

And with this shot he fled, to see what transformation he could effect with the aid of a whiskbroom, a tin pan of alkali water and a roller towel.

When she met him at the supper table her first question was, "Did Miss Messiter say I was an old maid?"

"Sho! I wouldn't let that trouble me if I was y'u. A woman ain't any older than she looks. Your age don't show to speak of."

"But did she?"

"I reckon she laid a trap for me and I shoved my paw in. She wanted to give me a pleasant surprise."

"Oh!"

"Don't y'u grow anxious about being an old maid. There ain't any in Wyoming to speak of. If y'u like I'll tell the boys you're worried and some of them will be Johnnie-on-the-Spot. They're awful gallant, cow-punchers are."

"Some of them may be," she differed. "If you want to know I'm just twenty-one."

He sawed industriously at his steak. "Y'u don't say! Just old enough to vote—like this steer was before they massacreed him."

She gave him one look, and thereafter punished him with silence.

They left Gimlet Butte early next morning and reached the Lazy D shortly after noon on the suc-ceeding day. McWilliams understood perfectly that strenuous competition would inevitably ensue as soon as the Lazy D beheld the attraction he had brought into their midst. Nor did he need a phrenologist to tell him that Nora was a born flirt and that her shy slant glances were meant to penetrate tough hides to tender hearts. But this did not discourage him, and he set about making his individual impression while he had her all to himself. He wasn't at all sure how deep this went, but he had the satisfaction of hearing his first name, the one she had told him she had no need of, fall tentatively from her pretty lips before the other boys caught a glimpse of her.

Shortly after his arrival at the ranch Mac went to make his report to his mistress of some business mat-ters connected with the trip.

"I see you got back safely with the old lady," she laughed when she caught sight of him.

His look reproached her. "Y'u said spinster."

"But it was you that insisted on the rheumatism. By the way, did you ask her about it?"

"We didn't get that far," he parried.

"Oh! How far did you get?" She perched herself on the porch railing and mocked him with her friendly eyes. Her heart was light within her and she was ready for anything in the way of fun, for the doctor had just pronounced her patient out of danger if he took proper care of himself.

"About as fur as I got with y'u, ma'am," he audaciously retorted.

"We might disagree as to how far that is," she flung back gayly with heightened color.

"No, ma'am, I don't think we would."

"But, gracious! You're not a Mormon. You don't want us both, do you?" she demanded, her eyes sparkling with the exhilaration of the tilt.

"Could I get either one of y'u, do y'u reckon? That's what's worrying me."

"I see, and so you intend to keep us both on the string."

His joyous laughter echoed hers. "I expaict y'u would call that presumption or some other dictionary word, wouldn't y'u?"

"In anybody else perhaps, but surely not in Mr. McWilliams."

"I'm awful glad to be trotting in a class by myself."

"And you'll let us know when you have made your mind up which of us it is to be?"

"Well, mine ain't the only mind that has to be made up," he drawled.

She took this up gleefully. "I can't answer for Nora, but I'll jump at the chance—if you decide to give it to me."

He laughed delightedly into the hat he was momentarily expecting to put on. "I'll mill it over a spell and let y'u know, ma'am."

"Yes, think it over from all points of view, Of course she is prettier, but then I'm not afflicted with rheumatism and probably wouldn't flirt as much afterward. I have a good temper, too, as a rule, but then so has Nora."

"Oh, she's prettier, is she?" With boyish audacity he grinned at her.

"What do you think?"

He shook his head. "I'll have to go to the foot of the class on that, ma'am. Give me an easier one."

"I'll have to choose another subject then. What did you do about that bunch of Circle 66 cows you looked at on your way in?"

They discussed business for a few minutes, after which she went back to her patient and he to his work.

"Ain't she a straight-up little gentleman for fair?" the foreman asked himself in rhetorical and exuberant question, slapping his hat against his leg as he strode toward the corral. "Think of her coming at me like she did, the blamed little thoroughbred. Y'u bet she knows me down to the ground and how sudden I got over any fool notions I might a-started to get in my cocoanut. But the way she came back at me, quick as lightning and then some, pretendin' all that foolishness and knowin' all the time I'd savez the game."

Both McWilliams and his mistress had guessed right in their surmise as to Nora Darling's popularity in the cow country. She made an immediate and pronounced hit. It was astonishing how many errands the men found to take them to "the house," as they called the building where the mistress of the ranch dwelt. Bannister served for a time as an excellent excuse. Judging from the number of the inquiries which the men found it necessary to make as to his progress, Helen would have guessed him exceedingly popular with her riders. Having a sense of humor, she mentioned this to McWilliams one day.

He laughed, and tried to turn it into a compliment to his mistress. But she would have none of it.

"I know better, sir. They don't come here to see me. Nora is the attraction, and I have sense enough to know it. My nose is quite out of joint," she laughed.

Mac looked with gay earnestness at the feature she had mentioned. "There's a heap of difference in noses," he murmured, apparently apropos of nothing.

"That's another way of telling me that Nora's pug is the sweetest thing you ever saw," she charged.

"I ain't half such a bad actor as some of the boys," he deprecated.

"Meaning in what way?"

"The Nora Darling way."

He pronounced her name so much as if it were a caress that his mistress laughed, and he joined in it.

"It's your fickleness that is breaking my heart, though I knew I was lost as soon as I saw your beatific look on the day you got back with Nora. The first week I came none of you could do enough for me. Now it's all Nora, darling." She mimicked gayly his intonation.

"Well, ma'am, it's this way," explained the foreman with a grin. "Y'u're right pleasant and friendly, but the boys have got a savvy way down deep that y'u'd shuck that friendliness awful sudden if any of them dropped around with 'Object, Matrimony' in their manner. Consequence is, they're loaded down to the ground with admiration of their boss, but they ain't presumptuous enough to expaict any more. I had notions, mebbe, I'd cut more ice, me being not afflicted with bashfulness. My notions faded, ma'am, in about a week."

"When Nora came?" she laughed.

"No, ma'am, they had gone glimmering long before she arrived. I was just convalescent enough to need being cheered up when she drapped in."

"And are you cheered up yet?" his mistress asked.

He took off his dusty hat and scratched his head. "I ain't right certain, yet, ma'am. Soon as I know I'm consoled, I'll be round with an invite to the wedding."

"That is, if you are."

"If I am—yes. Y'u can't most always tell when they have eyes like hers."

115

"You're quite an authority on the sex considering your years."

"Yes, ma'am." He looked aggrieved, thinking himself a man grown. "How did y'u say Mr. Bannister was?"

"Wait, and I'll send Nora out to tell you," she flashed, and disappeared in the house.

Conversation at the bunkhouse and the chuck-tent sometimes circled around the young women at the house, but its personality rarely grew pronounced. References to Helen Messiter and the housemaid were usually by way of repartee at each other. For a change had come over the spirit of the Lazy D men, and, though a cheerful profanity still flowed freely when they were alone together, vulgarity was largely banished.

The morning after his conversation with Miss Messiter, McWilliams was washing in the foreman's room when the triangle beat the call for breakfast, and he heard the cook's raucous "Come and get it." There was the usual stampede for the tent, and a minute later Mac flung back the flap and entered. He took the seat at the head of the table, along the benches on both sides of which the punchers were plying busy knives and forks.

"A stack of chips," ordered the foreman; and the cook's "Coming up" was scarcely more prompt than the plate of hot cakes he set before the young man.

"Hen fruit, sunny side up," shouted Reddy, who was further advanced in his meal.

"Tame that fog-horn, son," advised Wun Hop; but presently he slid three fried eggs from a frying-pan into the plate of the hungry one.

116

"I want y'u boys to finish flankin' that bunch of hill calves today," said the foreman, emptying half a jug of syrup over his cakes.

"Redtop, he ain't got no appetite these days," grinned Denver, as the gentleman mentioned cleaned up a second loaded plate of ham, eggs and fried potatoes. "I see him studying a Wind River Bible* yesterday. Curious how in the spring a young man's fancy gits to wandering on house furnishing. Red, he was taking the catalogue alphabetically. Carpets was absorbin' his attention, chairs on deck, and chandeliers in the hole, as we used to say when we was baseball kids."

"Ain't a word of truth in it," indignantly denied the assailed, his unfinished nose and chin giving him a pathetic, whipped puppy look. "Sho! I was just looking up saddles. Can't a fellow buy a new saddle without asking leave of Denver?"

"Cyarpets used to begin with a C in my spelling-book, but saddles got off right foot fust with a S," suggested Mac amiably.

"He was ce'tainly trying to tree his saddle among the C's. He was looking awful loving at a Turkish rug. Reckon he thought it was a saddle-blanket," derided Denver cheerfully.

"Huh! Y'u're awful smart, Denver," retaliated Reddy, his complexion matching his hair. "Y'u talk a heap with your mouth. Nobody believes a word of what y'u say."

Denver relaxed into a range song by way of repartee:

"I want mighty bad to be married,

117

To have a garden and a home;
I ce'tainly aim to git married,
And have a gyurl for my own."

"Aw! Y'u fresh guys make me tired. Y'u don't devil me a bit, not a bit. Whyfor should I care what y'u say? I guess this outfit ain't got no surcingle on me." Nevertheless, he made a hurried end of his breakfast and flung out of the tent.

"Y'u boys hadn't ought to wound Reddy's tender feelings, and him so bent on matrimony," said Denver innocently. "Get a move on them fried spuds and sashay them down this way, if there's any left when y'u fill your plate, Missou."

Nor was Reddy the only young man who had dreams those days at the Lazy D. Cupid must have had his hands full, for his darts punctured more than one honest plainsman's heart. The reputation of the young women at the Lazy D seemed to travel on the wings of the wind, and from far and near Cattleland sent devotees to this shrine of youth and beauty. So casually the victims drifted in, always with a good business excuse warranted to endure raillery and sarcasm, that it was impossible to say they had come of set purpose to sun themselves in feminine smiles.

As for Nora, it is not too much to say that she was having the time of her life. Detroit, Michigan, could offer no such field for her expansive charms as the Bighorn country, Wyoming. Here she might have her pick of a hundred, and every one of them picturesquely

118

begirt with flannel shirt, knotted scarf at neck, an arsenal that bristled, and a sun-tan that could be achieved only in the outdoors of the Rockies. Certainly these knights of the saddle radiated a romance with which even her floorwalker "gentleman friend" could not compete.

CHAPTER X

A SHEPHERD OF THE DESERT

It had been Helen Messiter's daily custom either to take a ride on her pony or a spin in her motor car, but since Bannister had been quartered at the Lazy D her time had been so fully occupied that she had given this up for the present. The arrival of Nora Darling, however, took so much work off her hands that she began to continue her rides and drives.

Her patient was by this time so far recovered that he did not need her constant attendance and there were reasons why she decided it best to spend only a minimum of her time with him. These had to do with her increasing interest in the man and the need she felt to discourage it. It had come to a pretty pass, she told herself scornfully, when she found herself inventing excuses to take her into the room where this most picturesque of unhanged scamps was lying. Most good women are at heart puritans, and if Helen was too liberal to judge others narrowly she could be none the less rigid with herself. She might talk to him of her duty, but it was her habit to be frank in thought and she knew that something nearer than that abstraction had moved her efforts in his behalf. She had fought for his life because she loved him. She could deny it no longer. Nor was the shame with which she confessed it unmingled with pride. He was a man to compel love, one of the mood imperative, chain-armored in the outdoor virtues of strength and endurance and stark courage. Her abasement began only where his superlation ended. That a being so godlike in equipment should have been fashioned without a soul, and that she should have given her heart to him. This was the fount of her degradation.

It was of these things she thought as she drove in the late afternoon toward those Antelope Peaks he had first pointed out to her. She swept past the scene of the battle and dipped down into the plains for a run to that western horizon behind the jagged mountain line of which the sun was radiantly setting in a splash of glorious colors. Lost in thought, space slipped under her wheels unnoticed. Not till her car refused the spur and slowed to a despondent halt did she observe that velvet night was falling over the land.

She prowled round the machine after the fashion of the motorist, examining details that might be the cause of the trouble. She discovered soon enough with instant dismay that the gasoline tank was empty. Reddy, always unreliable, must have forgotten to fill it when she told him to.

By the road she must be thirty miles from home if she were a step; across country as the crow flies, perhaps twenty. She was a young woman of resolution, and she wasted no time in tears or regrets. The XIX ranch, owned by a small "nester" named Henderson, could not be more than five or six miles to the southeast. If she struck across the hills she would be sure to run into one of the barblines. At the XIX she could get a horse and reach the Lazy D by midnight. Without any hesitation she struck out. It was unfortunate that she did not have on her heavy laced high boots, but she realized that she must take things as she found them. Things might have been a good deal worse, she reflected philosophically.

And before long they were worse, for the increasing darkness blotted out the landmarks she was using as guides and she was lost among the hill waves that rolled one after another across the range. Still she did not give way, telling herself that it would be better after the moon was up. She could then tell north from south, and so have a line by which to travel. But when at length the stars came out, thousands upon thousands of them, and looked down on a land magically flooded with chill moonlight, the girl found that the transformation of Wyoming into this scence of silvery loveliness had toned the distant mountain line to an indefinite haze that made it impossible for her to distinguish one peak from another.

She wandered for hours, hungry and tired and frightened, though this last she would not confess.

"There's nothing to be afraid of," she told herself over and over. "Even if I have to stay out all night it will do me no harm. There's no need to be a baby about it."

But try to evade it as she would, there was something in the loneliness of this limitless stretch of hilltop that got on her nerves. The very shadows cast by the moonshine seemed too fantastic for reality. Something eerie and unearthly hovered over it all, and before she knew it a sob choked up her throat.

Vague fancies filtered through her mind, weird imaginings born of the night in a mind that had been swept from the moorings of reason. So that with no sensible surprise there came to her in that moonlit sea of desert the sound of a voice, a clear sweet tenor swelling bravely in song with the very ecstacy of pathos.

It was the prison song from "Il Trovatore," and the desolation of its lifted appeal went to the heart like water to the roots of flowers.

> Ah! I have sigh'd to rest me
> Deep in the quiet grave.

The girl's sob caught in her breast, stilled with the awe of that heavenly music. So for an instant she waited before it was borne in on her that the voice was a human one, and that the heaven from which it descended was the hilltop above her.

A wild laugh, followed by an oath, cut the dying echoes of the song. She could hear the swish of a quirt falling again and again, and the sound of trampling hoofs thudding on the hard, sun-cracked ground. Startled, she sprang to her feet, and saw silhouetted against the skyline a horse and his rider fighting for mastery.

The battle was superb while it lasted. The horse had been a famous outlaw, broken to the saddle by its owner out of the sheer passion for victory, but there were times when its savage strength rebelled at abject submission, and this was one of them. It swung itself skyward, and came down like a pile-driver, camel-backed, and without joints in the legs. Swiftly it rose again, lunging forward and whirling in the air, then jarred down at an angle. The brute did its malevolent best, a fury incarnate. But the rider was a match, and more than a match, for it. He sat the saddle like a Centaur, with the perfect, unconscious grace of a born master, swaying in his seat as need was, and spurring the horse to a blinder fury.

Sudden as had been the start, no less sudden was the finish of the battle. The bronco pounded to a stiff-legged standstill, trembled for a long minute like an aspen, and sank to a tame surrender, despite the sharp spurs roweling its bloody sides.

"Ah, my beauty. You've had enough, have you?" demanded the cruel, triumphant voice of the rider. "You would try that game, would you? I'll teach you."

"Stop spurring that horse, you bully."

The man stopped, in sheer amazement at this apparition which had leaped out of the ground almost at his feet. His wary glance circled the hills to make sure she was alone.

"Ce'tainly, ma'am. We're sure delighted to meet up with you. Ain't we, Two-step?"

For himself, he spoke the simple truth. He lived in his sensations, spurring himself to fresh ones as he had but just now been spurring his horse to sate the greed of conquest in him. And this high-spirited, gallant creature—he could feel her vital courage in the very ring of her voice—offered a rare fillip to his jaded appetite. The dusky, long-lashed eyes which always give a woman an effect of beauty, the splendid fling of head, and the piquant, finely cut features, with their unconscious tale of Brahmin caste, the long lines of the supple body, willowy and yet plump as a partridge— they went to his head like strong wine. Here was an adventure from the gods—a stubborn will to bend, the pride of a haughty young beauty to trail in the dust, her untamed heart to break if need be. The lust of the battle was on him already. She was a woman to dream about,

"Sweeter than the lids of Juno's eyes,
Or Cytherea's breath,"

he told himself exultantly as he slid from his horse and stood bowing before her.

And he, for his part, was a taking enough picture of devil-may-care gallantry gone to seed. The touch of jaunty impudence in his humility, not less than the daring admiration of his handsome eyes and the easy, sinuous grace of his flexed muscles, labeled him what he was—a man bold and capable to do what he willed, and a villain every inch of him.

Said she, after that first clash of stormy eyes with bold, admiring ones:

"I am lost—from the Lazy D ranch."

"Why, no, you're found," he corrected, white teeth flashing in a smile.

"My motor ran out of gasoline this afternoon. I've been"—there was a catch in her voice—"wandering ever since."

"You're played out, of course, and y'u've had no supper," he said, his quiet close gaze on her.

"Yes, I'm played out and my nerve's gone." She laughed a little hysterically. "I expect I'm hungry and thirsty, too, though I hadn't noticed it before."

He whirled to his saddle, and had the canteen thongs unloosed in a moment. While she drank he rummaged from his saddle-bags some sandwiches of jerky and a flask of whiskey. She ate the sandwiches, he the while watching her with amused sympathy in his swarthy countenance.

"You ain't half-bad at the chuck-wagon, Miss Messiter," he told her.

She stopped, the sandwich part way to her mouth. "I don't remember your face. I've met so many people since I came to the Lazy D. Still, I think I should remember you."

He immediately relieved of duty her quasi apology. "You haven't seen *my face* before," he laughed, and, though she puzzled over the double meaning that seemed to lurk behind his words and amuse him, she could not find the key to it.

It was too dark to make out his features at all clearly, but she was sure she had seen him before or somebody that looked very much like him.

125

"Life on the range ain't just what y'u can call exciting," he continued, "and when a young lady fresh from back East drops among us while six-guns are popping, breaks up a likely feud and mends right neatly all the ventilated feudists it's a corollary to her fun that's she is going to become famous."

What he said was true enough. The unsolicited notoriety her exploit had brought upon her had been its chief penalty. Garbled versions of it had appeared with fake pictures in New York and Chicago Sunday supplements, and all Cattleland had heard and discussed it. No matter into what unfrequented cañon she rode, some silent cowpuncher would look at her as they met with admiring eyes behind which she read a knowledge of the story. It was a lonely desolate country, full of the wide deep silences of utter emptiness, yet there could be no footfall but the whisper of it was bruited on the wings of the wind.

"Do you know where the Lazy D ranch is from here?" she asked.

He nodded.

"Can you take me home?"

"I surely can. But not tonight. You're more tired than y'u know. We'll camp here, and in the mo'ning we'll hit the trail bright and early."

This did not suit her at all. "Is it far to the Lazy D?" she inquired anxiously.

"Every inch of forty miles. There's a creek not more than two hundred yards from here. We'll stay there till mo'ning," he made answer in a matter of course voice, leading the way to the place he had mentioned.

She followed, protesting. Yet though it was not in accord with her civilized sense of fitness, she knew that what he proposed was the common sense solution. She was tired and worn out, and she could see that his broncho had traveled far.

Having reached the bank of the creek, he unsaddled, watered his horse and picketed it, and started a fire. Uneasily she watched him.

"I don't like to sleep out. Isn't there a ranch-house near?"

"Y'u wouldn't call it near by the time we had reached it. What's to hinder your sleeping here? Isn't this room airy enough? And don't y'u like the system of lighting? 'Twas patented I forget how many million years ago. Y'u ain't going to play parlor girl now after getting the reputation y'u've got for gameness, are y'u?"

But he knew well enough that it was no silly school-girl fear she had, but some deep instinct in her that distrusted him and warned her to beware. So, lightly he took up the burden of the talk while he gathered cottonwood branches for the fire.

"Now if I'd only thought to bring a load of lumber and some carpenters—and a chaperon," he chided himself in burlesque, his bold eyes closely on the girl's face to gloat on the color that flew to her cheeks at his suggestion.

She hastened to disclaim lightly the feeling he had unmasked in her. "It is a pity, but it can't be helped now. I suppose I am cross and don't seem very grateful. I'm tired out and nervous, but I am sure that I'll enjoy sleeping out. If I don't I shall not be so ungenerous as to blame you."

He soon had a cup of steaming coffee ready for her, and the heat of it made a new woman of her. She sat in the warm fire glow, and began to feel stealing over her a delightful reaction of languor. She told herself severely it was ridiculous to have been so foolishly prim about the inevitable.

"Since you know my name, isn't it fair that I should know yours?" she smilingly asked, more amiably than she had yet spoken to him.

"Well, since I have found the lamb that was lost, y'u may call me a shepherd of the desert."

"Then, Mr. Shepherd, I'm very glad to meet you. I don't remember when I ever was more glad to meet a stranger." And she added with a little laugh: "It's a pity I'm too sleepy to do my duty by you in a social way."

"We'll let that wait till tomorrow. Y'u'll entertain me plenty then. I'll make your bunk up right away."

She was presently lying with her feet to the fire, snugly rolled in his saddle blankets. But though her eyes were heavy, her brain was still too active to permit her to sleep immediately. The excitement of her adventure was too near, the emotions of the day too poignantly vivid, to lose their hold on her at once. For the first time in her life she lay lapped in the illimitable velvet night, countless unwinking stars lighting the blue-black dream in which she floated. The enchantment of the night's loveliness swept through her sensitive pulses and thrilled her with the mystery of the great life of which she was an atom. Awe held her a willing captive.

She thought of many things, of her past life and its incongruity with the present, of the man who lay wounded at the Lazy D, of this other wide-shouldered vagabond who was just now in the shadows beyond the firelight, pacing up and down with long, light even strides as he looked to his horse and fed the fire. She watched him make an end of the things he found to do and then take his place opposite her. Who and what was he, this fascinating scamp who one moment flooded the moonlit desert with inspired snatches from the opera sung in the voice of an angel, and the next lashed at his horse like a devil incarnate? How reconcile the out-standing inconsistencies in him? For his every inflec-tion, every motion, proclaimed the strain of good blood gone wrong and trampled under foot of set, sardonic purpose, indicated him a man of culture in a hell of his own choosing. Lounging on his elbow in the flickering shadows, so carelessly insouciant in every picturesque inch of him, he seemed to radiate the melodrama of the untamed frontier, just as her guest of tarnished reputa-tion now at the ranch seemed to breathe forth its romance.

"Sleep well, little partner. Don't be afraid; nothing can harm you," this man had told her. Promptly she had answered, "I'm not afraid, thank you, in the least"; and after a moment had added, not to seem hostile, "Good night, big partner."

129

But despite her calm assurance she knew she did not feel so entirely safe as if it had been one of her own ranch boys on the other side of the fire, or even that other vagabond who had made so direct an appeal to her heart. If she were not afraid, at least she knew some vague hint of anxiety.

She was still thinking of him when she fell asleep, and when she awakened the first sound that fell on her ears was his tuneful whistle. Indeed she had an indistinct memory of him in the night, wrapping the blankets closer about her when the chill air had half stirred her from her slumber. The day was still very young, but the abundant desert light dismissed sleep summarily. She shook and brushed the wrinkles out of her clothes and went down to the creek to wash her face with the inadequate facilities at hand. After redressing her hair she returned to the fire, upon which a coffee pot was already simmering.

She came up noiselessly behind him, but his trained senses were apprised of her approach.

"Good mo'ning! How did y'u find your bedroom?" he asked, without turning from the bacon he was broiling on the end of a stick.

"Quite up to the specifications. With all Wyoming for a floor and the sky for a ceiling, I never had a room I liked better. But have you eyes in the back of your head?"

He laughed grimly. "I have to be all eyes and ears in my business."

"Is your business of a nature so sensitive?"

"As much so as stocks on Wall Street. And we haven't any ticker to warn us to get under cover. Do you take cream in your coffee, Miss Messiter?"

She looked round in surprise. "Cream?"

"We're in tin-can land, you know, and live on air-tights. I milk my cow with a can-opener. Let me recommend this quail on toast." He handed her a battered tin plate, and prepared to help her from the frying-pan.

"I suppose that is another name for pork?"

"No, really. I happened to bag a couple of hooters before you wakened."

"You're a missionary of the good-foods movement. I shall name your mission St. Sherry's-in-the-Wilderness."

"Ah, Sherry's! That's since my time. I don't suppose I should know my way about in little old New York now."

She found him eager to pick up again the broken strands that had connected him with the big world from which he had once come. It had been long since she had enjoyed a talk more, for he expressed himself with wit and dexterity. But through her enjoyment ran a note of apprehension. He was for the moment a resurrected gentleman. But what would he be next? She had an insistent memory of a heavenly flood of music broken by a horrible discord of raucous oaths.

It was he that lingered over their breakfast, loath to make the first move to bring him back into realities; and it was she that had to suggest the need of setting out. But once on his feet, he saddled and packed swiftly, with a deftness born of experience.

"We'll have to ask Two-step to carry double today," he said, as he helped her to a place behind him.

Two-step had evidently made an end of the bronco spree upon which he had been the evening before, for he submitted sedately to his unusual burden. The first hilltop they reached had its surprise to offer the girl. In a little valley below them, scarce a mile away, nestled a ranch with its corrals and buildings.

"Look!" she exclaimed; and then swiftly, "Didn't you know it was there?"

"Yes, that's the Hilke place," he answered with composure. "It hasn't been occupied for years."

"Isn't that some one crossing to the corral now?"

"No. A stray cow, I reckon."

They dropped into a hollow between the hills and left the ranch on their left. She was not satisfied, and yet she had not grounds enough upon which to base a suspicion. For surely the figure she had seen had been that of a man.

He let his horse take it easy, except when some impulse of mischief stirred him to break into a canter so as to make the girl put her arm round his waist for support. They stopped about noon by a stream in a cañon defile to lunch and rest the pony.

"I don't remember this place at all. Are we near home?" she asked.

"About five miles. I reckon you're right tired. It's an unhandy way to ride."

Every mile took them deeper into the mountains,

through winding cañons and over unsuspected trails, and the girl's uneasiness increased with the wildness of the country.

"Are you *sure* we're going the right way? I don't think we can be," she suggested more than once.

"Dead sure," he answered the last time, letting Two-step turn into a blind draw opening from sheer cañon walls.

A hundred feet from the entrance they rode round a great slide of rock into a tiny valley containing a group of buildings.

He swung from the horse and offered a hand to help her dismount.

A reckless, unholy light burned in his daring eyes.

"Home at last, Miss Messiter. Let me offer you a thousand welcomes."

An icy hand seemed to clutch at her heart. "Home! What do you mean? This isn't the Lazy D."

"Not at all. The Lazy D is sixty miles from here. This is where I hang out—and you, for the present."

"But—I don't understand. How dare you bring me here?"

"The desire for your company, Miss Messiter, made of me a Lochinvar."

She saw, with a shiver, that the ribald eyes were mocking her.

"Take me back this instant—this instant," she commanded, but her imperious voice was not very sure of itself. "Take me home at once, you liar."

"I expect you don't quite understand," he exclaimed,

with gentle derision. "You're a prisoner of war, Miss Messiter."

"And who are you?" she faltered.

But before he spoke she found an answer to her question, found it by a flash of divination she could never afterward explain.

"You're the man I met at Fraser's dance—the man they call the King of the Bighorn country."

He accepted identification with an elaborate bow. "Correct, ma'am. I'm Ned Bannister the king."

An instant before she had been sitting rigid with a face of startled fear, but as he spoke a great wave of joy beat into her heart. For if this man were the terror of the country the one she had left wounded at her house could not be. She forgot that she was herself in peril, forgot everything in the swift conviction that the man she loved was an honest gentleman and worthy of her.

The man standing by the horse could not understand the light that had so immediately leaped to her eyes. Even *his* vanity hesitated at the obvious deduction that she had already succumbed to his attractions.

"But I don't understand—that isn't your real name, is it? I know another man who calls himself Ned Bannister."

He laughed scornfully. "My cousin, the sheepherder. Yes, that's his name, too. We both have a right to it."

"Your cousin?"

The familiarity in him that had been haunting her all day and that had deceived her at the dance was now explained. It was her lover of which this man reminded her. Now that she had been given the clue she could trace kinship in manner, gait and appearance.

"I'm not proud of my mealy-mouthed namesake," he replied.

"Nor he of you, I am sure," she quickly answered.

"I dare say not. But won't y'u 'light, Miss Messiter?"

She slipped immediately to the ground beside him. Her eyes looked him over with quiet scorn.

"From first to last you have done nothing but lie to me. When we were out last night you knew that ranch was close at hand. You lied to me again when you said it was deserted."

"Very well. We'll say I lied, though it's not a nice word in so pretty a mouth as yours, Miss Messiter. Y'u ought to read up again the fable about the toads dropping from the beautiful lady's lips."

"What's your object? What do you expect to gain by it?"

"Up to date I've gained a right interesting guest. Y'u will be diverting enough. With so charming a lady visiting me I'm not worrying about getting bored."

"So you war on women, you coward."

The change in him was instantaneous. It was as if a thousand years of civilization had been sponged out in an eyebeat. He stood before her a savage primeval, his tight-lipped smile cruel in its triumph.

"Did I begin this fight? Didn't y'u and your punchers try to balk me by taking that sheepherder from me after I had bagged him? That was your hour. By God, this is mine! I'll teach y'u it isn't safe to interfere with me.

What I want I get one way or another, and don't y'u forget it, my girl."

She was afraid to the very marrow of her. But she would not show her fear, nor could he read it in the slim superb erectness with which she gave him defiance.

"You coward!"

"That's twice you've called me that," he cried, his face flushing darkly and his eyes glittering. "Y'u'll crawl on your knees to me and beg pardon before I'm through with y'u, my beauty. Y'u'll learn to lick the hand that strikes y'u. You're mine—mine to do with as I please. Don't forget that for a moment. I'll break your spirit or I'll break your heart."

His ferocity appalled her, but her brave eyes held their own. With an oath he turned on his heel and struck the palms of his hands together. An Indian squaw came running from one of the cabins. He flung at her a sentence or two in the native tongue and pointed at his captive. She asked a question impassively and he jabbed out a threat. The squaw nodded her head, and motioned to the girl to follow her.

When Helen Messiter was alone in the room that was to serve as her prison she sank into a chair and covered her face with her hands in a despair that was for the moment utter.

CHAPTER XI

A RESCUE

Helen Messiter was left alone until darkness fell, when the Cheyenne squaw brought in a kerosene lamp and shortly afterward her supper. The woman either could not or would not speak English, and her only answer to her captive's advances was by sullen grunts. At the expiration of half an hour she returned for the dishes, locking the door after her when she left.

The room itself was comfortable enough. It was evidently Bannister's own, judging from its contents. Two or three rifles hung in racks. On top of the bookcase was a half-filled tobacco pouch and several pipes, all of them lying carelessly on a pile of music which ran from Verdi to ragtime. In his books she found the same shallow catholicity. Side by side with Montaigne's "Essays," a well-worn Villon in the original, Stevenson's "Letters" and "Anna Karenina," dozens of paper-covered novels, mostly the veriest trash, held their disreputable own. Some of them were French, others detective stories, still others melodramatic tales of love. The piano was an expensive one, but not in the best of tune. Everything in the room contributed to the effect of capacity untempered by discipline and discrimination. Plainly he was a man of taste who had outraged and deadened his power of differentiation by abuse.

For Helen the silent night was alive with alarms. The moaning of the wind, the slightest rustle outside, the creaking of a board, were enough to set her heart wildly beating. She did not undress, but by the light of her dim, ragged wick sought for composure from the pages of Montaigne and Stevenson. When the first gray day streaks came she was still reading, but with their coming she blew out her light and lay down. She fell asleep at once, and it was five hours later that the knock of her attendant awakened her from heavy slumber.

With the bright sunlit day she was again mistress of her nerves, prepared to meet resolutely whatever danger might confront her. But the morning passed quietly enough, and after lunch the Indian woman led her into the little valley promenade in front of the buildings and sat down on a rock while her captive enjoyed the sunshine.

The course of Helen's saunterings took her toward the rock slide that made the gateway of the valley. She was wondering if it could have been left unguarded, when a rough voice warned her back. Looking round, she caught sight of a man seated cross-legged on a great boulder. It took only a second glance to certify that the man was her former foreman, Judd Morgan.

She had never seen anything more malevolent than his triumph.

"Better stay in the valley, Miss Messiter. Y'u might right easily get lost outside," he jeered.

Without reply she turned her back on him and began

to retrace her way to the house. Stung by her contempt, he sprang up and strode after her.

"So y'u won't speak to me, eh? Think yourself too good to speak to a common everyday God damned white man, do y'u?"

Apparently she did not know he was on the map. In a fury he caught at her shoulder and whirled her round.

"Now, by God, do y'u see me? I'm Judd Morgan, the man y'u kicked off the Lazy D. I told y'u then y'u were going to be sorry long as y'u lived."

"Don't you dare touch me, you hound!" Her blazing eyes menaced him so fiercely that he hesitated.

There was the sound of a quick, light step running toward them. Morgan half turned, was caught in a grip of steel and hurled headlong among a pile of broken rocks.

"Y'u would dare, would y'u?" panted his assailant, passionately, ready to obliterate the offender if he showed fight.

Morgan got up slowly, his head bleeding from contact with the sharp rocks. There was murder in his blood-shot eye, but he knew his master, and after trying vainly to face him down he swung away with an oath.

"I'll have to apologize for that coyote, Miss Messiter. These fellows need a hint occasionally as to how to behave," said Bannister.

"Your hints are rather forceful, are they not?"

"I ain't running a Sunday school," he admitted.

"So I have gathered. I wonder where he learned to bully women," she mused aloud.

"Putting it another way, you think there ought to be some one to apologize for his master."

He was smiling at her without the least rancor, and it came on her with a woman's swift instinct that safety lay in humoring his volatile moods and diverting him from those that were dangerous.

"Since I'm a prisoner of war I wouldn't dare think that—not aloud, at least. You might starve me," she told him, saucily.

"Still, down in your heart y'u think—"

"That there is a great deal of difference between master and man. One is a gentleman in his best moments; the other is always a ruffian."

She had touched his vanity. As he walked beside her she could almost see his complacency purr.

"I'm a miscreant, I reckon, but I was a gentleman first."

Fortunately he did not see the flash of veiled scorn she shot at him under her long lashes.

With her breakfast next morning the Cheyenne woman brought a note signed "Shepherd-of-the-Desert." In it Bannister asked permission to pay his respects. The girl divined that he was in his better mood, and penciled on his note the favor she could scarce refuse.

But she was scarcely prepared for the impudent air of jocund spring he brought into her prison, the gay assumption of *camaraderie* so inconsistent with the facts. Yet since safety lay in an avoidance of the tragic, she set herself to match his mood.

140

At sight of the open Tennyson on the table he laughed and quoted:

> "She only said, 'The day is dreary,
> He cometh not,' she said."

"But, you see, he comes," he added. "What say, Mariana of the Robbers' Roost, to making a picnic day of it? We'll climb the Crags and lunch on the summit."

"The Crags?"

"That Matterhorn-shaped peak that begins at our back door. Are you for it?"

While this mood was uppermost in him she felt reasonably safe. It was a phase of him she certainly did not mean to discourage. Besides, she had a youthful confidence in her powers that she was loath to give up without an effort to find the accessible side of his ruthless heart.

"I'll try it; but you must help me when we come to the bad places," she said.

"Sure thing! It's a deal. You're a right good mountaineer, I'll bet."

"Thank you; but you had better save your compliments till I make good," she told him, with the most piquant air of gayety in the world.

They started on horseback, following a mountain trail that zigzagged across the foothills toward the Crags. He had unearthed somewhere a boy's saddle that suited her very well, and the pony she rode was one of the easiest she had ever mounted. At the end of an hour's ride they left the horses and began the ascent on foot. It was a stiff climb, growing steeper as they ascended, but Helen Messiter had not tramped over golf links for nothing. She might grow leg weary, but she would not cry "Enough!" And he, on his part, showed the tactful consideration for the resources of her strength he had already taught her to expect from that other day's experience on the plains. It was a very rare hand of assistance that he offered her, but often he stopped to admire the beautiful view that stretched for many miles below them, in order that she might get a minute's breathing space.

Once he pointed out, far away on the horizon, a bright gleam that caught the sunlight like a heliograph.

"That's the big rock slide back of the Lazy D," he explained.

She drew a long breath, and flashed a stealthy look at him.

"It's a long way from here, isn't it?"

"I didn't find it so far last time I took the trip—not the last half of the journey, anyhow," he answered.

"You're very complimentary. I was only wondering whether I could find it if I should manage to escape."

He stroked his black mustache and smiled gallantly at her. "I reckon I won't let so pretty a prisoner escape."

"Do you expect me to burden your hospitality forever and a day? Wouldn't that be a little too much of Mariana of the Robbers' Roost?" she asked, lightly.

"I'm willing to risk it."

He looked with half-shut smoldering eyes at her

slender exquisiteness, so instinct with the vital charm of sex. There was veiled passion in his eyes, but there was in them, too, a desire to stand well with her. He meant to win her, but if possible he would win with her own reluctant consent. She must bring him with hesitant feet a heart surrendered in spite of her pride and flinty puritanism. The vanity of the man craved a victory that should be of the spirit as well as of the flesh.

Deftly she guided the conversation back to less dangerous channels. In this the increasing difficulty of the climb assisted her, for after they reached the last ascent sustained talk became impossible.

"See that trough above us near the summit? Y'u'll have to hang on by your eyelashes, pardner." He always burlesqued the word of comradeship a little to soften its familiarity.

"Dear me! Is it that bad?"

"It is so bad that at the top y'u have to jump for a grip and draw yourself up by your arms."

"I'll never be able to do it."

"I'm here to help."

"But if one should miss?"

He shrugged. "Ah! That's a theological question. If the sky pilots guess right, for y'u heaven and for me hell."

They negotiated the trough successfully to its uptilted end. She had a bad moment when he leaped for the rock rim above from the narrow ledge on which they stood. But he caught it, drew himself up without the least trouble and turned to assist her. He sat down on the rock edge facing the abyss beneath them, and told her to lock her hands together above his left foot. Then slowly, inch by inch, he drew her up till with one of his hands he could catch her wrist. A moment later she was standing on his rigid toes, from which position she warily edged to safety above.

"Well done, little pardner. You're the first woman ever climbed the Crags." He offered a hand to celebrate the achievement.

"If I am it is all due to you, big pardner. I could never have made that last bit alone." They ate lunch merrily in the pleasant sunlight, and both of them seemed as free from care as a schoolboy on a holiday.

"It's good to be alive, isn't it?" he asked her after they had eaten, as he lay on the warm ground at her feet. "And what a life it is here! To be riding free, with your knees pressing a saddle, in the wind and the sun. There's something in a man to which the wide spaces call. I'd rather lie here in the sunbeat with you beside me than be a king. You remember the 'Last Ride' that fellow Browning tells about? I reckon he's dead right. If a man could only capture his best moments and hold them forever it would be heaven to the nth degree."

She studied her sublimated villain with that fascination his vagaries always excited in her. Was ever a more impossible combination put together than this sentimental scamp with the long record of evil?

"Say it," he laughed. "Whang it out! Ask anything you like, pardner."

Pluckily daring, she took him at his word. "I was only

wondering at the different men I find in you. Before I have known you a dozen hours I discover in you the poet and the man of action, the schoolboy and the philosopher, the sentimentalist and the cynic, and— may I say it?—the gentleman and the blackguard. One feels a sense of loss. You should have specialized. You would have made such a good soldier, for instance. Pity you didn't go to West Point."

"Think so?" He was immensely flattered at her interest in him.

"Yes. You surely missed your calling. You were born for a soldier; cavalry, I should say. What an ornament to society you would have been if your energies had found the right vent! But they didn't find it—and you craved excitement, I suppose. Perhaps you had to go the way you did."

"Therefore I am what I am? Please particularize."

"I can't, because I don't understand you. But I think this much is true, that you have set yourself against all laws of God and man. Yet you are not consistent, since you are better than your creed. You tell yourself there shall be no law for you but your own will, and you find there is something in you stronger than desire that makes you shrink at many things. You can kill in fair fight, but you can't knife a man in the back, can you?"

"I never have."

"You have a dreadfully perverted set of rules, but you play by them. That's why I know I'm safe with you, even when you are at your worst." She announced this boldly, just as if she had no doubts.

"Oh, you know you're safe, do you?"

"Of course I do. You were once a gentleman and you can't forget it entirely. That's the weakness in your philosophy of total depravity."

"You speak with an assurance you don't always feel, I reckon. And I expect I wouldn't bank too much on those divinations of yours, if I were you." He rolled over so that he could face her more directly. "You've been mighty frank, Miss Messiter, and I take off my hat to your sand. Now I'm going to be frank awhile. You interest me. I never met a woman that interested me so much. But you do a heap more than interest me. No, you sit right there and listen. Your cheeky pluck and that insolent, indifferent beauty of yours made a hit with me the first minute I saw you that night. I swore I'd tame you, and that's why I brought you to the ranch. Your eye flashed a heap too haughty for me to give you the go-by. Mind you, I meant to be master. I meant to make you mine as much as that dog that licked my hand before we started. What I meant then I still mean, but in a different way.

"That's as far as it went with me then, but before we reached here next day I knew the thing cut deeper with me. I ain't saying that I love you, because I'm a sweep and it's just likely I don't know passion from love. But I'll tell you this—there hasn't been a waking moment since then I haven't been on fire to be with you. That's why I stayed away until I knew I wasn't so likely to slop over. But here, I'm doing it right this minute. I care more for you than I do for anything else on this earth.

146

But that makes it worse for you. I never cared for anybody without bringing ruin on them. I broke my mother's heart and spoiled the life of a girl I was going to marry. That's the kind of scoundrel I am. Even if I can make you care for me—and I reckon I can if y'u are like other women—I'll likely drag you through hell after me."

The simulation of despair in his beautiful eyes spoke more impressively than his self-scorning words. She was touched in spite of herself, despite, too, his colossal egotism. For there is an appeal about the engaging sinner that drums in a woman's head and calls to her heart. All good women are missionaries in the last analysis, and Miss Messiter was not an exception to her sex. Even though she knew he was half a fraud and that his emotion was theatric, she could not let the moment pass.

She leaned forward, a sweet, shy dignity in her manner. "Is it too late to change? Why not begin now? There is still a tomorrow, and it need not be the slave of yesterday. Life for all of us is full of milestones."

"And how shall I begin my new career of saintliness?" he asked, with a swift return to blithe irony.

"The nearest duty. Take me back to my ranch. Begin a life of rigid honesty."

"Give you up now that I have found you? That is just the last thing I would do," he cried, with glancing eyes. "No—no. The clock can't be turned back. I have sowed and I must reap."

He leaped to his feet. "Come! We must be going."

She rose sadly, for she knew the mood of sentimental regret for his wasted life had passed, and she had failed.

They descended the trough and reached the boulder field that had marked the terminal of the glacier. At the farther edge of it the outlaw turned to point out to the girl a great bank of snow on a mountainside fifteen miles away.

He changed his weight as he turned, when a rock slipped under his foot and he came down hard. He was up again in an instant, but Helen Messiter caught the sharp intake of his breath when he set foot to the ground.

"You've sprained your ankle!" she cried.

"Afraid so. It's my own rotten carelessness." He broke into a storm of curses and limped forward a dozen steps, but he had to set his teeth to stand the pain.

"Lean on me," she said, gently.

"I reckon I'll have to," he grimly answered.

They covered a quarter of a mile, with many stops to rest the swollen ankle. Only by the irregularity of his breathing and the damp moisture on his forehead could she tell the agony he was enduring.

"It must be dreadful," she told him once.

"I've got to stand for it, I reckon."

Again she said, when they had reached a wooded grove where pines grew splendid on a carpet of grass: "Only two hundred yards more. I think I can bring your pony as far as the big cottonwood."

She noticed that he leaned heavier and heavier on her. However, when they reached the cottonwood he leaned no more, but pitched forward in a faint. The water bottle was empty, but she ran down to where the ponies had been left, and presently came back with his canteen. She had been away perhaps twenty minutes, and when she came back he waved a hand airily at her.

"First time in my life that ever happened," he apologized, gayly. "But why didn't y'u get on Jim and cut loose for the Lazy D while you had the chance?"

"I didn't think of it. Perhaps I shall next time."

"I shouldn't. Y'u see, I'd follow you and bring you back. And if I didn't find you there would be a lamb lost again in these hills."

"The sporting thing would be to take a chance."

"And leave me here alone? Well, I'm going to give you a show to take it." He handed her his revolver. "Y'u may need this if you're going traveling."

"Are you telling me to go?" she asked, amazed.

"I'm telling you to do as you think best. Y'u may take a hike or y'u may bring back Two-step to me. Suit yourself."

"I tell you plainly, I sha'n't come back."

"And I'm sure y'u will."

"But I won't. The thing's absurd. Would you?"

"No, I shouldn't. But y'u will."

"I won't. Good-bye." She held out her hand.

He shook his head, looking steadily at her. "What's the use? You'll be back in half an hour."

"Not I. Did you say I must keep the Antelope Peaks in a line to reach the Lazy D?"

"Yes, a little to the left. Don't be long, little pardner."

149

"I hate to leave you here. Perhaps I'll send a sheriff to take care of you."

"Better bring Two-step up to the south of that bunch of cottonwoods. It's not so steep that way."

"I'll mention it to the sheriff. I'm not coming myself."

She left him apparently obstinate in the conviction that she would return. In reality he was taking a gambler's chance, but it was of a part with the reckless spirit of the man that the risk appealed to him. It was plain he could not drag himself farther. Since he must let her go for the horse alone, he chose that she should go with her eyes open to his knowledge of the opportunity of escape.

But Helen Messiter had not the slightest intention of returning. She had found her chance, and she meant to make the most of it. As rapidly as her unaccustomed fingers would permit she saddled and cinched her pony. She had not ridden a hundred yards before Two-step came crashing through the young cottonwood grove after her. Objecting to being left alone, he had broken the rein that tied him. The girl tried to recapture the horse in order that the outlaw might not be left entirely without means of reaching camp, but her efforts were unsuccessful. She had to give it up and resume her journey.

Of course the men at his ranch would miss their chief and search for him. There could be no doubt but that they would find him. She bolstered up her assurance of this as she rode toward the Antelope Peaks, but her hope lacked buoyancy, because she doubted if they had any idea of where he had been going to spend the day.

She rode slower and slower, and finally came to a long halt for consideration. Vividly there rose before her a picture of the miscreant waiting grimly for death or rescue. Well, she was not to blame. If she deserted him it was to save herself. But to leave him helpless—

No, she could not leave a crippled man to die alone, even though he were her enemy. That was the goal to which her circling thoughts came always home, and with a sob she turned her horse's head. It was a piece of soft-headed folly, she confessed, but she could not help it.

So back she went and found him lying just where she had left him. His derisive smile offered her no thanks. She doubted, indeed, whether he felt any sense of gratitude.

"Y'u didn't break your neck hurrying," he said.

She made her confession with a palpable chagrin. "I meant to ride away. I rode a mile or two, But I had to come back. I couldn't leave you here alone."

His eyes sparkled triumphantly. She saw that he had misunderstood the reason of her return, that he was pluming himself on a conquest of his fascinated victim.

"One couldn't leave even a broken-legged dog without help," she added, quietly.

"So how could we expect a woman to leave the man she's getting ready to love?"

She let her contemptuous eyes rest on him in silence.

"That's right. Look at me as if I were dirt under your feet. Hate me, if it makes y'u feel better. But y'u'll have to come to loving me just the same."

"Can you get on without help?" she asked, ranging the pony alongside him.

"Yes." He dragged himself to the saddle and smiled down at her. "So y'u better make up your mind to that soon as convenient."

Disdaining answer, she walked in front of the pony down the trail. She was tired, but her elastic tread would not admit it to him. For she was dramatizing unconsciously, with firmly clenched fingers that bit into her palms, the march of the unconquerable.

Evening had fallen before they reached the ranch. It was beautifully still, except for the call of the quails. The hazy violet outline of the mountains came to silhouette against the skyline with a fine edge.

As they passed the pony corral he spoke again. "I'll never forget today. I've got it fenced from all the yesterdays and tomorrows. I have surely enjoyed our little picnic."

"Nor will I forget it," she flung back quickly, as she followed him into the house. "For I never before met a man wholly incapable of gratitude and entirely lacking in all the elements that go to distinguish a human being from a wolf."

He turned to speak to her, and as he did so a quiet voice cautioned him:

"Don't move, seh, except to throw up your hands."

At the sound of that pleasant drawl Helen's heart jumped to her throat. Jim McWilliams, half seated on the edge of the table, was looking intently at Bannister, and there was a revolver in his hand. On the other side of the room sat Morgan and the Cheyenne woman, apparently in charge of the young giant Denver.

Bannister's hands went up, even as he whirled with a snarl toward the man Morgan.

"I told y'u to watch out, y'u muttonhead!"

"But y'u clean forgot to remember to watch out your own self," spoke up McWilliams, unbuckling the belt from the waist of his new captive.

"Oh, Mac, you blessed boy!" cried Helen, with an hysterical laugh that was half a sob. "How did you ever find me?"

"Followed the track of the gas wagon to where it ran out of juice. We lost your trail after that, but Denver and me had the good luck to pick it up again where y'u'd camped that night. We mislaid it again up in the hills, and Denver he knew about this place. We dropped in just casual for information, but when we set our peepers on Judd we allowed we would stay awhile, him being so anxious to have us."

"You dear boys! I'm so glad! You don't know," she sobbed, dropping weakly into the nearest chair.

"We can guess, ma'am," her foreman answered grimly, his eyes on Bannister. "And if either of these scoundrels have treated y'u so they need their light put out all y'u have got to do is to say so."

"No, no, Mac. Let us go away from here and leave them. Can't we go now—this very minute?"

The foreman's eyes found those of Denver and the latter nodded. Neither of them had had a bite to eat since the previous evening, and they were naturally ravenous.

"All right. We'll go right now, ma'am. Denver, I'll take care of these beauties while y'u step into the pantry with Mrs. Lo-the-poor-Indian and put up a lunch. Y'u don't want to forget we're hungry enough to eat the wool off a pair of chaps."

"I ain't likely to forget it, am I?" grinned Denver, as he rose.

"You poor boys! I know you are starved. I'll see about the lunch if one of you will get the horses round," Helen broke in. "Only let us hurry and get away from here."

Ten minutes later they were in the saddle. For the sake of precaution Mac walked two of his captives with them for about a mile before releasing them. Bannister, unable to travel, they left behind.

"We'll get down out of the hills and then cut acrost to the Meeker ranch," said McWilliams, after they had ridden forward a few miles. "I'll telephone from there to Slauson's and have the old man send a boy over to the Lazy D with the good word. We'll get an early start from Meeker's and make it home in the afternoon."

"How did you leave Mr. Bannister?" asked Helen, in a carefully careless voice.

She had held back this question for nearly an hour till Denver, who was guiding the party, had passed out of earshot.

"Left him with two of the boys holding him down. He was plumb anxious to commit suicide by joining the hunt for y'u, but I had other thoughts," grinned Mac.

She felt herself flushing in the darkness. "We've made a great mistake about him, Mac, It's his cousin of the same name that is the desperado—the man we just left."

"Yes, that's what Judd let out before y'u and the King arrived. It made me plumb glad to my gizzard to hear it."

"I was pleased, too."

"Somehow I suspicioned that," he made answer, with banter in his dry tones.

"Of course I would be glad to know that he is not a villain," she defended.

"Sure!"

"Well, one doesn't like to think that a friend—"

"He's your friend, is he?" chuckled Mac.

"Why shouldn't he be?"

"I'm offering no objections, ma'am."

"You act as if—"

"Sho! Don't pay any attention to me. Sometimes I get these spells of laughing in to myself. They just come. Doctors never could find a reason."

"Oh, well!"

"He was your enemy and now he's your friend. Course since I'm your foreman I got to keep posted on how we stand with our neighbors. If your feelings change to him again y'u'll let me know, I expect."

"Why should they change?" she asked in a cold voice that her rising color belied.

"Search *me!* I just thought mebbe—"

155

"You think too much," she cut in, shortly.

"Yes, ma'am," admitted the youth, meekly, but from time to time as they rode she could hear faint sounds of mirth from his direction. McWilliams telephoned from the Meeker ranch to Slauson's, and inside of two hours the Lazy D knew that its owner had been found. As one puncher after another reported there on jaded ponies to get the latest word they heard that all was well. Each one at once unsaddled, ate and turned in for the first night's sleep he had had since his mistress had been missing. Next morning they rode in a body to meet her.

She saw them galloping toward her in a cloud of dust, and presently she was the centre of a circle of her happy family. They were like boys—exuberant in their joy at her deliverance and eager to set out at once to avenge her wrongs.

Ned Bannister, from his window, saw them coming. When the group separated at the corral and she rode from among them with McWilliams toward the house the sheepman could sit still no longer. He limped to the front door and waved the American flag which he had unearthed for the occasion.

CHAPTER XII

MISTRESS AND MAID

N ow that it was safely concluded, Helen thought the adventure almost worth while for the spontaneous expressions of good will it had drawn forth from her adherents. Mrs. Winslow and Nora had taken her to their arms and wept and laughed over her in turn, and in their silent undemonstrative way she had felt herself hedged in by unusual solicitude on the part of her riders. It was good—none but she knew how good—to be back among her own, to bask in a friendliness she could not doubt. It was best of all to sit opposite Ned Bannister again with no weight on her heart from the consciousness of his unworthiness.

She could affect to disregard the gray eyes that followed her with such magnetized content about the living room, but beneath her cool self-containment she knew the joyous heart in her was strangely buoyant. He loved her, and she had a right to let herself love him. This was enough for the present.

"They're so plumb glad to see y'u they can't let y'u alone," laughed Bannister at the sound of a knock on the door that was about the fifth in as many minutes.

This time it proved to be Nora, come to find out what her mistress would like for supper. Helen turned to the invalid.

"What would you like, Mr. Bannister?"

"I should like a porterhouse with mushrooms," he announced promptly.

"You can't have it. You know what the doctor said." Very peremptorily she smiled this at him.

"He's an old granny, Miss Messiter."

"You may have an egg on toast."

"Make it two," he pleaded. "Excitement's just like caviar to the appetite, and seeing y'u safe—"

"Very well—two," she conceded.

They ate supper together in a renewal of the pleasant intimacy so delightful to both. He lay on the lounge, propped up with sofa cushions, the while he watched her deft fingers butter the toast and prepare his egg. It was surely worthwhile to be a convalescent, given so sweet a comrade for a nurse; and after he had moved over to the table he enjoyed immensely the gay firmness with which she denied him what was not good for him.

"I'll bet y'u didn't have supper like this at Robbers' Roost," he told her, enthusiastically.

"It wasn't so bad, considering everything." She was looking directly at him as she spoke. "Your cousin is rather a remarkable man in some ways. He manages to live on the best that can be got in tin-can land."

"Did he tell y'u he was my cousin?" he asked, slowly.

"Yes, and that his name was Ned Bannister, too?"

"Did that explain anything to y'u?"

"It explained a great deal, but it left some things not clear yet."

"For instance?"

"For one thing, the reason why you should bear the odium of his crimes. I suppose you don't care for him, though I can see how you might in a way."

"I don't care for him in the least, though I used to when we were boys. As to letting myself be blamed for his crimes, I did it because I couldn't help myself. We look more or less alike, and he was cunning enough to manufacture evidence against me. We were never seen together, and so very few know that there are two Bannisters. At first I used to protest, but I gave it up. There wasn't the least use. I could only wait for him to be captured or killed. In the meantime it didn't make me any more popular to be a sheepman."

"Weren't you taking a long chance of being killed first? Some one with a grudge against him might have shot you."

"They haven't yet," he smiled.

"You might at least have told *me* how it was," she reproached.

"I started to tell y'u that first day, but it looked so much of a fairy tale to unload that I passed it up."

"Then you ought not to blame me for thinking you what you were not."

"I don't remember blaming y'u. The fact is I thought it awful white of y'u to do your Christian duty so thorough, me being such a miscreant," he drawled.

"You gave me no chance to think well of you."

"But yet y'u did your duty from A to Z."

"We're not talking about my duty," she flashed back. "My point is that you weren't fair to me. If I thought ill of you how could I help it?"

"I expaict your Kalamazoo conscience is worryin' y'u because y'u misjudged me."

"It isn't," she denied instantly.

"I ain't of a revengeful disposition. I'll forgive y'u for doing your duty and saving my life twice," he said, with a smile of whimsical irony.

"I don't want your forgiveness."

"Well, then for thinking me a 'bad man.'"

"You ought to beg *my* pardon. I was a friend—at least you say I acted like one—and you didn't care enough to right yourself with me."

"Maybe I cared too much to risk trying it. I knew there would be proof some time, and I decided to lie under the suspicion until I could get it. I see now that wasn't kind or fair to you. I am sorry I didn't tell y'u all about it. May I tell y'u the story now?"

"If you wish."

It was a long story, but the main points can be told in a paragraph. The grandfather of the two cousins, General Edward Bannister, had worn the Confederate gray for four years, and had lost an arm in the service of the flag with the stars and bars. After the war he returned to his home in Virginia to find it in ruins, his slaves freed and his fields mortgaged. He had pulled himself together for another start, and had practiced law in the little town where his family had lived for generations. Of his two sons, one was a ne'er-do-well. He was one of those brilliant fellows of whom much is expected that never develops. He had a taste for low company, married beneath him, and, after a career that was a continual mortification and humiliation to his father, was killed in a drunken brawl under disgraceful circumstances, leaving behind a son named for the general. The second son of General Bannister also died young, but not before he had proved his devotion to his father by an exemplary life. He, too, was married and left an only son, also named for the old soldier. The boys were about of an age and were well matched in physical and

160

mental equipment. But the general, who had taken them both to live with him, soon discovered that their characters were as dissimilar as the poles. One grandson was frank, generous, open as the light; the other was of a nature almost degenerate. In fact, each had inherited the qualities of his father. Tales began to come to the old general's ears that at first he refused to credit. But eventually it was made plain to him that one of the boys was a rake of the most objectionable type.

There were many stormy scenes between the general and his grandson, but the boy continued to go from bad to worse. After a peculiarly flagrant case, involving the character of a respectable young girl, young Ned Bannister was forbidden his ancestral home. It had been by means of his cousin that this last iniquity of his had been unearthed, and the boy had taken it to his grandfather in hot indignation as the last hope of protecting the reputation of the injured girl. From that hour the evil hatred of his cousin, always dormant in the heart, flamed into active heat. The disowned youth swore to be revenged. A short time later the general died, leaving what little property he had entirely to the one grandson. This stirred again the bitter rage of the other. He set fire to the house that had been willed his cousin, and took a train that night for Wyoming. By a strange irony of fate they met again in the West years later, and the enmity between them was renewed, growing every month more bitter on the part of the one who called himself the King of the Bighorn Country.

She broke the silence after his story with a gentle

"Thank you. I can understand why you don't like to tell the story."

"I am very glad of the chance to tell it to you," he answered.

"When you were delirious you sometimes begged some one you called Ned not to break his mother's heart. I thought then you might be speaking to yourself as ill people do. Of course I see now it was your cousin that was on your mind."

"When I was out of my head I must have talked a lot of nonsense," he suggested, in the voice of a question. "I expect I had opinions I wouldn't have been scattering around so free if I'd known what I was saying."

He was hardly prepared for the tide of color that swept her cheeks at his words nor for the momentary confusion that shuttered the shy eyes with long lashes cast down.

"Sick folks do talk foolishness, they say," he added, his gaze trained on her suspiciously.

"Do they?"

"Mrs. Winslow says I did. But when I asked her what it was I said she only laughed and told me to ask y'u. Well, I'm askin' now."

She became very busy over the teapot. "You talked about the work at your ranch—sheep dipping and such things."

"Was that all?"

"No, about lots of other things—football and your early life. I don't see what Mrs. Winslow meant. Will you have some more tea?"

"No, thank y'u. I have finished. Yes, that ce'tainly seems harmless. I didn't know but I had been telling secrets." Still his unwavering eyes rested quietly on her.

"Secrets?" She summoned her aplomb to let a question rest lightly in the face she turned toward him, though she was afraid she met his eyes hardly long enough for complete innocence.

"Why, yes, secrets." He measured looks with her deliberately before he changed the subject. and he knew again the delightful excitement of victory. "Are y'u going to read to me this evening?"

She took his opening so eagerly that he smiled, at which her color mounted again.

"If y'u like. What shall I read?"

"Some more of Barrie's books, if y'u don't mind. When a fellow is weak as a kitten he sorter takes to things that are about kids."

Nora came in and cleared away the supper things. She was just beginning to wash them when McWilliams and Denver dropped into the kitchen by different doors. Each seemed surprised and disappointed at the presence of the other. Nora gave each of them a smile and a dishcloth.

"Reddy, he's shavin' and Frisco's struggling with a biled shirt—I mean with a necktie," Denver hastily amended. "They'll be along right soon, I shouldn't wonder."

"Y'u better go tell the boys Miss Nora don't want her kitchen littered up with so many of them," suggested his rival.

"Y'u're foreman here. I don't aim to butt into your business, Mac," grinned back the other, polishing a tea plate with the towel.

"I want to get some table linen over to Lee Ming tonight," said Nora, presently.

"Denver, he'll be glad to take it for y'u, Miss Nora. He's real obliging," offered Mac, generously.

"I've been in the house all day, so I need a walk. I thought perhaps one of you gentlemen—" Miss Nora looked from one to the other of them with deep innocence.

"Sure, I'll go along and carry it. Just as Mac says, I'll be real pleased to go," said Denver, hastily.

Mac felt he had been a trifle precipitate in his assumption that Nora did not intend to go herself. Lee Ming had established a laundry some half mile from the ranch, and the way thereto lay through most picturesque shadow and moonlight. The foreman had conscientious scruples against letting Denver escort her down such a veritable lovers' lane of romantic scenery.

"I don't know as y'u ought to go out in the night air with that cold, Denver. I'd hate a heap to have y'u catch pneumony. It don't seem to me I'd be justified in allowin' y'u to," said the foreman, anxiously.

"You're *that* thoughtful, Mac. But I expect mebbe a little saunter with Miss Nora will do my throat good. We'll walk real slow, so's not to wear out my strength."

"Big, husky fellows like y'u are awful likely to drop off with pneumony. I been thinkin' I got some awful good medicine that would be the right stuff for y'u. It's

164

in the drawer of my washstand. Help yourself liberal and it will surely do y'u good. Y'u'll find it *in a bottle*."

"I'll bet it's good medicine, Mac. After we get home I'll drop around. In the washstand, y'u said?"

"I hate to have y'u take such a risk," Mac tried again. "There ain't a bit of use in y'u exposing yourself so careless. Y'u take a hot footbath and some of that medicine, Denver, then go right straight to bed, and in the mo'ning y'u'll be good as new. Honest, y'u won't know yourself."

"Y'u got the *best* heart, Mac."

Nora giggled.

"Since I'm foreman I got to be a mother to y'u boys, ain't I?"

"Y'u're liable to be a grandmother to us if y'u keep on," came back the young giant.

"Y'u plumb discourage me, Denver," sighed the foreman.

"No, sir! The way I look at it, a fellow's got to take some risk. Now, y'u cayn't tell some things. I figure I ain't half so likely to catch pneumony as y'u would be to get heart trouble if y'u went walking with Miss Nora," returned Denver.

A perfect gravity sat on both their faces during the progress of most of their repartee.

"If your throat's so bad, Mr. Halliday, I'll put a kerosene rag round it for you when we get back," Nora said, with a sweet little glance of sympathy that the foreman did not enjoy.

Denver, otherwise "Mr. Halliday," beamed. "Y'u're

real kind, ma'am. I'll bet that will help it on the outside much as Mac's medicine will inside."

"What'll y'u do for my heart, ma'am, if it gits bad the way Denver figures it will?"

Y'u might try a mustard plaster," she gurgled, with laughter.

For once the deboniar foreman's ready tongue had brought him to defeat. He was about to retire from the field temporarily when Nora herself offered first aid to the wounded.

"We would like to have you come along with us, Mr. McWilliams. I want you to come if you can spare the time."

The soft eyes telegraphed an invitation with such a subtle suggestion of a private understanding that Mac was instantly encouraged to accept. He knew, of course, that she was playing them against each other and sitting back to enjoy the result, but he was possessed of the hope common to youths in his case that he really was on a better footing with her than the other boys. This opinion, it may be added, was shared by Denver, Frisco and even Reddy as regards themselves. Which is merely another way of putting the regrettable fact that this very charming young woman was given to coquetting with the hearts of her admirers.

"Any time y'u get oneasy about that cough y'u go right on home, Denver. Don't stay jest out of politeness. We'll never miss y'u, anyhow," the foreman assured him.

"Thank y'u, Mac. But y'u see I got to stay to keep

Miss Nora from getting bored."

"Was it a phrenologist strung y'u with the notion y'u was a cure for lonesomeness?"

"Shucks! I don't make no such claims. The only thing is it's a comfort when you're bored to have company. Miss Nora, she's so polite. But, y'u see, if I'm along I can take y'u for a walk when y'u get too bad."

They reached the little trail that ran up to Lee Ming's place, and Denver suggested that Mac run in with the bundle so as to save Nora the climb.

"I'd like to, honest I would. But since y'u thought of it first I won't steal the credit of doing Miss Nora a good turn. We'll wait right here for y'u till y'u come back."

"We'll all go up together," decided Nora, and honors were easy.

In the pleasant moonlight they sauntered back, two of them still engaged in lively badinage, while the third played chorus with appreciative little giggles and murmurs of "Oh, Mr. Halliday!" and "You know you're just flattering me, Mr. McWilliams."

If they had not been so absorbed in their gay foolishness the two men might not have walked so innocently into the trap waiting for them at their journey's end. As it was, the first intimation they had of anything unusual was a stern command to surrender.

"Throw up your hands. Quick, you blank fools!"

A masked man covered them, in each hand a six-shooter, and at his summons the arms of the cow-punchers went instantly into the air.

Nora gave an involuntary little scream of dismay.

"Y'u don't need to be afraid, lady. Ain't nobody going to hurt you, I reckon," the masked man growled.

"Sure they won't," Mac reassured her, adding ironically: "This gun-play business is just a neighborly frolic. Liable to happen any day in Wyoming."

A second masked man stepped up. He, too, was garnished with an arsenal.

"What's all this talking about?" he demanded, sharply.

"We just been having a little conversation, seh?" returned McWilliams, gently, his vigilant eyes searching through the disguise of the other. "Just been telling the lady that your call is in a friendly spirit. No objections, I suppose?"

The swarthy newcomer, who seemed to be in command, swore sourly.

"Y'u put a knot in your tongue, Mr. Foreman."

"Ce'tainly, if y'u prefer," returned the indomitable McWilliams.

"Shut up or I'll pump lead into you!"

"I'm padlocked, seh."

Nora Darling interrupted the dialogue by quietly fainting. The foreman caught her as she fell.

"See what y'u done, y'u blamed chump!" he snapped.

CHAPTER XIII

THE TWO COUSINS

The sheepman lay at his ease, the strong supple lines of him stretched lazily on the lounge. Helen was sitting beside him in an easy chair, and he watched the play of her face in the lamplight as she read from "The Little White Bird." She was very good to see, so vitally alive and full of a sweet charm that half revealed and half concealed her personality, The imagination with which she threw herself into a discussion of the child fancies portrayed by the Scotch writer captured his fancy. It delighted him to tempt her into discursions that told him by suggestion something of what she thought and was.

They were in animated debate when the door opened to admit somebody else. He had stepped in so quietly that he stood there a little while without being observed, smiling down at them with triumphant malice behind the mask he wore. Perhaps it was the black visor that was responsible for the Mephisto effect, since it hid all the face but the leering eyes. These, narrowed to slits, swept the room and came back to its occupants. He was a tall man and well-knit, dressed incongruously in up-to-date riding breeches and boots, in combination with the usual gray shirt, knotted kerchief and wide-brimmed felt hat of the horseman of the plains. The dust of the desert lay thick on him, without in the least obscuring a certain ribald elegance, a distinction of wickedness that rested upon him as his due. To this result his debonair manner contributed, though it carried with it no suggestion of weakness. To the girl who looked up and found him there he looked indescribably sinister.

She half rose to her feet, dilated eyes fixed on him.

"Good evenin'. I came to make sure y'u got safe home, Miss Messiter," he said.

The eyes of the two men clashed, the sheepman's stern and unyielding, his cousin's lit with the devil of triumph. But out of the faces of both men looked the inevitable conflict, the declaration of war that never ends till death.

"I've been a heap anxious about y'u—couldn't sleep for worrying. So I saddled up and rode in to find out if y'u were all right and to inquire how Cousin Ned was getting along."

The sheepman, not deigning to move an inch from his position, looked in silence his steady contempt.

"This conversation sounds a whole lot like a monologue up to date," he continued. "Now, maybe y'u don't know y'u have the honor of entertaining the King of the Bighorn." The man's brown hand brushed the mask from his eyes and he bowed with mocking deference. "Miss Messiter, allow me to introduce myself again— Ned Bannister, train robber, rustler, kidnapper and general bad man. But I ain't told y'u the worst yet. I'm cousin to a sheepherder, and that's the lowest thing that walks."

170

He limped forward a few steps and sat down. "Thank you, I believe I will stay a while since y'u both ask me so urgent. It isn't often I meet with a welcome so hearty and straight from the heart."

It was not hard to see how the likeness between them contributed to the mistake that had been current concerning them. Side by side, no man could have mistaken one for the other. The color of their eyes, the shade of hair, even the cut of their features, were different. But beneath all distinctions in detail ran a family resemblance not to be denied. This man looked like his cousin, the sheepman, as the latter might have done if all his life he had given a free rein to evil passions. The height, the build, the elastic tread of each, made further contributions to this effect of similarity.

"What are you doing here?" They were the first words spoken by the man on the lounge and they rang with a curt challenge.

"Come to inquire after the health of my dear cousin," came the prompt silken answer.

"You villain!"

"My dear cousin, y'u speak with such conviction that y'u almost persuade me. But of course if I'm a villain I've got to live up to my reputation. Haven't I, Miss Messiter?"

"Wouldn't it be better to live it down?" she asked with a quietness that belied her terror. For there had been in his manner a threat, not against her but against the man whom her heart acknowledged as her lover.

He laughed. "Yu're still hoping to make a Sunday

school superintendent out of me, I see. Y'u haven't forgot all your schoolmarm ways yet, but I'll teach y'u to forget them."

The other cousin watched him with a cool, quiet glance that never wavered. The outlaw was heavily armed, but his weapons were sheathed, and, though there was a wary glitter behind the vindictive exultation in his eyes, his capable hands betrayed no knowledge of the existence of his revolvers. It was, he knew, to be a moral victory, if one at all.

"Hope I'm not disturbing any happy family circle," he remarked, and, taking two limping steps forward, he lifted the book from the girl's unresisting hands. H'm! Barrie. I don't go much on him. He's too sissy for me. But I could have guessed the other Ned Bannister would be reading something like that," he concluded, a flicker of sneering contempt crossing his face.

"Perhaps y'u'll learn some time to attend to your own business," said the man on the couch quietly.

Hatred gleamed in the narrowed slits from which the soul of the other cousin looked down at him. "I'm a philanthropist, and my business is attending to other people's. They raise sheep, for instance, and I market them."

The girl hastily interrupted. She had not feared for herself, but she knew fear for the indomitable man she had nursed back to life. "Won't you sit down, Mr. Bannister? Since you don't approve our literature, perhaps we can find some other diversion more to your taste." She smiled faintly.

172

The man turned in smiling divination of her purpose, and sat down to play with her as a cat does with a mouse.

"Thank y'u, Miss Messiter, I believe I will. I called to thank y'u for your kindness to my cousin as well as to inquire about you. The word goes that y'u pulled my dear cousin back when death was reaching mighty strong for him. Of course I feel grateful to y'u. How is he getting along now?"

"He's doing very well, I think."

"That's ce'tainly good hearing," was his ironical response. "How come he to get hurt, did y'u say?"

His sleek smile was a thing hateful to see.

"A hound bit me," explained the sheepman.

"Y'u don't say! I reckon y'u oughtn't to have got in its way. Did y'u kill it?"

"Not yet."

"That was surely a mistake, for it's liable to bite again."

The girl felt a sudden sickness at his honeyed cruelty, but immediately pulled herself together. For whatever fiendish intention might be in his mind she meant to frustrate it.

"I hear you are of a musical turn, Mr. Bannister. Won't you play for us?"

She had by chance found his weak spot. Instantly his eyes lit up. He stepped across to the piano and began to look over the music, though not so intently that he forgot to keep under his eye the man on the lounge.

"H'm! Mozart, Grieg, Chopin, Raff, Beethoven. Y'u

ce'tainly have the music here; I wonder if y'u have the musician." He looked her over with a bold, unscrupulous gaze. "It's an old trick to have classical music on the rack and ragtime in your soul. Can y'u play these?"

"You will have to be the judge of that," she said.

He selected two of Grieg's songs and invited her to the piano. He knew instantly that the Norwegian's delicate fancy and lyrical feeling had found in her no inadequate medium of expression. The peculiar emotional quality of the song "I Love Thee" seemed to fill the room as she played. When she swung round on the stool at its conclusion it was to meet a shining-eyed, musical enthusiast instead of the villain she had left five minutes earlier.

"Y'u *can* play," was all he said, but the manner of it spoke volumes.

For nearly an hour he kept her at the piano, and when at last he let her stop playing he seemed a man transformed.

"You have given me a great pleasure, a very great pleasure, Miss Messiter," he thanked her warmly, his Western idiom sloughed with his villainy for the moment. "It has been a good many months since I have heard any decent music. With your permission I shall come again."

Her hesitation was imperceptible. "Surely, if you wish." She felt it would be worse than idle to deny the permission she might not be able to refuse.

With perfect grace he bowed, and as he wheeled away met with a little shock of remembrance the gaze of his

174

cousin. For a long moment their eyes bored into each other. Neither yielded the beat of an eyelid, but it was the outlaw that spoke.

"I had forgotten y'u. That's strange, too, because it was for y'u I came. I'm going to take y'u home with me."

"Alive or dead?" asked the other serenely.

"Alive, dear Ned."

"Same old traits cropping out again. There was always something feline about y'u. I remember when y'u were a boy y'u liked to torment wild animals y'u had trapped."

"I play with larger game now—and find it more interesting."

"Just so. Miss Messiter, I shall have to borrow a pony from y'u, unless—" He broke off and turned indifferently to the bandit.

"Yes, I brought a hawss along with me for y'u," replied the other to the unvoiced question. "I thought maybe y'u might want to ride with us."

"But he can't ride. He couldn't possibly. It would kill him," the girl broke out.

"I reckon not." The man from the Shoshones glanced at his victim as he drew on his gauntlets. "He's a heap tougher than y'u think."

"But it will. If he should ride now, why—It would be the same as murder," she gasped. "You wouldn't make him ride now?"

"Didn't y'u hear him order his hawss, ma'am? He's keen on this ride. Of course he don't have to go unless

175

he wants to." The man turned his villainous smile on his cousin, and the latter interpreted it to mean that if he preferred, the point of attack might be shifted to the girl. He might go or he might stay. But if he stayed the mistress of the Lazy D would have to pay for his decision.

"No, I'll ride," he said at once.

Helen Messiter had missed the meaning of that Marconied message that flashed between them. She set her jaw with decision. "Well, you'll not. It's perfectly ridiculous. I won't hear of such a thing."

"Y'u seem right welcome. Hadn't y'u better stay, Ned?" murmured the outlaw, with smiling eyes that mocked.

"Of course he had. He couldn't ride a mile—not half a mile. The idea is utterly preposterous."

The sheepman got to his feet unsteadily. "I'll do famously."

"I won't have it. Why are you so foolish about going? He said you didn't need to go. You can't ride any more than a baby could chop down that pine in the yard."

"I'm a heap stronger than y'u think."

"Yes, you are!" she derided. "It's nothing but obstinacy. Make him stay," she appealed to the outlaw.

"Am I my cousin's keeper?" he drawled. "I can advise him to stay, but I can't make him."

"Well, I can. I'm his nurse, and I say he sha'n't stir a foot out of this house—not a foot."

The wounded man smiled quietly, admiring the splendid energy of her. "I'm right sorry to leave y'u so unceremoniously."

"You're not going." She wheeled on the outlaw "I don't understand this at all. But if you want him you can find him here when you come again. Put him on parole and leave him here. I'll not be a party to murder by letting him go."

"Y'u think I'm going to murder him?" he smiled.

"I think he cannot stand the riding. It would kill him."

"A haidstrong man is bound to have his way. He seems hell-bent on riding. All the docs say the outside of a hawss is good for the inside of a man. Mebbe it'll be the making of him."

"I won't have it. I'll rouse the whole countryside against you. Why don't you parole him till he is better?"

"All right. We'll leave it that way," announced the man. "I'd hate to hurt your tender feelings after such a pleasant evening. Let him give his parole to come to me whenever I send for him, no matter where he may be, to quit whatever he is doing right that instant, and come on the jump. If he wants to leave it that way, we'll call it a bargain."

Again the rapier-thrust of their eyes crossed. The sheepman was satisfied with what he saw in the face of his foe.

"All right. It's a deal," he agreed, and sank weakly back to the couch.

There are men whose looks are a profanation to any good woman. Ned Bannister, of the Shoshones, was one of them. He looked at his cousin, and his ribald eyes coasted back to bold scrutiny of this young woman's charming, buoyant youth. There was something in his face that sent a flush of shame coursing through her rich blood. No man had ever looked at her like that before.

"Take awful good care of him," he sneered, with so plain an implication of evil that her clean blood boiled. "But I know y'u will, and don't let him go before he's real strong."

"No," she murmured, hating herself for the flush that bathed her.

He bowed like a Chesterfield, and went out with elastic heels, spurs clicking.

Helen turned fiercely on her guest. "Why did you make me insist on your staying? As if I want you here, as if—" She stopped, choking with anger; presently flamed out, "I hate you," and ran from the room to hide herself alone with her tears and her shame.

CHAPTER XIV

FOR THE WORLD'S CHAMPIONSHIP

The scene on which Helen Messiter's eyes rested that mellow Fourth of July was vivid enough to have interested a far more jaded mind than hers. Nowhere outside of Cattleland could it have been duplicated. Wyoming is sparsely populated, but the riders of the plains think nothing of traveling a hundred miles in the saddle to be present at a "bronco-busting" contest. Large delegations, too, had come in by railroad from Caspar, Billings, Sheridan, Cheyenne and a score of other points, so that the amphitheatre that looked down on the arena was filled to its capacity.

All night the little town had rioted with its guests. Everything was wide open at Gimlet Butte. Saloons were doing a land-office business and gambling-houses coining money. Great piles of gold had passed to and fro during the night at the roulette wheel and the faro table. But with the coming of day interest had centered on the rough-riding contest for the world's championship. Saloons and dance halls were deserted, and the universal trend of travel had been toward the big grand stands, from which the sport could be best viewed.

It was afternoon now. The preliminaries had been ridden, and half a dozen of the best riders had been chosen by the judges to ride again for the finals. Helen was wonderfully interested, because in the six who were to ride again were included the two Bannister cousins, her foreman, McWilliams, the young man "Texas," whom she had met the day of her arrival at Gimlet Butte, and Tom Sanford, who had last year won the championship.

She looked down on the arena, and her heart throbbed with the pure joy of life. Already she loved her West and its picturesque, chap-clad population. Their jingling spurs and their colored kerchiefs knotted round sunburned necks, their frank, whole-hearted abandon to the interest of the moment, led her to regard these youths as schoolboys. Yet they were a hard-bitten lot, as one could see, burned to a brick-red by the untempered sun of the Rockies; with muscles knit like steel, and hearts toughened to endure any blizzard they might meet. Only the humorous wrinkles about the corners of their eyes gave them away for the cheerful sons of mirth that they were.

"Bob Austin on Two-step," annnounced the megaphone man, and a little stir eddied through the group gathered at the lane between the arena and the corral.

A meek-looking buckskin was driven into the arena. The embodiment of listlessness, it apparently had not ambition enough to flick a fly from its flank with its tail. Suddenly the bronco's ears pricked, its sharp eyes dilated. A man was riding forward, the loop of a lariat circling about his head. The rope fell true, but the wily pony side-stepped, and the loop slithered to the ground. Again the rope shot forward, dropped over the pony's head and tightened. The roper's mustang braced its forefeet, and brought the buckskin up short. Another rope swept over its head. It stood trembling, unable to move without strangling itself.

A picturesque youth in flannel shirt and chaps came forward, dragging blanket, saddle and bridle. At sight of him the horse gave a spasmodic fling, then trembled again violently. A blind was coaxed over its eyes and the bridle slipped on. Quickly and warily, with deft fingers, the young man saddled and cinched. He waved a hand jauntily to the ropers. The lariats were thrown off as the puncher swung to the saddle. For an instant the buckskin stood bewildered, motionless as a statue. There was a sudden leap forward high in air, and Bob

180

Austin, alias "Texas,' swung his sombrero with a joyous whoop.

"Fan him! Fan him!" screamed the spectators, and the rider's quirt went up and down like a piston-rod.

Round and round went Two-step in a vicious circle, "swapping ends" with dizzying rapidity. Suddenly he went forward as from a catapult, and came to sudden halt in about five seconds. But Texas's knees still clung, viselike, to the sides of the pony. A series of quick bucks followed, the buckskin corning down with back humped, all four legs stiff as iron posts. The jar on the rider would have been like a pile-driver falling on his head had he not let himself grow limp. The buckskin plunged forward again in frenzied leaps, ending in an unexpected jump to one side. Alas for Texas! One moment he was jubilantly plying quirt and spurs, the next he found himself pitching sideways. To save himself he caught at the saddle-horn.

"He's hunting leather," shouted a hundred voices.

One of the judges rode out and waved a hand. Texas slipped to the ground disqualified, and made his dejected way back to his deriding comrades. Some of them had endured similar misfortunes earlier in the day. Therefore they found much pleasure in condoling with him.

"If he'd only recollected to saw off the horn of his saddle, then he couldn't 'a' found it when he went to hunt leather," mournfully commented one puncher in a shirt of robin's egg blue.

" 'Twould have been most as good as to take the dust,

wouldn't it?" retorted Texas gently, and the laugh was on the gentleman in blue, because he had been thrown earlier in the day.

"A fellow's hands sure get in his way sometimes. I reckon if you'd tied your hands, Tex, you'd been riding that rocking-hawss yet," suggested Denver amiably.

"Sometimes it's his foot he puts in it. There was onct a gent disqualified for riding on his spurs," said Texas reminiscently.

At which hit Denver retired, for not three hours before he had been detected digging his spurs into the cinch to help him stick to the saddle.

"Jim McWilliams will ride Dead Easy," came the announcement through the megaphone, and a burst of cheering passed along the grand stand, for the sunny smile of the foreman of the Lazy D made him a general favorite. Helen leaned forward and whispered something gaily to Nora, who sat in the seat in front of her. The Irish girl laughed and blushed, but when her mistress looked up it was her turn to feel the mounting color creep into her cheeks. For Ned Bannister, arrayed in all his riding finery, was making his way along the aisle to her.

She had not seen him since he had ridden away from the Lazy D ten days before, quite sufficiently recovered from his wounds to take up the routine of life again. They had parted not the best of friends, for she had not yet forgiven him for his determination to leave with his cousin on the night that she had been forced to insist on his remaining. He had put her in a false position, and he

182

had never explained to her why. Nor could she guess the reason—for he was not a man to harvest credit for himself by explaining his own chivalry.

Since her heart told her how glad she was he had come to her box to see her, she greeted him with the coolest little nod in the world.

"Good morning, Miss Messiter. May I sit beside y'u?" he asked.

"Oh, certainly!" She swept her skirts aside carelessly and made room for him. "I thought you were going to ride soon."

"No, I ride last except for Sanford, the champion. My cousin rides just before me. He's entered under the name of Jack Holloway."

She was thinking that he had no business to be riding, that his wounds were still too fresh, but she did not intend again to show interest enough in his affairs to interfere even by suggestion. Her heart had been in her mouth every moment of the time this morning while he had been tossed hither and thither on the back of his mount. In his delirium he had said he loved her. If he did, why should he torture her so? It was well enough for sound men to risk their lives, but—

A cheer swelled in the grand stand and died breathlessly away. McWilliams was setting a pace it would take a rare expert to equal. He was a trick rider, and all the spectacular feats that appealed to the onlooker were his. While his horse was wildly pitching, he drank a bottle of pop and tossed the bottle away. With the reins in his teeth he slipped off his coat and vest, and concluded a splendid exhibition of skill by riding with his feet out of the stirrups. He had been smoking a cigar when he mounted. Except while he had been drinking the pop it had been in his mouth from beginning to end, and, after he had vaulted from the pony's back, he deliberately puffed a long smoke-spiral into the air, to show that his cigar was still alight. No previous rider had earned so spontaneous a burst of applause.

"He's ce'tainly a pure when it comes to riding," acknowledged Bannister. "I look to see him get either first or second."

"Whom do you think is his most dangerous rival?" Helen asked.

"My cousin is a straight-up rider, too. He's more graceful than Mac, I think, but not quite so good on tricks. It will be nip and tuck."

"How about your cousin's cousin?" she asked, with bold irony.

"He hopes he won't have to take the dust," was his laughing answer.

The next rider suffered defeat irrevocably before he had been thirty seconds in the saddle. His mount was one of the most cunning of the outlaw ponies of the Northwest, and it brought him to grief by jamming his leg hard against the fence. He tried in vain to spur the bronco into the middle of the arena, but after it drove at a post for the third time and ground his limb against it, he gave up to the pain and slipped off.

"That isn't fair, is it?" Helen asked of the young man sitting beside her.

He shrugged his lean, broad shoulders. "He should have known how to keep the horse in the open. Mac would never have been caught that way."

"Jack Holloway on Rocking Horse," the announcer shouted.

It took four men and two lariats to subdue this horse to a condition sufficiently tame to permit of a saddle being slipped on. Even then this could not be accomplished without throwing the bronco first. The result was that all the spirit was taken out of the animal by the preliminary ordeal, so that when the man from the Shoshone country mounted, his steed was too jaded to attempt resistance.

"Thumb him! Thumb him!" the audience cried, referring to the cowboy trick of running the thumbs along a certain place in the shoulder to stir the anger of the bucker.

But the rider slipped off with disgust. "Give me another horse," he demanded, and after a minute's consultation among the judges a second pony was driven out from the corral. This one proved to be a Tartar. It went off in a frenzy of pitching the moment its rider dropped into the saddle.

"Y'u'll go a long way before you see better ridin' than his and Mac's. Notice how he gives to its pitching," said Bannister, as he watched his cousin's perfect ease in the cyclone of which he was the center.

"I expect it depends on the kind of a 'hawss,'" she mocked. "He's riding well, isn't he?"

"I don't know any that ride better."

The horse put up a superb fight, trying everything it knew to unseat this demon clamped to its back. It possessed in combination all the worst vices, was a weaver, a sunfisher and a fence-rower, and never had it tried so desperately to maintain its record of never having been ridden. But the outlaw in the saddle was too much for the outlaw underneath. He was master, just as he was first among the ruffians whom he led, because there was in him a red-hot devil of wickedness that would brook no rival.

The furious bronco surrendered without an instant's warning, and its rider slipped at once to the ground. As he sauntered through the dust toward the grand stand, Helen could not fail to see how his vanity sunned itself in the applause that met his performance. His equipment was perfect to the least detail. The reflection from a lady's looking-glass was no brighter than the silver spurs he jingled on his sprightly heels, Strikingly handsome in a dark, sinister way, one would say at first sight, and later would chafe at the justice of a verdict not to be denied.

Ned Bannister rose from his seat beside Helen. "Wish me luck," he said, with his gay smile.

"I wish you all the luck you deserve," she answered.

"Oh, wish me more than that if y'u want me to win."

"I didn't say I wanted you to win. You take the most unaccountable things for granted."

"I've a good mind to win, then, just to spite y'u," he laughed.

"As if you could," she mocked; but her voice took a

softer intonation as she called after him in a low murmur: "Be careful, please."

His white teeth flashed a smile of reassurance at her. "I've never been killed yet."

"Ned Bannister on Steamboat," sang out the megaphone man.

"I'm ce'tainly in luck. Steamboat's the worst hawss on the range," he told himself, as he strode down the grand stand to enter the arena.

The announcement of his name created for the second time that day a stir of unusual interest. Everybody in that large audience had heard of Ned Bannister; knew of his record as a "bad man" and his prowess as the king of the Shoshone country; suspected him of being a train and bank robber as well as a rustler. That he should have the boldness to enter the contest in his own name seemed to show how defiant he was of the public sentiment against him, and how secure he counted himself in flaunting this contempt. As for the sheepman, the notoriety that his cousin's odorous reputation had thrust upon him was extremely distasteful as well as dangerous, but he had done nothing to disgrace his name, and he meant to use it openly. He could almost catch the low whispers that passed from mouth to mouth about him.

"Ain't it a shame that a fellow like that, leader of all the criminals that hide in the mountains, can show himself openly before ten thousand honest folks?" That he knew to be the purport of their whispering, and along with it went a recital of the crimes he had committed.

How he was a noted "waddy," or cattle-rustler; how he and his gang had held up three trains in eighteen months; how he had killed Tom Mooney, Bob Carney and several others—these were the sorts of things that were being said about him, and from the bottom of his soul he resented his impotency to clear his name.

There was something in Bannister's riding that caught Helen's fancy at once. It was the unconscious grace of the man, the ease with which he seemed to make himself a very part of the horse. He attempted no tricks, rode without any flourishes. But the perfect poise of his lithe body as it gave with the motions of the horse, proclaimed him a born rider; so finished, indeed, that his very ease seemed to discount the performance. Steamboat had a malevolent red eye that glared hatred at the oppressor man, and today it lived up to its reputation of being the most vicious and untamed animal on the frontier. But, though it did its best to unseat the rider and trample him underfoot, there was no moment when the issue seemed in doubt save once. The horse flung itself backward in a somersault, risking its own neck in order to break its master's. But he was equal to the occasion; and when Steamboat staggered again to its feet Bannister was still in the saddle. It was a daring and magnificent piece of horsemanship, and, though he was supposed to be a desperado and a ruffian, his achievement met with a breathless gasp, followed by thunderous applause.

The battle between horse and man was on again, for the animal was as strong almost in courage as the rider.

But Steamboat's confidence had been shaken as well as its strength. Its efforts grew less cyclonic. Foam covered its mouth and flecked its sides. The pitches were easy to foresee and meet. Presently they ceased altogether.

Bannister slid from the saddle and swayed unsteadily across the arena. The emergency past, he had scarce an ounce of force left in him. Jim McWilliams ran out and slipped an arm around his shoulders, regardless of what his friends might think of him for it.

"You're all in, old man. Y'u hadn't ought to have ridden, even though y'u did skin us all to a finish."

"Nonsense, Mac. First place goes to y'u or—or Jack Holloway."

"Not unless the judges are blind."

But Bannister's prediction proved true. The champion, Sanford, had been traveling with a Wild West show, and was far too soft to compete with these lusty cowboys, who had kept hard from their daily life on the plains. Before he had ridden three minutes it was apparent that he stood no chance of retaining his title, so that the decision narrowed itself to an issue between the two Bannisters and McWilliams. First place was awarded to the latter, the second prize to Jack Holloway and the third to Ned Bannister.

But nearly everybody in the grand stand knew that Bannister had been discriminated against because of his unpopularity. The judges were not local men, and had nothing to fear from the outlaw. Therefore they penalized him on account of his reputation. It would never do for the Associated Press dispatches to send word all over the East that a murderous desperado was permitted, unmolested, to walk away with the championship belt.

"It ain't a square deal," declared McWilliams promptly.

He was sitting beside Nora, and he turned round to express his opinion to the two sitting behind him in the box.

"We'll not go behind the returns. Y'u won fairly. I congratulate y'u, Mr. Champion-of-the-world," replied the sheepman, shaking hands cordially.

"I told you to bring that belt to the Lazy D," smiled his mistress, as she shook hands.

But in her heart she was crying out that it was an outrage.

CHAPTER XV

JUDD MORGAN PASSES

Gimlet Butte devoted the night of the Fourth to a high old time. The roping and the other sports were to be on the morrow, and meanwhile the night hours were filled with exuberance. The cowboy's spree comes only once in several months, but when it does come he enters into the occasion with such whole-hearted enthusiasm as to make up swiftly for lost time. A traveling midway had cast its tents in a vacant square in competition with the regular attractions of the town, and everywhere the hard-riding punchers were "night herding" in full regalia.

There was a big masked ball in the street, and another in the Masonic Hall, while here and there flared the lights of the faker with something to sell. Among these last was "Soapy" Sothern, doing a thriving business in selling suckers and bars wrapped with greenbacks. Crowds tramped the streets blowing horns and throwing confetti, and everywhere was a large sprinkling of men in high-heeled boots, swinging along with the awkward, stiff-legged gait of the cowboy. Sometimes a girl was hanging on his arm, and again he was "whooping it up with the boys"; but in either case the range-rider's savings were burning a hole through his pockets with extreme rapidity.

Jim McWilliams and the sheepman Bannister had that day sealed a friendship that was to be as enduring as life. The owner of the sheep ranch was already under heavy obligation to the foreman of the Lazy D, but debt alone is not enough on which to found soul brotherhood. There must be qualities of kinship in the primeval elements of character. Both men had suspected that this kinship existed, but today they had proved it in the way that one had lost and the other had won the coveted championship. They had made no vows and no professions. The subject had not even been touched in words; a meeting of the eyes, followed by the handshake with which Bannister had congratulated the winner. That had been all. But it was enough.

With the casual democracy of the frontier they had

together escorted Helen Messiter and Nora Darling through a riotous three hours of carnival, taking care to get them back to their hotel before the night really began "to howl."

But after they had left the young women, neither of them cared to sleep yet. They were still in costume, Mac dressed as a monk, and his friend as a Stuart cavalier, and the spirit of frolic was yet strong in them.

"I expaict, mebbe, we better hunt in couples if we're going to help paint the town," smiled Mac, and his friend had immediately agreed.

It must have been well after midnight that they found themselves "bucking the tiger" in a combination saloon and gambling-house, whose patrons were decidedly cosmopolitan in character. Here white and red and yellow men played side by side, the Orient and the Occident and the aboriginal alike intent on the falling cards and the little rolling ball. A good many of them were still in their masks and dominos, though these, for the most part, removed their visors before playing.

Neither McWilliams nor his friend were betting high, and the luck had been so even that at the end of two hours' play neither of them had at any time either won or lost more than fifteen dollars. In point of fact, they were playing not so much to win as just to keep in touch with the gay, youthful humor of the night.

They were getting tired of the game when two men jingled in for a drink. They were talking loudly together, and it was impossible to miss the subject of their conversation.

McWilliams gave a little jerk of his head toward one of them. "Judd Morgan," his lips framed without making a sound.

Bannister nodded.

"Been tanking up all day," Mac added. "Otherwise his tongue would not be shooting off so reckless."

A silence had fallen over the assembly save for the braggarts at the bar. Men looked at each other, and then furtively at Bannister. For Morgan, ignorant of who was sitting quietly with his back to him at the faro-table, was venting his hate of Bannister and McWilliams.

"Both in the same boat. Did y'u see how Mac ran to help him today? Both waddies. Both rustlers. Both train robbers. Sho! I got through putting a padlock on me mouth. Man to man, I'm as good as either of them—damn sight better. I wisht they was here, one or both; I wisht they would step up here and fight it out. Bannister's a false alarm, and that foreman of the Lazy D—" His tongue stumbled over a blur of villification that ended with a foul mention of Miss Messiter.

Instantly two chairs crashed to the floor. Two pair of gray eyes met quietly.

"My quarrel, Bann," said Jim, in a low, even voice.

The other nodded. "I'll see y'u have a clear field."

The man who was with Morgan suddenly whispered in his ear, and the latter slewed his head in startled fear. Almost instantly a bullet clipped past McWilliams's shoulder. Morgan had fired without waiting for the challenge he felt sure was at hand. Once—twice the foreman's revolver made answer. Morgan staggered, slipped down to the floor, a bullet crashing through the chandelier as he fell. For a moment his body jerked. Then he rolled over and lay still.

The foreman's weapon covered him unwaveringly, but no more steadily than Bannister's gaze the man who had come in with him who lay lifeless on the floor. The man looked at the lifeless thing, shuddered, and backed out of the saloon.

"I call y'u all to witness that my friend killed him in self-defense," said Bannister evenly. "Y'u all saw him fire first. Mac did not even have his gun out."

"That's right," agreed one, and another added: "He got what was coming to him."

"He sure did," was the barkeeper's indorsement. "He came in hunting trouble, but I reckon he didn't want to be accommodated so prompt."

"Y'u'll find us at the Gimlet Butte House if we're wanted for this," said Bannister. "We'll be there till mo'ning."

But once out of the gambling-house McWilliams drew his friend to one side. "Do y'u know who that was I killed?"

"Judd Morgan, foreman before y'u at the Lazy D."

"Yes, but what else?"

"What do y'u mean?"

"I mean that next to your cousin Judd was leader of that Shoshone-Teton bunch."

"How do y'u know?"

"I suspected it a long time, but I knew for sure the day that your cousin held up the ranch. The man that was in charge of the crowd outside was Morgan. I could swear to it. I knew him soon as I clapped eyes to him, but I was awful careful to forget to tell him I recognized him."

"That means we are in more serious trouble than I had supposed."

"Y'u bet it does. We're in a hell of a hole, figure it out any way y'u like. Instead of having shot up a casual idiot, I've killed Ned Bannister's right-hand man. That will be the excuse—shooting Morgan. But the real trouble is that I won the championship belt from your cousin. He already hated y'u like poison, and he don't love me any too hard. He will have us arrested by his sheriff here. Catch the point. *Y'u're Ned Bannister, the outlaw, and I'm his right-bower.* That's the play he's going to make, and he's going to make it right soon."

"I don't care if he does. We'll fight him on his own ground. We'll prove that he's the miscreant and not us."

"Prove nothing," snarled McWilliams. "Do y'u reckon he'll give us a chance to prove a thing? Not on your life. He'll have us jailed first thing; then he'll stir up a sentiment against us, and before morning there will be a lynching-bee, and y'u and I will wear the neckties. How do y'u like the looks of it?"

"But y'u have a lot of friends. They won't stand for anything like that."

"Not if they had time to stop it. Trouble is, a fellow's friends think awful slow. They'll arrive in time to cut us down and be the mourners. No, sir! It's a hike for

Jimmie Mac on the back of the first bronc he can slap a saddle on."

Bannister frowned. "I don't like to run before the scurvy scoundrels."

"Do y'u suppose I'm enjoying it? Not to any extent, I allow. But that sweet relative of yours holds every ace in the deck, and he'll play them, too. He owns the law in this man's town, and he owns the lawless. But the best card he holds is that he can get a thousand of the best people here to join him in hanging the 'king' of the Shoshone outlaws. Explanations nothing! Y'u *rode* under the name of Bannister, didn't y'u? He's Jack Holloway."

"It does make a strong combination," admitted the sheepman.

"Strong! It's invincible. I can see him playing it, laughing up his sleeve all the time at the honest fools he is working. No, sir! I draw out of a game like that. Y'u don't get a run for your money."

"Of course he knows already what has happened," mused Bannister.

"Sure he knows. That fellow with Morgan made a bee-line for him. Just about now he's routing the sheriff out of his bed. We got no time to lose. Thing is, to burn the wind out of this town while we have the chance."

"I see. It won't help us any to be spilling lead into a sheriff's posse. That would ce'tainly put us in the wrong."

"Now y'u're shouting. If we're honest men, why don't we surrender peaceable? That's the play the

196

'king' is going to make in this town. Now if we should spoil a posse and bump off one or two of them, we couldn't pile up evidence enough to get a jury to acquit. No, sir! We can't surrender and we can't fight. Consequence is, we got to roll our tails immediate."

"We have an appointment with Miss Messiter and Nora for tomorrow morning. We'll have to leave word we can't keep it."

"Sure. Denver and Missou are playing the wheel down at the Silver Dollar. I reckon we better make those boys jump and run errands for us while we lie low. I'll drop in casual and give them the word. Meet y'u here in ten minutes. Whatever y'u do, keep that mask on your face."

"Better meet farther from the scene of trouble. Suppose we say the north gate of the grand stand?"

"Good enough. So-long."

The first faint streaks of day were beginning to show on the horizon when Bannister reached the grand stand. He knew that inside of another half-hour the little frontier town would be blinking in the early morning sunlight that falls so brilliantly through the limpid atmosphere. If they were going to leave without fighting their way out there was no time to lose.

Ten minutes slowly ticked away.

He glanced at his watch. "Five minutes after four. I wish I had gone with Mac. He may have been recognized."

But even as the thought flitted through his mind, the

semi-darkness opened to let a figure out of it.

"All quiet along the Potomac, seh?" asked the foreman's blithe voice. "Good. I found the boys and got them started." He flung down a Mexican vaquero's gaily trimmed costume. "Get into these, seh. Denver shucked them for me. That coyote must have noticed what we wore before he slid out. Y'u can bet the orders are to watch for us as we were dressed then."

"What are y'u going to do?"

"Me? I'm scheduled to be Aaron Burr, seh. Missou swaps with me when he gets back here. They're going to rustle us some white men's clothes, too, but we cayn't wear them till we get out of town on account of showing our handsome faces."

"What about horses?"

"Denver is rustling some for us. Y'u better be scribbling your billy-doo to the girl y'u leave behind y'u, seh."

"Haven't y'u got one to scribble?" Bannister retorted. "Seems to me y'u better get busy, too."

So it happened that when Missou arrived a few minutes later he found this pair of gentlemen, who were about to flee for their lives, busily inditing what McWilliams had termed facetiously *billets-doux*. Each of them was trying to make his letter a little warmer than friendship allowed without committing himself to any chance of a rebuff. Mac got as far as Nora Darling, absent-mindedly inserted a comma between the words, and there stuck hopelessly. He looked enviously across at Bannister, whose pencil

198

was traveling rapidly down his note-book.

"My, what a swift trail your pencil leaves on that paper. That's going some. Mine's bogged down before it got started. I wisht y'u would start me off."

"Well, if you ain't up and started a business college already. I had ought to have brought a typewriter along with me," murmured Missou ironically.

"How are things stacking? Our friends the enemy getting busy yet?" asked Bannister, folding and addressing his note.

"That's what. Orders gone out to guard every road so as not to let you pass. What's the matter with me rustling up the boys and us holding down a corner of this town ourselves?"

The sheepman shook his head. "We're not going to start a little private war of our own. We couldn't do that without spilling a lot of blood. No, we'll make a run for it."

"That y'u, Denver?" the foreman called softly, as the sound of approaching horses reached him.

"Bet your life. Got your own broncs, too. Sheriff Burns called up Daniels not to let any horses go out from his corral to anybody without his O.K. I happened to be cinching at the time the 'phone message came, so I concluded that order wasn't for me, and lit out kinder unceremonious."

Hastily the fugitives donned the new costumes and dominos, turned their notes over to Denver, and swung to their saddles.

"Good luck!" the punchers called after them, and

Denver added an ironical promise that the foreman had no doubt he would keep. "I'll look out for Nora—Darling." There was a drawling pause between the first and second names. "I'll ce'tainly see that she don't have any time to worry about y'u, Mac."

"Y'u go to Halifax," returned Mac genially over his shoulder as he loped away.

"I doubt if we can get out by the roads. Soon as we reach the end of the street we better cut across that hayfield," suggested Ned.

"That's whatever. Then we'll slip past the sentries without being seen. I'd hate to spoil any of them if we can help it. We're liable to get ourselves disliked if our guns spatter too much."

They rode through the main street, still noisy with the shouts of late revelers returning to their quarters. Masked men were yet in evidence occasionally, so that their habits caused neither remark nor suspicion. A good many of the punchers, unable to stay longer, were slipping out of town after having made a night of it. In the general exodus the two friends hoped to escape unobserved.

They dropped into a side street, galloped down it for two hundred yards, and dismounted at a barb-wire fence which ran parallel with the road. The foreman's wire-clippers severed the strands one by one, and they led their horses through the gap. They crossed an alfalfa-field, jumped an irrigation ditch, used the clippers again, and found themselves in a large pasture. It was getting lighter every moment, and while they were still in the pasture a voice hailed them from the road in an unmistakable command to halt.

They bent low over the backs of their ponies and gave them the spur. The shot they had expected rang out, passing harmlessly over them. Another followed, and still another.

"That's right. Shoot up the scenery. Y'u don't hurt us none," the foreman said, apostrophizing the man behind the gun.

The next clipped fence brought them to the open country. For half an hour they rode swiftly without halt. Then McWilliams drew up.

"Where are we making for?"

"How about the Wind River country?"

"Won't do. First off, they'll strike right down that way after us. What's the matter with running up Sweetwater Creek and lying out in the bad lands around the Roubideaux?"

"Good. I have a sheep-camp up that way. I can arrange to have grub sent there for us by a man I can trust."

"All right. The Roubideaux goes."

While they were nooning at a cow-spring, Bannister, lying on his back, with his face to the turquoise sky, became aware that a vagrant impulse had crystallized to a fixed determination. He broached it at once to his companion.

"One thing is a cinch, Mac. Neither y'u nor I will be safe in this country now until we have broken up the gang of desperadoes that is terrorizing this country. If we don't get them they will get us. There isn't any doubt about that. I'm not willing to lie down before these miscreants. What do y'u say?"

"I'm with y'u, old man. But put a name to it. What are y'u proposing?"

"I'm proposing that y'u and I make it our business not to have any other business until we clean out this nest of wolves. Let's go right after them, and see if we can't wipe out the Shoshone-Teton outfit."

"How? They own the law, don't they?"

"They don't own the United States Government. When they held up a mail-train they did a fool thing, for they bucked up against Uncle Sam. What I propose is that we get hold of one of the gang and make him weaken. Then, after we have got hold of some evidence that will convict, we'll go out and run down my namesake, Ned Bannister. If people once get the idea that his hold isn't so strong there's a hundred people that will testify against him. We'll have him in a Government prison inside of six months."

"Or else he'll have us in a hole in the ground," added the foreman, dryly.

"One or the other," admitted Bannister. "Are y'u in on this thing?"

"I surely am. Y'u're the best man I've met up with in a month of Sundays, seh. Y'u ain't got but one fault; and that is y'u don't smoke cigareets. Feed yourself about a dozen a day and y'u won't have a blamed trouble left. Match, seh?" The foreman of the Lazy D, already following his own advice, rolled deftly his smoke, moistened it and proceeded to blow away his troubles.

Bannister looked at his debonair insouciance and laughed. "Water off a duck's back," he quoted. "I know some folks that would be sweating fear right now. It's ce'tainly an aggravating situation, that of being an honest man hunted as a villain by a villain. But I expaict my cousin's enjoying it."

"He ain't enjoying it so much as he would if his plans had worked out a little smoother. He's holding the sack right now and cussing right smaht over it being empty, I reckon."

"He *did* lock the stable door a little too late," chuckled the sheepman. But even as he spoke a shadow fell over his face. "My God! I had forgotten. Y'u don't suppose he would take it out of Miss Messiter."

"Not unless he's tired of living," returned her foreman, darkly. "One thing, this country won't stand for is that. He's got to keep his hands off women or he loses out. He dassent lay a hand on them if they don't want him to. That's the law of the plains, isn't it?"

"That's the unwritten law for the bad man, but I notice it doesn't seem to satisfy y'u, my friend. Y'u and I know that my cousin, Ned Bannister, doesn't acknowledge any law, written or unwritten. He's a devil and he has no fear. Didn't he kidnap her before?"

"He surely would never dare touch those young ladies. But—I don't know. Bann, I guess we better roll along toward the Lazy D country, after all."

"I think so." Ned looked at his friend with smiling drollery. "I thought y'u smoked your troubles away, Jim. This one seems to worry y'u."

McWilliams grinned sheepishly. "There's one trouble won't be smoked away. It kinder dwells." Then, apparently apropos of nothing, he added, irrelevantly: "Wonder what Denver's doing right now?"

"Probably keeping that appointment y'u ran away from," bantered his friend.

"I'll bet he is. Funny how some men have all the luck," murmured the despondent foreman.

CHAPTER XVI

HUNTING BIG GAME

In point of fact, Denver's occupation at that moment was precisely what they had guessed it to be. He was sitting beside Nora Darling in the grand stand, explaining to her the fine points of "roping." Mr. Bob Austin, commonly known as "Texas," was meanwhile trying to make himself agreeable to Helen Messiter. Truth to tell, both young women listened with divided interest to their admirers. Both of them had heard the story of the night, and each of them had tucked away in her corsage a scribbled note she wanted to get back to her room and read again. That the pursuit was still on everybody knew, and those on the inside were aware that the "King," masquerading under the name of Jack Holloway, was the active power behind the sheriff stimulating the chase.

It was after the roping had begun, and Austin had been called away to take his turn, that the outlaw chief sauntered along the aisle of the grand stand to the box in which was seated the mistress of the Lazy D.

"Beautiful mo'ning, isn't it? Delightfully crisp and clear," he said by way of introduction, stopping at her box.

She understood the subtle jeer in his manner, and her fine courage rose to meet it. There was a daring light in her eye, a buoyant challenge in her voice as she answered:

"It is a splendid morning. I'm not surprised you are enjoying it."

"Did I say I was enjoying it?" He laughed as he lifted the bar, came into her box and took a seat.

"Of course not. How careless of me! I had forgotten you were in mourning for a deceased friend."

His dark eyes flashed. "I'll not mourn for him long. He was a mighty trifling fellow, anyhow. Soon as I catch and hang his murderers I'll quit wearing black."

"You may wear out several suits before then," she hit back.

"Don't y'u believe it; when I want a thing I don't quit till it's done."

She met his gaze, and the impact of eyes seemed to shock her physically. The wickedness in him threatened, gloated, dominated. She shivered in the warm sunlight, and would not have had him know it for worlds.

"Dear me! How confident you talk. Aren't you some-times disappointed?"

"Temporarily. But when I want a thing I take it in the end."

She knew he was serving notice on her that he meant to win her; and again the little spinal shiver raced over her. She could not look at his sardonic, evil face without fear, and she could not look away without being aware of his eyes possessing her. What was the use of courage against such a creature as this?

"Yes, I understand you take a good deal that isn't yours," she retorted carelessly, her eyes on the arena.

"I make it mine when I take it," he answered coolly, admiring the gameness which she wore as a suit of chain armor against his thrusts.

"Isn't it a little dangerous sometimes?" her even voice countered. "When you take what belongs to others you run a risk, don't you?"

"That's part of the rules. Except for that I shouldn't like it so well. I hunt big game, and the bigger the game the more risk. That's why y'u guessed right when y'u said I was enjoying the mo'ning."

"Meaning—your cousin?"

"Well, no. I wasn't thinking of him, though he's some sizable. But I'm hunting bigger game than he is, and I expect to bag it."

She let her scornful eyes drift slowly over him. "I might pretend to misunderstand you. But I won't. You may have your answer now. I am not afraid of you, for since you are a bully you must be a coward. I saw a rat-

206

tlesnake last week in the hills. It reminded me of some one I have seen. I'll leave you to guess who."

Her answer drew blood. The black tide raced under the swarthy tan of his face. He leaned forward till his beady eyes were close to her defiant ones. "Y'u have forgotten one thing, Miss Messiter. A rattlesnake can sting. I ask nothing of you. Can't I break your heart without your loving me? You're only a woman—and not the first I have broken, by God!"

His slim, lithe body was leaning forward so that it cut off others, and left them to all intents alone. At a touch of her fingers the handbag in her lap flew open and a little ivory-hilted revolver lay in her hand.

"You may break me, but you'll never bend me an inch."

He looked at the little gun and laughed ironically. "Sho! If y'u should hit me with that and I should find it out I might get mad at y'u."

"Did I say it was for you?" she said coldly; and again the shock of joined eyes ended in drawn battle.

"Have y'u the nerve?" He looked her over, so dainty and so resolute, so silken strong; and he knew he had his answer.

His smoldering eyes burned with desire to snatch her to him and ride away into the hills. For he was a man who lived in his sensations. He had won many women to their hurt, but it was the joy of conflict that made the pursuit worth while to him; and this young woman, who could so delightfully bubble with little laughs ready to spill over and was yet possessed of a spirit so

207

finely superior to the tenderness of her soft, round, maidenly curves, allured him mightily to the attack.

She dropped the revolver back into the bag and shut the clasp with a click, "And now I think, Mr. Bannister, that I'll not detain you any longer. We understand each other sufficiently."

He rose with a laugh that mocked. "I expaict to spend quite a bit of time understanding y'u one of these days. In the meantime this is to our better acquaintance."

Deliberately, without the least haste, he stooped and kissed her before she could rally from the staggering surprise of the intention she read in his eyes too late to elude. Then, with the coolest bravado in the world, he turned on his heel and strolled away.

Angry sapphires gleamed at him from under the long, brown lashes. She was furious, aghast, daunted. By the merest chance she was sitting in a corner of the box, so screened from observation that none could see. But the insolence of him, the reckless defiance of all standards of society, shook her even while it enraged her. He had put forth his claim like a braggart, but he had made good with an audacity superb in its effrontery. How she hated him! How she feared him! The thoughts were woven inseparably in her mind. Mephisto himself could not have impressed himself more imperatively than this strutting, heartless master artist in vice.

She saw him again presently down in the arena, for it was his turn to show his skill at roping. Texas had done well; very well, indeed. He had made the throw and tie in thirty-seven seconds, which was two seconds faster than the record of the previous year. But she knew instinctively, as her fascinated eyes watched the outlaw preparing for the feat, that he was going to win. He would use his success as a weapon against her; as a means of showing her that he always succeeded in whatever he undertook. So she interpreted the look he flung her as he waited at the chute for the wild hill steer to be driven into the arena.

It takes a good man physically to make a successful roper. He must be possessed of nerve, skill and endurance far out of the ordinary. He must be quick-eyed, strong-handed, nimble of foot, expert of hand and built like a wildcat. So Denver explained to the two young women in the box, and the one behind him admitted reluctantly that the long, lean, supple Centaur waiting impassively at the gateway fitted the specifications.

Out flashed the rough-coated hill steer, wild and fleet as a hare, thin and leggy, with muscles of whipcord. Down went the flag, and the stopwatches began to tick off the seconds. Like an arrow the outlaw's pony shot forward, a lariat circling round and round the rider's head. At every leap the cow pony lessened the gap as it pounded forward on the heels of the flying steer.

The loop swept forward and dropped over the horns of the animal. The pony, with the perfect craft of long practice, swerved to one side with a rush. The dragging rope swung up against the running steer's legs, grew suddenly taut. Down went the steer's head, and next moment its feet were swept from under it as it went heavily to the ground. Man and horse were perfect in their team work. As the supple rider slid from the back of the pony it ran to the end of the rope and braced itself to keep the animal from rising. Bannister leaped on the steer, tie-rope in hand. Swiftly his deft hands passed to and fro, making the necessary loops and knots. Then his hands went into the air. The steer was hog-tied.

For a few seconds the judges consulted together. "Twenty-nine seconds," announced their spokesman, and at the words a great cheer went up. Bannister had made his tie in record time.

Impudently the scoundrel sauntered up to the grand stand, bowed elaborately to Miss Messiter, and perched himself on the fence, where he might be the observed of all observers. It was curious, she thought, how his vanity walked hand in hand with so much power and force. He was really extraordinarily strong, but no debutante's self-sufficiency could have excelled his. He was so frankly an egotist that it ceased to be a weakness.

Back in her room at the hotel an hour later Helen paced up and down under a nervous strain foreign to her temperament. She was afraid; for the first time in her life definitely afraid. This man pitted against her had deliberately divorced his life from morality. In him lay no appeal to any conscience court of last resort. But the terror of this was not for herself principally, but for her flying lover. With his indubitable power, backed by the unpopularity of the sheepman in this cattle country, the King of the Bighorn could destroy his cousin if he set himself to do so. Of this she was convinced, and her conviction carried a certainty that he had the will as well as the means. If he had lacked anything in motive she herself had supplied one. For she was afraid that this villain had read her heart.

And as her hand went fluttering to her heart she found small comfort in the paper lying next it that only a few hours before had brought her joy. For at any moment a messenger might come in to tell her that the writer of it had been captured and was to be dealt with summarily in frontier fashion. At best her lover and her friend were but fugitives from justice. Against them were arrayed not only the ruffian followers of their enemy, but also the lawfully constituted authorities of the county. Even if they should escape today the net would tighten on them, and they would eventually be captured.

For the third time since coming to Wyoming Helen found refuge in tears.

CHAPTER XVII

RUN TO EARTH

When word came to Denver and the other punchers of the Lazy D that Reddy had been pressed into service as a guide for the posse that was pursuing the fugitives they gave vent to their feelings in choice profanity.

"Now, ain't that like him? Had to run around like a locoed calf telling all he knowed and more till Burns ropes him in," commented the disgusted Missou.

"Trouble with Reddy is he sets his mouth to working and then goes away and leaves it," mourned Jim Henson.

"I'd hate to feel as sore as Reddy will when the boys get through playing with him after he gets back to the ranch," Denver contributed, when he had exhausted his vocabulary.

Meanwhile Reddy, unaware of being a cause of offense, was cheerfully happy in the unexpected honor that had been thrust upon him. His will was of putty, molded into the opinion of whomever he happened at the moment to be with. Just now, with the ironic eye of Sheriff Burns upon him, he was strong for law enforcement.

"A feller hadn't ought to be so promiscuous with his hardware. This here thing of shooting up citizens don't do Wyoming no good these days. Capital ain't a-going to come in when such goings-on occur," he sagely opined, unconsciously parroting the sentiment Burns had just been instilling into him.

"That's right, sir. If that ain't horse sense I don't know any. You got a head on you, all right," answered the admiring sheriff.

The flattered Reddy pleaded guilty to being wiser than most men. "Jest because I punch cows ain't any reason why I'm anybody's fool. I'll show them smart boys at the Lazy D I don't have to take the dust of any of the bunch when it comes to using my think tank."

"I would," sympathized Burns. "You bet they'll all be

almighty jealous when they learn how you was chosen out of the whole outfit on this job."

All day they rode, and that night camped a few miles from the Lazy D. Early next morning they hailed a solitary rider, as he passed. The man turned out to be a cowman, with a small ranch not far from the one owned by Miss Messiter.

"Hello, Henderson! Y'u seen anything of Jim McWilliams and another fellow riding acrost this way?" asked Reddy.

"Nope," answered the cowman promptly. But immediately he modified his statement to add that he had seen two men riding toward Dry Creek a couple of hours ago. "They was going kinder slow. Looked to me sorter like one of them was hurt and the other was helping him out," he volunteered.

The sheriff looked significantly at one of his men and nodded.

"You didn't recognize the horses, I reckon?"

"Come to think of it, one of the ponies did look like Jim's roan. What's up, boys? Anything doing?"

"Nothing particular. We want to see Jim, that's all. So long."

What Henderson had guessed was the truth. The continuous hard riding had been too much for Bannister and his wound had opened anew. They were at the time only a few miles from a shack on Dry Creek, where the Lazy D punchers sometimes put up. McWilliams had attended the wound as best he could, and after a few hours' rest had headed for the cabin in the hills. They were compelled to travel very slowly, since the motion kept the sheepman's wound continually bleeding. But about noon they reached the refuge they had been seeking and Bannister lay down on the bunk with their saddle blankets under him. He soon fell asleep, and Mac took advantage of this to set out on a foraging expedition to a ranch not far distant. Here he got some bread, bacon, milk and eggs from a man he could trust and returned to his friend.

It was dark by the time he reached the cabin. He dismounted, and with his arms full of provisions pushed into the hut.

"Awake, Bann?" he asked in a low voice.

The answer was unexpected. Something heavy struck his chest and flung him back against the wall. Before he could recover his balance he was pinioned fast. Four men had hurled themselves upon him.

"We've got you, Jim. Not a mite o' use resisting," counseled the sheriff.

"Think I don't savez that? I can take a hint when a whole Methodist church fails on me. Who are y'u, anyhow?"

"Somebody light a lantern," ordered Burns.

By the dim light it cast Mac made them out, land saw Ned Bannister gagged and handcuffed on the bed. He knew a moment of surprise when his eyes fell on Reddy.

"So it was y'u brought them here, Red?" he said quietly.

Contrary to his own expectations, the gentleman

named was embarrassed. "The sheriff, he summoned me to serve," was his lame defense.

"And so y'u threw down your friends. Good boy!"

"A man's got to back the law up, ain't he?"

Mac turned his shoulder on him rather pointedly. "There isn't any need of keeping that gag in my friend's mouth any longer," he suggested to Burns.

"That's right, too. Take it out, boys. I got to do my duty, but I don't aim to make any gentleman more uncomfortable than I can help. I want everything to be pleasant all round."

"I'm right glad to hear that, Burns, because my friend isn't fit to travel. Y'u can take me back and leave him out here with a guard," the foreman replied quickly.

"Sorry I can't accommodate you, Jim, but I got to take y'u both with me."

"Those are the orders of the King, are they?"

Burns flushed darkly. "It ain't going to do you any good to talk that way. You know mighty well this here man with you is Bannister. I ain't going to take no chances on losing him now I've got my hand on him."

"Y'u ce'tainly deserve a re-election, and I'll bet y'u get it all right. Any man so given over to duty, so plumb loaded down to the hocks with conscience as y'u, will surely come back with a big majority next November."

"I ain't askin' for *your* vote, Mac."

"Oh, y'u don't need votes. Just get the King to O.K. your nomination and y'u'll win in a walk."

"My friend, y'u better mind your own business. Far as I can make out y'u got troubles enough of your own," retorted the nettled sheriff.

"Y'u don't need to tell me that, Tom Burns. Y'u ain't a man—nothing but a stuffed skin worked by a string. When that miscreant Bannister pulls the string y'u jump. He's jerked it now, so y'u're taking us back to him. I can prove that coyote Morgan shot at me first, but that doesn't cut any ice with you."

"What made you light out so sudden, then?" demanded the aggrieved Burns triumphantly.

"Because I knew *you.* That's a plenty good reason. I'm not asking anything for myself. All I say is that my friend isn't fit to travel yet. Let him stay here under a guard till he is."

"He was fit enough to get here. By thunder, he's fit to go back!"

"Y'u've said enough, Mac," broke in Bannister. "It's awfully good of y'u to speak for me, but I would rather see it out with you to a finish. I don't want any favors from this yellow dog of my cousin."

The "yellow dog" set his teeth and swore vindictively behind them. He was already imagining an hour when these insolent prisoners of his would sing another tune.

CHAPTER XVIII

PLAYING FOR TIME

They've got 'em. Caught them on Dry Creek, just below Green Forks."

Helen Messiter, just finishing her breakfast at the

hotel preparatory to leaving in her machine for the ranch, laid down her knife and fork and looked with dilated eyes at Denver, who had broken in with the news.

"Are you sure?" The color had washed from her face and left her very white, but she fronted the situation quietly without hysterics or fuss of any kind.

"Yes, ma'am. They're bringing them in now to jail. Watch out and y'u'll see them pass here in a few minutes. Seems that Bannister's wound opened up on him and he couldn't go any farther. 'Course Mac wouldn't leave him. Sheriff Burns and his posse dropped in on them and had them covered before Mac could chirp."

"You are sure this man—this desperado Bannister—will do nothing till night?"

"Not the way I figure it. He'll have the jail watched all day. But he's got to work the town up to a lynching. I expect the bars will be free for all today. By night the worst part of this town will be ready for anything. The rest of the citizens are going to sit down and do nothing just because it is Bannister."

"But it isn't Bannister—not the Bannister they think it is."

He shook his head. "No use, ma'am. I've talked till my throat aches, but it don't do a mite of good. Nobody believes a word of what I say. Y'u see, we ain't got any proof."

"Proof! We have enough, God knows! Didn't this villain—this outlaw that calls himself Jack Holloway—attack and try to murder him?"

217

"That's what we believe, but the report out is that one of us punchers shot him up for crossing the dead-line."

"Didn't this fellow hold up the ranch and try to take Ned Bannister away with him?"

"Yes, ma'am. But that doesn't look good to most people. They say he had his friends come to take him away so y'u wouldn't hold him and let us boys get him. This cousin business is a fairy tale the way they size it up. How come this cousin to let him go if he held up the ranch to put the sick man out of business? No, miss. This country has made up its mind that your friend is the original Ned Bannister. My opinion is that nothing on earth can save him."

"I don't want your opinion. I'm going to save him, I tell you; and you are going to help. Are his friends nothing but a bunch of quitters?" she cried, with sparkling eyes.

"I didn't know I was such a great friend of his," answered the cowboy sulkily.

"You're a friend of Jim McWilliams, aren't you? Are you going to sneak away and let these curs hang him?"

Denver flushed. "Y'u're dead right, Miss Helen. I guess I'll see it out with you. What's the orders?"

"I want you to help me organize a defense. Get all Mac's friends stirred up to make a fight for him. Bring as many of them in to see me during the day as you can. If you see any of the rest of the Lazy D boys send them in to me for instructions. Report yourself every hour to me. And make sure that at least three of your friends that you can trust are hanging round the jail all day so as to be ready in case any attempt is made to storm it before dark."

"I'll see to it." Denver hung on his heel a moment before leaving. "It's only square to tell y'u, Miss Helen, that this means war here tonight. These streets are going to run with blood if we try to save them."

"I'm taking that responsibility," she told him curtly; but a moment later she added gently, "I have a plan, my friend, that may stop this outrage yet. But you must do your best for me." She smiled sadly at him. "You're my foreman, today, you know."

"I'm going to do my level best, y'u may tie to that," he told her earnestly.

"I know you will." And their fingers touched for an instant.

Through a window the girl could see a crowd pouring down the street toward the hotel. She flew up the stairs and out upon the second-story piazza that looked down upon the road.

From her point of vantage she easily picked them out—the two unarmed men riding with their hands tied behind their backs, encircled by a dozen riders armed to the teeth. Bannister's hat had apparently fallen off farther down the street, for the man beside him was dusting it. The wounded prisoner looked about him without fear, but it was plain he was near the limit of endurance. He was pale as a sheet, and his fair curls clung moistly to his damp forehead.

McWilliams caught sight of her first, and she could see him turn and say a word to his comrade. Bannister looked up, caught sight of her, and smiled. That smile, so pale and wan, went to her heart like a knife. But the message of her eyes was hope. They told the prisoners silently to be of good cheer, that at least they were not deserted to their fate.

"What is it about—the crowd?" Nora asked of her mistress as the latter was returning to the head of the stairs.

In as few words as she could Helen told her, repressing sharply the tears the girl began to shed. "This is not the time to weep—not yet. We must save them. You can do your part. Mr. Bannister is wounded. Get a doctor over the telephone and see that he attends him at once. Don't leave the 'phone until you have got one to promise to go immediately."

"Yes, miss. Is there anything else?"

"Ask the doctor to call you up from the prison and tell you how Mr. Bannister is. Make it plain to him that he is to give up his other practice, if necessary, and is to keep us informed through the day about his patient's condition. I will be responsible for his bill."

Helen herself hurried to the telegraph office at the depot. She wrote out a long dispatch and handed it to the operator. "Send this at once, please."

He was one of those supercilious young idiots that make the most of such small power as ever drifts down to them. Taking the message, he tossed it on the table. "I'll send it when I get time."

"You'll send it now."

"What—what's that?"

220

Her steady eyes caught and held his shifting ones. "I say you are going to send it now—this very minute."

"I guess not. The line's busy," he bluffed.

"If you don't begin sending that message this minute I'll make it my business to see that you lose your position," she told him calmly.

He snatched up the paper from the place where he had tossed it. "Oh, well, if it's so darned important," he conceded ungraciously.

She stood quietly above him while he sent the telegram, even though he contrived to make every moment of her stay an unvoiced insult. Her wire was to the wife of the Governor of the State. They had been close friends at school, and the latter had been urging Helen to pay a visit to Cheyenne. The message she sent was as follows:

Battle imminent between outlaws and cattlemen here. Bloodshed certain tonight. My foreman last night killed in self-defense a desperado. Bannister's gang, in league with town authorities, mean to lynch him and one of my other friends after dark this evening. Sheriff will do nothing. Can your husband send soldiers immediately? Wire answer.

The operator looked up sullenly after his fingers had finished the last tap. "Well?"

"Just one thing more," Helen told him. "You understand the rules of the company about secrecy. Nobody but you knows I am sending this message. If by any chance it should leak out, I shall know through whom. If you want to hold your position, you will keep quiet."

"I know my business," he growled. Nevertheless, she had spoken in season, for he had had it in his mind to give a tip where he knew it would be understood to hasten the jail delivery and accompanying lynching.

When she returned to the hotel, Helen found Missou waiting for her. She immediately sent him back to the office, and told him to wait there until the answer was received. "I'll send one of the boys up to relieve you so that you may come with the telegram as soon as it arrives. I want the operator watched all day. Oh, here's Jim Henson! Denver has explained the situation to you, I presume. I want you to go up to the telegraph office and stay there all day. Go to lunch with the operator when he goes. Don't let him talk privately to anybody, not even for a few seconds. I don't want you to seem to have him under guard before outsiders, but let him know it very plainly. He is not to mention a wire I sent or the answer to it—not to anybody, Jim. Is that plain?"

"Y'u bet! He's a clam, all right, till the order is countermanded." And the young man departed with a cheerful grin that assured Helen she had nothing to fear from official leaks.

Nora, from answering a telephone call, came to report to the general in charge. "The doctor says that he has looked after Mr. Bannister, and there is no immediate danger. If he keeps quiet for a few days he ought to do well. Mr. McWilliams sent a message by him to say that we aren't to worry about him. He said he would—would—rope a heap of cows—on the Lazy D yet."

Nora, bursting into tears, flung herself into Helen's arms. "They are going to kill him. I know they are, and—and 'twas only yesterday, ma'am, I told him not to—to get gay, the poor boy. When he tried to—to—" She broke down and sobbed.

Her mistress smiled in spite of herself, though she was bitterly aware that even Nora's grief was only superficially ludicrous.

"We're going to save him, Nora, if we can. There's hope while there's life. You see, Mac himself is full of courage. *He* hasn't given up. We must keep up our courage, too."

"Yes, ma'am, but this is the first gentleman friend I ever had hanged, and—" She broke off, sobbing, leaving the rest as a guess.

Helen filled it out aloud. "And you were going to say that you care more for him than any of the others. Well, you must stop coquetting and tell him so when we have saved him."

"Yes, ma'am," agreed Nora, very repentant for the moment of the fact that it was her nature to play with the hearts of those of the male persuasion. Irrelevantly she added: "He was *that* kind, ma'am, and tender-hearted."

Helen, whose own heart was breaking, continued to soothe her. "Don't say *was,* child. You are to be brave, and not think of him that way."

"Yes, ma'am. He told me he was going to buy cows

223

with the thousand dollars he won yesterday. I knew he meant—"

"Yes, of course. It's a cowboy's way of saying that he means to start housekeeping. Have you the telegram, Missou?" For that young man was standing in the doorway.

He handed her the yellow slip. She ripped open the envelope and read:

Company B en route. Railroad connections uncertain. Postpone crisis long as possible. May reach Gimlet Butte by ten-thirty.

Her first thought was of unspeakable relief. The militia was going to take a hand. The boys in khaki would come marching down the street, and everything would be all right. But hard on the heels of her instinctive gladness trod the sober second thought. Ten-thirty at best, and perhaps later! Would they wait that long, or would they do their cowardly work as soon as night fell? She must contrive to delay them till the train drew in. She must play for those two lives with all her woman's wit; must match the outlaw's sinister cunning and fool him into delay. She knew he would come if she sent for him. But how long could she keep him? As long as he was amused at her agony, as long as his pleasure in tormenting her was greater than his impatience to be at his ruffianly work. Oh, if she ever needed all her power it would be tonight.

Throughout the day she continued to receive hourly

reports from Denver, who always brought with him four or five honest cowpunchers from up-country to listen to the strange tale she unfolded to them. It was, of course, in part, the spell of her sweet personality, of that shy appeal she made to the manhood in them; but of those who came, nearly all believed, for the time at least, and aligned themselves on her side in the struggle that was impending. Some of these were swayed from their allegiance in the course of the day, but a few she knew would remain true.

Meanwhile, all through the day, the enemy was busily at work. As Denver had predicted, free liquor was served to all who would drink. The town and its guests were started on a grand debauch that was to end in violence that might shock their sober intelligence. Everywhere poisoned whispers were being flung broadcast against the two men waiting in the jail for what the night would bring forth.

Dusk fell on a town crazed by bad whiskey and evil report. The deeds of Bannister were hashed and rehashed at every bar, and nobody related them with more ironic gusto than the man who called himself Jack Holloway. There were people in town who knew his real name and character, but of these the majority were either in alliance with him or dared not voice their, knowledge. Only Miss Messiter and her punchers told the truth, and their words were blown away like chaff.

From the first moment of darkness Helen had the outlaw leader dogged by two of her men. Since neither of these were her own riders this was done without suspicion. At intervals of every quarter of an hour they reported to her in turn. Bannister was beginning to drink heavily, and she did not want to cut short his dissipation by a single minute. Yet she had to make sure of getting his attention before he went too far.

It was close to nine when she sent him a note, not daring to delay a minute longer. For the reports of her men were all to the same effect, that the crisis would not now be long postponed. Bannister, or Holloway, as he chose to call himself, was at the bar with his lieutenants in evil when the note reached him. He read it with a satisfaction he could not conceal. So! He had brought her already to her knees. Before he was through with her she should grovel in the dust before him.

"I'll be back in a few minutes. Do nothing till I return," he ordered, and went jingling away to the Elk House.

The young woman's anxiety was pitiable, but she repressed it sternly when she went to meet the man she feared; and never had it been more in evidence than in this hour of her greatest torture. Blithely she came forward to meet him, eye challenging eye gayly. No hint of her anguish escaped into her manner. He read there only coquetry, the eternal sex conflict, the winsome defiance of a woman hitherto the virgin mistress of all assaults upon her heart's citadel. It was the last thing he had expected to see, but it was infinitely more piquant, more intoxicating, than desperation. She seemed to give the lie to his impression of her love for his cousin; and that, too, delighted his pride.

"You will sit down?"

Carelessly, almost indolently, she put the question, her raised eyebrows indicating a chair with perfunctory hospitality. He had not meant to sit, had expected only to gloat a few minutes over her despair; but this situation called for more deliberation. He had yet to establish the mastery his vanity demanded. Therefore he took a chair.

"This is ce'tainly an unexpected honor. Did y'u send for me to explain some more about that sufficient understanding between us?" he sneered.

It was a great relief to her to see that, though he had been drinking, as she had heard, he was entirely master of himself. Her efforts might still be directed to Philip sober.

"I sent for you to congratulate you," she answered, with a smile. "You are a bigger man than I thought. You have done what you said you would do, and I presume you can very shortly go out of mourning."

He radiated vanity, seemed to visibly expand. "Do y'u go in when I go out?" he asked brutally.

She laughed lightly. "Hardly. But it does seem as if I'm unlucky in my foremen. They all seem to have engagements across the divide."

"I'll get y'u another."

"Thank you. I was going to ask as much of you. Can you suggest one now?"

"I'm a right good cattle man myself."

"And—can you stay with me a reasonable time?"

He laughed. "I have no engagements across the Styx, ma'am."

"My other foremen thought *they* were permanent fixtures here, too."

"We're all liable to mistakes."

"Even you, I suppose."

"I'll sign a lease to give y'u possession of my skill for as long as y'u like."

She settled herself comfortably back in an easy chair, as alluring a picture of buoyant, radiant youth as he had seen in many a day. "But the terms. I am afraid I can't offer you as much as you make at your present occupation."

"I could keep that up as a side-line."

"So you could. But if you use my time for your own profit, you ought to pay me a royalty on your intake."

His eyes lit with laughter. "I reckon that can be arranged. Any percentage you think fair. It will all be in the family, anyway."

"I think that is one of the things about which we don't agree," she made answer softly, flashing him the proper look of inviting disdain from under her silken lashes.

He leaned forward, elbow on the chair-arm and chin in hand. "We'll agree about it one of these days."

"Think so?" she returned airily.

"I don't think. I know."

Just an eyebeat her gaze met his, with that hint of shy questioning, of puzzled doubt that showed a growing interest. "I wonder," she murmured, and recovered herself with a hurried little laugh.

How she hated her task, and him! She was a singularly honest woman, but she must play the siren; must allure this scoundrel to forgetfulness, and yet elude the very familiarity her manner invited. She knew her part, the heartless, enticing coquette, compounded half of passion and half of selfishness. It was a hateful thing to do, this sacrifice of her personal reticence, of the individual abstraction in which she wrapped herself as a cloak, in order to hint at a possibility of some intimacy of feeling between them. She shrank from it with a repugnance hardly to be overcome, but she held herself with an iron will and consummate art to the role she had undertaken. Two lives hung on her success. She must not forget that. She would not let herself forget that—and one of them that of the man she loved.

So, bravely she played her part, repelling always with a hint of invitation, denying with the promise in her fascinated eyes of ultimate surrender to his ardor. In the zest of the pursuit the minutes slipped away unnoticed. Never had a woman seemed to him more subtly elusive, and never had he felt more sure of himself. Her charm grew on him, stirred his pulses to a faster beat. For it was his favorite sport, and this warm, supple young creature, who was to be the victim of his bow and arrow, slowed herself worthy of his mettle.

The clock downstairs struck the half-hour, and Bannister, reminded of what lay before him outside, made a move to go. Her alert eyes had been expecting it, and she forestalled him by a change of tactics. Moved apparently by impulse, she seated herself on the piano-stool, swept the keys for an instant with her fingers, and plunged into the brilliant "Carmen" overture. Susceptible as this man was to the influence of music, he could not fail to be arrested by so perfect an interpretation of his mood. He stood rooted, was carried back again in imagination to a great artiste's rendering of that story of fierce passion and aching desire so brilliantly enacted under the white sunbeat of a country of cloudless skies. Imperceptibly she drifted into other parts of the opera. Was it the wild, gypsy seductiveness of *Carmen* that he felt, or, rather, this American girl's allurement? From "Love will like a birdling fly" she slipped into the exquisitely graceful snatches of song with which *Carmen* answers the officer's questions. Their rare buoyancy marched with his mood, and from them she carried him into the song "Over the hill," that is so perfect and romantic an expression of the *wanderlust*.

How long she could have held him she will never know, for, at that inopportune time came blundering one of his men into the room with a call for his presence to take charge of the situation outside.

"What do y'u want, Bostwick?" he demanded, with curt peremptoriness.

The man whispered in his ear.

"Can't wait any longer, can't they?" snapped his chief. "Y'u tell them they'll wait till I give the word. Understand?"

He almost flung the man out of the room, but Helen noticed that she had lost him. His interest was perfunctory, and, though he remained a little time longer, it was to establish his authority with the men rather than to listen to her. Twice he looked at his watch within five minutes.

He rose to go. "There is a little piece of business I have to put through. So I'll have to ask y'u to excuse me. I have had a delightful hour, and I hate to go." He smiled, and quoted with mock sentimentality:

> "The hours I spent with thee, dear heart,
>   Are as a string of pearls to me;
> I count them over, every one apart,
>   My rosary! My rosary!"

"Dear me! One certainly lives and learns. How could I have guessed that, with your reputation, you could afford to indulge in a rosary?" she mocked.

"Good night." He offered his hand.

"Don't go yet," she coaxed.

He shook his head. "Duty, y'u know."

"Stay only a little longer. Just ten minutes more."

His vanity purred, so softly she stroked it. "Can't. Wish I could. Y'u hear how noisy things are getting. I've got to take charge. So-long."

She stood close, looking up at him with a face of seductive appeal.

"Don't go yet. Please!"

The triumph of victory mounted to his head. "I'll come back when I've done what I've got to do."

"No, no. Stay a little longer—just a little."

231

"Not a minute, sweetheart."

He bent to kiss her, and a little clenched fist struck his face.

"Don't you dare!" she cried.

The outraged woman in her, curbed all evening with an iron bit, escaped from control. Delightedly he laughed. The hot spirit in her pleased him mightily. He took her little hands and held them in one of his while he smiled down at her. "I guess that kiss will keep, my girl, till I come back."

"My God! Are you going to kill your own cousin?"

All her terror, all her detestation and hatred of him, looked haggardly out of her unmasked face. His narrowed eyes searched her heart, and his countenance grew every second more sinister.

"Y'u have been fooling me all evening, then?"

"Yes, and hating you every minute of the time."

"Y'u dared?" His face was black with rage.

"You would like to kill me. Why don't you?"

"Because I know a better revenge. I'm going out to take it now. After your lover is dead, I'll come back and make love to y'u again," he sneered.

"Never!" She stood before him like a queen in her lissom, brave, defiant youth. "And as for your cousin, you may kill him, but you can't destroy his contempt for you. He will die despising you for a coward and a scoundrel."

It was true, and he knew it. In his heart he cursed her, while he vainly sought some weapon that would strike home through her impervious armor.

"Y'u love him. I'll remember that when I see him kick," he taunted.

"I make you a present of the information. I love him, and I despise you. Nothing can change those facts," she retorted whitely.

"Mebbe, but some day y'ull crawl on your knees to beg my pardon for having told me so."

"There is your overweening vanity again," she commented.

"I'm going to break y'u, my beauty, so that y'u'll come running when I snap my fingers."

"We'll see."

"And in the meantime I'll go hang your lover." He bowed ironically, swung on his jingling heel, and strode out of the room.

She stood there listening to his dying footfalls, then covered her face with her hands, as if to press back the dreadful vision her mind conjured.

CHAPTER XIX

WEST POINT TO THE RESCUE

It was understood that the sheriff should make a perfunctory defense against the mob in order to "square" him with the voters at the election soon to be held. But the word had been quietly passed that the bullets of the prison guards would be fired over the heads of the attackers. This assurance lent an added braggadocio to the Dutch courage of the lynchers. Many of them who would otherwise have hung back distinguished themselves by the enthusiasm which they displayed.

Bannister himself generaled the affair, detailing squads to batter down the outer door, to guard every side of the prison, and to overpower the sheriff's guard. That official, according to programme, appeared at a window and made a tittle speech, declaring his intention of performing his duty at whatever cost. He was hooted down with jeers and laughter, and immediately the attack commenced.

The yells of the attackers mingled with the sound of the axe-blows and the report of revolvers from inside the building. Among those nearest to the door being battered down were Denver and the few men he had with him. His plan offered merely a forlorn hope. It was that in the first scramble to get in after the way was opened he and his friends might push up the stairs in the van, and hold the corridor for as long as they could against the furious mob.

It took less than a quarter of an hour to batter down the door, and among the first of those who sprang across the threshold were Denver, Missou, Frisco and their allies. While others stopped to overpower the struggling deputies according to the arranged farce, they hurried upstairs and discovered the cell in which their friends were fastened.

Frisco passed a revolver through the grating to McWilliams, and another to Bannister. "Haven't got the keys, so I can't let y'u out, old hoss," he told the foreman. "But mebbe y'u won't feel so lonesome with these little toys to play with."

Meanwhile Denver, a young giant of seventy-six inches, held the head of the stairs, with four stalwart plainsmen back of him. The rush of many feet came up pell-mell, and he flung the leaders back on those behind.

"Hold on there. This isn't a free-lunch counter. Don't you see we're crowded up here already?"

"What's eating you? Whyfor, can't we come?" growled one of the foremost nursing an injured nose.

"I've just explained to you, son, that it's crowded. Folks are prevalent enough up here right now. Send up that bunch of keys and we'll bring your meat to you fast enough."

"What's that? What's that?" The outlaw chief pushed his way through the dense mob at the door and reached the stairway.

"He won't let us up," growled one of them.

"Who won't?" demanded Bannister sharply, and at once came leaping up the stairs.

"Nothing doing." drawled Frisco, and tossed him over the railing on to the heads of his followers below.

They carried Bannister into the open air, for his head had struck the newel-post in his descent. This gave the defense a few minutes' respite.

"They're going to come a-shooting next time," remarked Denver. "Just as soon as he comes back from bye-low land you'll see things hum."

"Y'u bet," agreed Missou. We'll last about three minutes when the stampede begins."

The scream of an engine pierced the night.

Denver's face lit. "Make it five minutes Missou, and Mac is safe. At least, I'm hoping so awful hard. Miss Helen wired for the militia from Sheridan this mo'ning. Chances are they're on that train. I couldn't tell you earlier, because she made me promise not to. She was afraid it might leak out and get things started sooner."

Weak but furious, the miscreant from the Shoshones returned to the attack. "Break in the back door and sneak up behind on those fellows. We'll have the men we want inside of fifteen minutes," he promised the mob.

"We'll rush them from both sides, and show those guys on the landing whether they can stop us," added Bostwick.

Suddenly some one raised the cry, "The soldiers!" Bannister looked up the street and swore a vicious oath. Swinging down the road at double time came a company of militia in khaki. He was mad with baffled fury, but he made good his retreat at once and disappeared promptly into the nearest dark alley.

The mob scattered by universal impulse; disintegrated so promptly that within five minutes the soldiers held the ground alone, save for the officials of the prison and Denver's little band.

A boyish lieutenant lately out of the Point, and just come in to a lieutenancy in the militia, was in command. "In time?" he asked anxiously, for this was his first independent expedition.

"Y'u bet," chuckled Denver. "We're right glad to see

you, and I'll bet those boys in the cage ain't regretting your arrival any. Fifteen minutes later and you would have been in time to hold the funeral services, I reckon."

"Where is Miss Messiter?" asked the young officer.

"She's at the Elk House, colonel. I expect some of us better drift over there and tell her it's all right. She's the gamest little woman that ever crossed the Wyoming line. Hadn't been for her these boys would have been across the divide hours ago. She's a plumb thorough-bred. Wouldn't give up an inch. All day she has gen-eraled this thing; played a mighty weak hand for a heap more than it was worth. Sand? Seh, she's grit clear through, if anybody asks you." And Denver told the story of the day, making much of her unflinching courage and nothing of her men's readiness to back whatever steps she decided upon.

It was ten minutes past eleven when a smooth young, apple-cheeked lad in khaki presented himself before Helen Messiter with a bow never invented outside of West Point.

"I am Lieutenant Beecher. Governor Raleigh presents his compliments by me, Miss Messiter, and is very glad to be able to put at your service such forces as are needed to quiet the town."

"You were in time?" she breathed.

"With about five minutes to spare. I am having the prisoners brought here for the night if you do not object. In the morning I shall investigate the affair, and take such steps as are necessary. In the meantime you may rest assured that there will be no further disturbance."

"Thank you. I am sure that with you in command everything will now be all right, and I am quite of your opinion that the prisoners had better stay here for the night. One of them is wounded, and ought to be given the best attention. But, of course, you will see to that, lieutenant."

The young man blushed. This was the right kind of appreciation. He wished his old classmates at the Point could hear how implicitly this sweet girl relied on him.

"Certainly. And now, Miss Messiter, if there is nothing you wish, I shall retire for the night. You may sleep with perfect confidence."

"I am sure I may, lieutenant." She gave him a broadside of trusting eyes full of admiration. "But perhaps you would like me to see my foreman first, just to relieve my mind. And, as you were about to say, his friend might be brought in, too, since they are together."

The young man promptly assented, though he had not been aware that he was about to say anything of the kind.

They came in together, Bannister supported by McWilliams's arm. The eyes of both mistress and maid brimmed over with tears when they saw them. Helen dragged forward a chair for the sheepman, and he sank into it. From its depths he looked up with his rare, sweet smile.

"I've heard about it," he told her, in a low voice. "I've heard how y'u fought for my life all day. There's nothing I can say. I owed y'u everything already twice, and now I owe it all over again. Give me a lifetime and I couldn't get even."

Helen's swift glance swept over Nora and the foreman. They were in a dark alcove, oblivious of anybody else. Also they were in each other's arms frankly. For some reason wine flowed into the cream of Helen's cheeks.

"Do you have to 'get even'? Among friends is that necessary?" she asked shyly.

"I hope not. If it is, I'm sure bankrupt. Even my thanks seem to stay at home. If y'u hadn't done so much for me, perhaps I could tell y'u how much y'u had done. But I have no words to say it."

"Then don't," she advised.

"Y'u're the best friend a man ever had. That's all I can say."

"It's enough, since you mean it, even though it isn't true," she answered gently.

Their eyes met, fastened for an instant, and by common consent looked away.

As it chanced they were close to the window, their shadows reflected on the blind. A man, slipping past in the street on horseback, stopped at sight of that lighted window, with the moving shadows, in an uncontrollable white fury. He slid from the saddle, threw the reins over the horse's head to the ground, and slipped his revolver from its holster and back to make sure that he could draw it easily. Then he passed springily across the road to the hotel and up the stairs. He trod lightly, stealthily, and by his very wariness defeated his purpose of eluding observation. For a pair of keen eyes from the hotel office glimpsed the figure stealing past so noiselessly, and promptly followed up the stairway.

"Hope I don't intrude at this happy family gathering."

Helen, who had been pouring a glass of cordial for the spent and wounded sheepman, put the glass down on the table and turned at sound of the silken, sinister voice. After one glance at the vindictive face, from the cold eyes of which hate seemed to smolder, she took an instinctive step toward her lover. The cold wave that drenched her heart accompanied an assurance that the man in the doorway meant trouble.

His sleek smile arrested her. He was standing with his feet apart, his hands clasped lightly behind his back, as natty and as well groomed as was his wont.

"Ah, make the most of what ye yet may spend,
Before ye, too, into the Dust descend;
 Dust into Dust, and under Dust to lie,
Sans Wine, sans Song, sans Singer, and—sans End!"

he misquoted, with a sneer; and immediately interrupted his irony to give way to one of his sudden blind rages.

With incredible swiftness his right hand moved forward and up, catching revolver from scabbard as it rose. But by a fraction of a second his purpose had been anticipated. A closed fist shot forward to the salient jaw in time to fling the bullets into the ceiling. An arm encircled the outlaw's neck, and flung him backward down the stairs. The railing broke his fall, and on it his body slid downward, the weapon falling from his hand. He pulled himself together at the foot of the stairs, crouched for an upward rush, but changed his mind instantly. The young officer who had flung him down had him covered with his own six-shooter. He could hear footsteps running toward him, and he knew that in a few seconds he would be in the hands of the soldiers. Plunging out of the doorway, the desperado vaulted to the saddle and drove his spurs home. For a minute hoofs pounded on the hard, white road. Then the night swallowed him and the echo of his disappearance.

"That was Bannister of the Shoshones and the Tetons," the girl's white lips pronounced to Lieutenant Beecher.

"And I let him get away from me," the disappointed lad groaned. "Why, I had him right in my hands. I could have throttled him as easy. But how was I to know he would have nerve enough to come rushing into a hotel full of soldiers hunting him?"

"Y'u have a very persistent cousin, Mr. Bannister," said McWilliams, coming forward from the alcove with shining eyes. "And I must say he's game. Did y'u ever hear the like? Come butting in here as cool as if he hadn't a thing to do but sing out orders like he was in his own home. He was that easy."

"It seems to me that a little of the praise is due Lieutenant Beecher. If he hadn't dealt so competently with the situation murder would have been done. Did you learn your boxing at the Academy, Lieutenant?" Helen

241

asked, trying to treat the situation lightly in spite of her hammering heart.

"I was the champion middleweight of our class," Beecher could not help saying boyishly, with another of his blushes.

"I can easily believe it," returned Helen.

"I wish y'u would teach me how to double up a man so prompt and immediate," said the admiring foreman.

"I expect I'm under particular obligations to that straight right to the chin, Lieutenant," chimed in the sheepman. "The fact is that I don't seem to be able to get out anything except thanks these days. I ought to send my cousin a letter thanking *him* for giving me a chance to owe so much kindness to so many people."

"Your cousin?" repeated the uncomprehending officer.

"This desperado, Bannister, is my cousin," answered the sheepman gravely.

"But if he was your cousin, why should he want to kill you?"

"That's a long story, Lieutenant. Will y'u hear it now?"

"If you feel strong enough to tell it."

"Oh, I'm strong enough." He glanced at Helen. "Perhaps we had better not tire Miss Messiter with it. If y'u'll come to my room—"

"I should like, above all things, to hear it again," interrupted that young woman promptly.

For the man she loved had just come back to her from

the brink of the grave and she was still reluctant to let him out of her sight.

So Ned Bannister told his story once more, and out of the alcove came the happy foreman and Nora to listen to the tale. While he told it his sweetheart's contented eyes were on him. The excitement of the night burnt pleasantly in her veins, for out of the nettle danger she had plucked safety for her sheepman.

CHAPTER XX

TWO CASES OF DISCIPLINE

The Fourth of July celebration at Gimlet Butte had been a thing of the past for four days and the Lazy D had fallen back into the routine of ranch life. The riders were discussing supper and the continued absence of Reddy when that young man drew back the flap and joined them.

He stood near the doorway and grinned with embarrassed guilt at the assembled company.

"I reckon I got too much Fourth of July at Gimlet Butte, boys. That's howcome I to be onpunctual getting back."

There was a long silence, during which those at the table looked at him with an expressionless gravity that did not seem to veil an unduly warm welcome.

"Hello, Mac! Hello, boys! I just got back," he further contributed.

Without comment the Lazy D resumed supper.

243

Apparently it had not missed Reddy or noticed his return. Casual conversation was picked up cheerfully. The return of the prodigal was quite ignored.

"Then that blamed cow gits its back up and makes a bee-line for Rogers. The old man hikes for his pony and—"

"Seems good to git my legs under the old table again," interrupted Reddy with cheerful unease.

"—loses by about half a second," continued Missou. "If Doc hadn't roped its hind laig—"

"Have some cigars, boys. I brought a box back with me." Reddy tossed a handful on the table, where they continued to lie unnoticed.

"—there's no telling what would have happened. As 'twas the old man got off with a—"

"Y'u bet, they're good cigars all right," broke in the propitiatory Reddy.

The interrupted anecdote went on to a finish and the men trooped out and left the prodigal alone with his hash. When that young man reached the bunkhouse Frisco was indulging in a reminiscence. Reddy got only the last of it, but that did not contribute to his serenity.

"Yep! When I was working on the Silver Dollar. Must a-been three years ago, I reckon, when Jerry Miller got that chapping."

"Threw down the outfit in a row they had with the Lafferty crowd, didn't he?" asked Denver.

Frisco nodded.

Mac got up, glanced round, and reached for his hat. "I

244

reckon I'll have to be going," he said, and forthright departed.

Reddy reached for *his* hat and rose. "I got to go and have a talk with Mac," he explained.

Denver got to the door first and his big frame filled it.

"Don't hurry, Reddy. It ain't polite to rush away right after dinner. Besides, Mac will be here all day. He ain't starting for New York."

"Y'u're gittin' blamed particular. Mac he went right out."

"But Mac didn't have a most particular engagement with the boys. There's a difference."

"Why, I ain't got—" Reddy paused and looked around helplessly.

"Gents, I move y'u that it be the horse sense of the Lazy D that our friend Mr. Reddy Reeves be given gratis one chapping immediately if not sooner. The reason for which same being that he played a lowdown trick on the outfit whose bread he was eating."

"Oh, quit your foolin', boys," besought the victim anxiously.

"And that Denver, being some able-bodied and having a good reach, be requested to deliver same to the gent needing it," concluded Missou.

Reddy backed in alarm to the wall. "Y'u boys don't want to get gay with me. Y'u can't monkey with—"

Motion carried unanimously.

Just as Reddy whipped out his revolver Denver's long leg shot out and his foot caught the wrist behind the weapon. When Reddy next took cognizance of his surroundings he was serving as a mattress for the anatomy of three stalwart riders. He was gently deposited face down on his bunk with a one-hundred-eighty-pound live peg at the end of each arm and leg.

"All ready, Denver," announced Frisco from the end of the left foot.

Denver selected a pair of plain leather chaps with care and proceeded to business. What he had to do he did with energy. It is safe to say that at least one of those present can still vividly remember this and testify to his thoroughness.

Mac drifted in after the disciplining. As foreman it was fitting that he should be discreetly ignorant of what had occurred, but he could not help saying:

"That y'u I heard singing, Reddy? Seems to me y'u had ought to take that voice into grand opera. The way y'u straddle them high notes is a caution for fair. What was it y'u was singing? Sounded like 'Would I were far from here, love.'"

"Y'u go to hell," choked Reddy, rushing past him from the bunkhouse.

McWilliams looked round innocently. "I judge some of y'u boys must a-been teasing Reddy from his manner. Seemed like he didn't want to sit down and talk."

"I shouldn't wonder but he'll hold his conversations standing for a day or two," returned Missou gravely.

At the end of the laugh that greeted this Mac replied: "Well, y'u boys want to be gentle with him."

"He's so plumb tender now that I reckon he'll get

along without any more treatment in that line from us," drawled Frisco.

Mac departed laughing. He had an engagement that recurred daily in the dusk of the evening, and he was always careful to be on time. The other party to the engagement met him at the kitchen door and fell with him into the trail that led to Lee Ming's laundry.

"What made you late?" she asked.

"I'm not late, honey. I seem late because you're so anxious," he explained.

"I'm not," protested Nora indignantly. "If you think you're the only man on the place, Jim McWilliams—"

"Sho! Hold your hawsses a minute, Nora, darling. A spinster like y'u—"

"You think you're awful funny—writing in my autograph album that a spinster's best friend is her powder box. I like Mr. Halliday's ways better. He's a perfect gentleman."

"I ain't got a word to say against Denver, even if he did write in your book,

> " 'Sugar is sweet,
> The sky is blue,
> Grass is green
> And so are you.'

"I reckon, being a perfect gentleman, he meant—"

"You know very well you wrote that in yourself and pretended it was Mr. Halliday, signing his name and everything. It wasn't a bit nice of you."

"Now do I look like a forger?" he wanted to know with innocence on his cherubic face.

"Anyway you know it was mean. Mr. Halliday wouldn't do such a thing. You take your arm down and keep it where it belongs, Mr. McWilliams."

"That ain't my name, Nora, darling, and I'd like to know where my arm belongs if it isn't round the prettiest girl in Wyoming. What's the use of being engaged if—"

"I'm not sure I'm going to stay engaged to you," announced the young woman coolly, walking at the opposite edge of the path from him.

"Now that ain't any way to talk—"

"You needn't lecture me. I'm not your wife and I don't think I'm going to be," cut in Nora, whose temper was ruffled on account of having had to wait for him as well as for other reasons.

"Y'u surely wouldn't make me sue y'u for breach of promise, would y'u?" he demanded, with a burlesque of anxiety that was the final straw.

Nora turned on her heel and headed for the house.

"Now don't y'u get mad at me, honey. I was only joking," he explained as he pursued her.

"You think you can laugh at me all you please. I'll show you that you can't," she informed him icily.

"Sho! I wasn't laughing at y'u. What tickled me—"

"I'm not interested in your amusement, Mr. McWilliams."

"What's the use of flying out about a little thing like that? Honest, I don't even know what you're mad at me

248

for," the perplexed foreman averred.

"I'm not mad at you, as you call it. I'm simply disgusted."

And with a final "Good night" flung haughtily over her shoulder Miss Nora Darling disappeared into the house.

Mac took off his hat and gazed at the door that had been closed in his face. He scratched his puzzled poll in vain.

"I ce'tainly got mine good and straight just like Reddy got his. But what in time was it all about? And me thinkin' I was a graduate in the study of the ladies. I reckon I never did get jarred up so. It's plumb discouraging."

If he could have caught a glimpse of Nora at that moment, lying on her bed and crying as if her heart would break, Mac might have found the situation less hopeless.

CHAPTER XXI

THE SIGNAL LIGHTS

In a little hill-rift about a mile back of the Lazy D Ranch was a deserted miner's cabin. The hut sat on the edge of a bluff that commanded a view of the buildings below, while at the same time the pines that surrounded it screened the shack from any casual observation. A thin curl of smoke was rising from the mud chimney, and inside the cabin two men lounged before the open fire.

"It's his move, and he is going to make it soon. Every night I look for him to drop down on the ranch. His hate's kind of volcanic, Mr. Ned Bannister's is, and it's bound to bubble over mighty sudden one of these days," said the younger of the two, rising and stretching himself.

"It did bubble over some when he drove two thousand of my sheep over the bluff and killed the whole outfit," suggested the namesake of the man mentioned.

"Yes, I reckon that's some irritating," agreed McWilliams. "But if I know him, he isn't going to be content with sheep so long as he can take it out of a real live man."

"Or woman," suggested the sheepman.

"Or woman," agreed the other. "Especially when he thinks he can cut y'u deeper by striking at her. If he doesn't raid the Lazy D one of these nights, I'm a blamed poor prophet."

Bannister nodded agreement. "He's near the end of his rope. He could see that if he were blind. When we captured Bostwick and they got a confession out of him, that started the landslide against him. It began to be noised abroad that the government was going to wipe him out. Folks began to lose their terror of him, and after that his whole outfit began to want to turn State's evidence. He isn't sure of one of them now; can't tell when he will be shot in the back by one of his own scoundrels for that two thousand dollars reward."

The foreman strolled negligently to the door. His eyes

drifted indolently down into the valley, and immediately sparkled with excitement.

"The signal's out, Bann," he exclaimed. "It's in your window."

The sheepman leaped to his feet and strode to the door. Down in the valley a light was gleaming in a window. Even while he looked another light appeared in a second window.

"She wants us both," cried the foreman, running to the little corral back of the house.

He presently reappeared with two horses, both saddled, and they took the downward trail at once.

"If Miss Helen can keep him in play till we arrive," murmured Mac anxiously.

"She can if he gives her a chance, and I think he will. There's a kind of cat instinct in him to play with his prey."

"Yes, but he missed his kill last time by letting her fool him. That's what I'm afraid of, that he won't wait."

They had reached lower ground now, and could put their ponies at a pounding gallop that ate up the trail fast. As they approached the houses, both men drew rein and looked carefully to their weapons. Then they slid from the saddles and slipped noiselessly forward.

What the foreman had said was exactly true. Helen Messiter did want them both, and she wanted them very much indeed.

After supper she had been dreamily playing over to herself one of Chopin's waltzes, when she became aware, by some instinct, that she was not alone in the

251

room. There had been no least sound, no slightest stir to betray an alien presence. Yet that some one was in the room she knew, and by some subtle sixth sense could even put a name to the intruder.

Without turning she called over her shoulder: "Shall I finish the waltz?" No faintest tremor in the clear, sweet voice betrayed the racing heart.

"Y'u're a cool hand, my friend," came his ready answer. "But I think we'll dispense with the music. I had enough last time to serve me for twice."

She laughed as she swung on the stool, with that musical scorn which both allured and maddened. "I did rather do you that time," she allowed.

"This is the return match. You won then. I win now," he told her, with a look that chilled.

"Indeed! But isn't that rather discounting the future?"

"Only the immediate future. Y'u're mine, my beauty, and I mean to take y'u with me."

Just a disdainful sweep of her eyes she gave him as she rose from the piano-stool and rearranged the lamps. "You mean so much that never comes to pass, Mr. Bannister. The road to the nether regions is paved with good intentions, we are given to understand. Not that yours can by any stretch of imagination be called 'good intentions.'"

"Contrariwise, then, perhaps the road to heaven may be paved with evil intentions. Since y'u travel the road with me, wherever it may lead, it were but gallant to hope so."

He took three sharp steps toward her and stood

looking down in her face, her sweet slenderness so close to him that the perfume mounted to his brain. Surely no maiden had ever been more desirable than this one, who held him in such contemptuous estimation that only her steady eyes moved at his approach. These held to his and defied him, while she stood leaning motionless against the table with such strong and supple grace. She knew what he meant to do, hated him for it, and would not give him the satisfaction of flying an inch from him or struggling with him.

"Your eyes are pools of splendor. That's right. Make them flash fire. I love to see such spirit, since it offers a more enticing pleasure in breaking," he told her, with an admiration half-ironic but wholly genuine. "Pools of splendor, my beauty! Therefore I salute them."

At the touch of his lips upon her eyelids a shiver ran through her, but still she made no movement, was cold to him as marble. "You coward!" she said softly, with an infinite contempt.

"Your lips," he continued to catalogue, "are ripe as fresh flesh of Southern fruit. No cupid ever possessed so adorable a mouth. A worshiper of Eros I, as now I prove."

This time it was the mouth he kissed, the while her unconquered spirit looked out of the brave eyes, and fain would have murdered him. In turn he kissed her cold cheeks, the tip of one of her little ears, the small, clenched fist with which she longed to strike him.

"Are you quite through?"

"For the present, and now, having put the seal of my

ownership on her more obvious charms, I'll take my bride home."

"I would die first."

"Nay, you'll die later, Madam Bannister, but not for many years, I hope," he told her, with a theatrical bow.

"Do you think me so weak a thing as your words imply?"

"Rather so strong that the glory of overcoming y'u fills me with joy. Believe me, madam, though your master I am not less your slave," he mocked.

"You are neither my master nor my slave, but a thing I detest," she said, in a low voice that carried extraordinary intensity.

"And obey," he added, suavely. "Come, madam, to horse, for our honeymoon."

"I tell you I shall not go."

"Then, in faith, we'll re-enact a modern edition of 'The Taming of the Shrew.' Y'u'll find me, sweet, as apt at the part as old *Petruchio*." He paced complacently up the room and back, and quoted glibly:

"And thus I'll curb her mad and headstrong humor.
He that knows better how to tame a shrew,
Now let him speak; 'tis charity to show."

"Would you take me against my will?"

"Y'u have said it. What's your will to me? What I want I take. And I sure want my beautiful shrew." His half-shuttered eyes gloated on her as he rattled off a couple more lines from the play he had mentioned.

254

"Kate, like the hazel-twig,
Is straight and slender, and as brown in hue
As hazel-nuts, and sweeter than the kernels."

She let a swift glance travel anxiously to the door. "You are in a very poetical mood today."

"As befits a bridegroom, my own." He stepped lightly to the window and tapped twice on the pane. "A signal to bring the horses round. If y'u have any preparations to make, any trousseau to prepare, y'u better set that girl of yours to work."

"I have no preparations to make."

"Coming to me simply as y'u are? Good! We'll lead the simple life."

Nora, as it chanced, knocked and entered at this moment. The sight of her vivid good looks struck him for the first time. At sight of him she stopped, gazing with parted lips, a double row of pearls shining through.

He turned swiftly to the mistress. "Y'u ought not to be alone there among so many men. It wouldn't be proper. We'll take the girl along with us."

"Where?" Nora's parted lips emitted.

"To Arden, my dear." He interrupted himself to look at his watch. "I wonder why that fellow doesn't come with the horses. They should pass this window."

Bannister, standing jauntily with his feet astride as he looked out of the window, heard some one enter the room. "Did y'u bring round the horses?" he snapped, without looking round.

"No, we allowed they wouldn't be needed."

At sound of the slow drawl the outlaw wheeled like a flash, his hand traveling to the hilt of the revolver that hung on his hip. But he was too late. Already two revolvers covered him, and he knew that both his cousin and McWilliams were dead shots. He flashed one venomous look at the mistress of the ranch.

"Y'u fooled me again. That lamp business was a signal, and I was too thick-haided to see it. My compliments to y'u, Miss Messiter."

"Y'u are under arrest," announced his cousin.

"Y'u don't say." His voice was full of sarcastic admiration. "And you done it with your little gun! My, what a wonder y'u are!"

"Take your hand from the butt of that gun. Y'u better relieve him of it, Mac. He's got such a restless disposition he might commit suicide by reaching for it."

"What do y'u think you're going to do with me now y'u have got me, Cousin Ned?"

"We're going to turn y'u over to the United States Government."

"Guess again. I have a thing or two to say to that."

"You're going to Gimlet Butte with us, alive or dead."

The outlaw intentionally misunderstood. "If I've got to take y'u, then we'll say y'u go dead rather than alive."

"He was going to take Nora and me with him," Helen explained to her friends.

Instantly the man swung round on her. "But now I've changed my mind, ma'am. I'm going to take my cousin with me instead of y'u ladies."

Helen caught his meaning first, and flashed it whitely to her lover. It dawned on him more slowly.

"I see y'u remember, Miss Messiter," he continued, with a cruel, silken laugh. "He gave me his parole to go with me whenever I said the word. I'm saying it now." He sat down astride a chair, put his chin on the back cross-bar, and grinned malevolently from one to another.

"What's come over this happy family? It don't look so joyous all of a sudden. Y'u don't need to worry, ma'am, I'll send him back to y'u all right—alive or dead. With his shield or on it, y'u know. Ha! ha!"

"You will not go with him?" It was wrung from Helen as a low cry, and struck her lover's heart.

"I must," he answered. "I gave him my word, y'u remember."

"But why keep it? You know what he is, how absolutely devoid of honor."

"That is not quite the question, is it?" he smiled.

"Would he keep his word to you?"

"Not if a lie would do as well. But that isn't the point, either."

"It's quixotic—foolish—worse than that—ridiculous," she implored.

"Perhaps, but the fact remains that I am pledged."

" 'I could not love thee, dear, so much
Loved I not honor more,' "

murmured the villain in the chair, apparently to the

ceiling. "Dear Ned, he always was the soul of honor. I'll have those lines carved on his tombstone."

"You see! He is already bragging that he means to kill you," said the girl.

"I shall go armed," the sheepman answered.

"Yes, but he will take you into the mountain fastnesses, where the men that serve him will do his bidding. What is one man among so many?"

"Two men, ma'am," corrected the foreman.

"What's that?" The outlaw broke off the snatch of opera he was singing to slew his head round at McWilliams.

"I said two. Any objections, seh?"

"Yes. That wasn't in the contract."

"We're giving y'u surplusage, that's all. Y'u wanted one of us, and y'u get two. We don't charge anything for the extra weight," grinned Mac.

"Oh, Mac, will you go with him?" cried Helen, with shining eyes.

"Those are my present intentions, Miss Helen," laughed her foreman.

Whereat Nora emerged from the background and flung herself on him. "Y'u can't go, Jim! I won't have you go!" she cried.

The young man blushed a beautiful pink, and accepted gladly this overt evidence of a reconciliation. "It's all right, honey. Don't y'u think two big, grown-up men are good to handle that scalawag? Sho! Don't y'u worry."

"Miss Nora can come, too, if she likes," suggested he

of the Shoshones. "Looks like we would have quite a party. Won't y'u join us, too, Miss Messiter, according to the original plan?" he said, extending an ironical invitation.

"I think we had better cut it down to me alone. We'll not burden your hospitality, sir," said the sheepman.

"No, sir, I'm in on this. Whyfor can't I go?" demanded Jim.

Bannister, the outlaw, eyed him unpleasantly. "Y'u certainly can so far as I am concerned. I owe y'u one, too, Mr. McWilliams. Only if y'u come of your own free will, as y'u are surely welcome to do, don't holler if y'u're not so welcome to leave whenever y'u take a notion."

"I'll try and look out for that. It's settled, then, that we ride together. When do y'u want to start?"

"We can't go any sooner than right now. I hate to take these young men from y'u, ladies, but, as I said, I'll send them back in good shape. *Adios, señorita.* Don't forget to whom y'u belong." He swaggered to the door and turned, leaning against the jamb with one hand against it. "I expect y'u can say those lovey-dovey good-byes without my help. I'm going into the yard. If y'u want to y'u can plug me in the back through the window," he suggested, with a sneer.

"As y'u would us under similar circumstances," retorted his cousin.

"Be with y'u in five minutes," said the foreman.

"Don't hurry. It's a long good-bye y'u're saying," returned his enemy placidly.

Nora and the young man who belonged to her followed him from the room, leaving Bannister and his hostess alone.

"Shall I ever see you again?" Helen murmured.

"I think so," the sheepman answered. "The truth is that this opportunity falls pat. Jim and I have been wanting to meet those men who are under my cousin's influence and have a talk with them. There is no question but that the gang is disintegrating, and I believe that if we offered to mediate between its members and the Government something might be done to stop the outrages that have been terrorizing this country. My cousin can't be reached, but I believe the rest of them, or, at least a part, can be induced either to surrender or to flee the country. Anyhow, we want to try it."

"But the danger?" she breathed.

"Is less than y'u think. Their leader has not anywhere nearly the absolute power he had a few months ago. They would hardly dare do violence to a peace envoy."

"Your cousin would. I don't believe he has any scruples."

"We shall keep an eye on him. Both of us will not sleep at the same time. Y'u may depend on me to bring your foreman safely back to y'u," he smiled.

"Oh, my foreman!"

"And your foreman's friend," he added. "I have the best of reasons for wanting to return alive. I think y'u know them. They have to do with y'u, Miss Helen."

It had come at last, but, womanlike, she evaded the issue her heart had sought. "Yes, I know. You think it would not be fair to throw away your life in this foolish manner after I have saved it for you—how many times was it you said?" The blue eyes lifted with deceptive frankness to the gray ones.

"No, that isn't my reason. I have a better one than that. I love y'u, girl, more than anything in this world."

"And so you try to prove it to me by running into a trap set for you to take your life. That's a selfish kind of love, isn't it? Or it would be if I loved you."

"*Do* y'u love me, Helen?"

"Why should I tell you, since you don't love me enough to give up this quixotic madness?"

"Don't y'u see, dear, I *can't* give it up?"

"I see you won't. You care more for your pride than for me."

"No, it isn't that. I've *got* to go. It isn't that I want to leave y'u, God knows. But I've given my word, and I must keep it. Do y'u want me to be a quitter, and y'u so game yourself? Do y'u want it to go all over this cattle country that I gave my word and took it back because I lost my nerve?"

"The boy that takes a dare isn't a hero, is he? There's a higher courage that refuses to be drawn into such foolishness, that doesn't give way to the jeers of the empty headed."

"I don't think that is a parallel case. I'm sorry we can't see this alike, but I've got to go ahead the way that seems to me right."

"You're going to leave me, then, to go with that man?"

261

"Yes, if that's the way y'u have to put it." He looked at her sorrowfully, and added gently: "I thought you would see it. I thought sure you would."

But she could not bear that he should leave her so, and she cried out after him. "Oh, I see it. I know you must go; but I can't bear it." Her head buried itself in his coat. "It isn't right—it isn't a—a square deal that you should go away now, the very minute you belong to me."

A happy smile shone in his eyes. "I belong to you, do I? That's good hearing, girl o' mine." His arm went round her and he stroked the black head softly. "I'll not be gone long, dear. Don't y'u worry about me. I'll be back with y'u soon; just as soon as I have finished this piece of work I have to do."

"But if you should get—if anything should happen to you?"

"Nothing is going to happen to me. There is a special providence looks after lovers, y'u know."

"Be careful, Ned, of yourself. For my sake, dear."

"I'll dry my socks every time I get my feet wet for fear of taking cold," he laughed.

"But you will, won't you?"

"I'll be very careful, Helen," he promises more gravely.

Even then she could hardly let him go, clinging to him with a reluctance to separate that was a new experience to her independent, vigorous youth. In the end he unloosened her arms, kissed her once, and hurried out of the room. In the hallway he met McWilliams, also

262

hurrying out from a tearful farewell on the part of Nora.

Bannister, the outlaw, already mounted, was waiting for them. "Y'u *did* get through at last," he drawled insolently. "Well, if y'u'll kindly give orders to your seven-foot dwarf to point that Winchester another way I'll collect my men and we'll be moving."

For, though the outlaw had left his men in command of the ranch when he went into the house, he found the situation reversed on his eturn. With the arrival of reinforcements, in the persons of McWilliams and his friend, it had been the turn of the raiders to turn over their weapons.

"All right, Denver," nodded the foreman.

The outlaw chief whistled for his men, and with their guests they rode into the silent, desert night.

CHAPTER XXII

EXIT THE "KING"

They bedded that night under the great vault-roof where twinkle a million stars.

There were three of the outlaw's men with him, and both McWilliams and his friend noticed that they slept a little apart from their chief. There were other indications among the rustlers of a camp divided against itself. Bannister's orders to them he contrived to make an insult, and their obedience was as surly as possible compatible with safety. For all of the men knew that he would not hesitate to shoot them down in one of his violent rages should they anger him sufficiently.

Throughout the night there was no time that at least two men were not awake in the camp. The foreman and the sheepman took turns keeping vigil; and on the other side of the fire sat one of the rustlers in silent watchfulness. To the man opposite him each of the sentinels were outposts of the enemy, but they fraternized after the manner of army sentries, exchanging tobacco and occasional casual conversation.

The foreman took the first turn, and opposite him sat a one-eyed old scoundrel who had rustled calves from big outfits ever since Wyoming was a territory and long before. Chalkeye Dave, he was called, and sometimes merely Chalkeye. What his real name was no man knew. Nor was his past a subject for conversation in his presence. It was known that he had been in the Nevada penitentiary, and that he had killed a man in Arizona, but these details of an active life were rarely resurrected. For Chalkeye was deadly on the shoot, and was ready for it at the drop of the hat, though he had his good points, too. One of these was a remarkable fondness for another member of the party, a mere lad, called by his companions Hughie. Generally surly and morose, to such a degree that even his chief was careful to humor him as a rule, when with Hughie all the softer elements of his character came to the surface. In his rough way he was even humorous and genial.

Jim McWilliams found him neither, however. He declined to engage in conversation, accepted a proffer of tobacco with a silent, hostile grunt, and relapsed into a long silence that lasted till his shift was ended.

"Hate to have y'u leave, old man. Yu're so darned good company I'll ce'tainly pine for you," the foreman suggested, with sarcasm, when the old man rolled up in his blankets preparatory to falling asleep immediately.

Chalkeye's successor was a blatant youth much impressed with his own importance. He was both foul-mouthed and foul-minded, so that Jim was constrained to interrupt his evil boastings by pretending to fall asleep.

It was nearly two o'clock when the foreman aroused his friend to take his turn. Shortly after this the lad Hughie relieved the bragging, would-be bad man.

Hughie was a flaxen-haired, rather good-looking boy of nineteen. In his small, wistful face was not a line of wickedness, though it was plain that he was weak. He seemed so unfit for the life he was leading that the sheepman's interest was aroused. For on the frontier it takes a strong, competent miscreant to be a bad man and survive. Ineffectives and weaklings are quickly weeded out to their graves or the penitentiaries.

The boy was manifestly under great fear of his chief, but the curly haired young Hermes who kept watch with him had a very winning smile and a charming manner when he cared to exert it. Almost in spite of himself the youngster was led to talk. It seemed that he had but lately joined the Teton-Shoshones outfit of des-peradoes, and between the lines Bannister easily read that his cousin's masterful compulsion had coerced the young fellow. All he wanted was an opportunity to withdraw in safety, but he knew he could never do this so long as the "King" was alive and at liberty.

Under the star-roof in the chill, breaking day Ned Bannister talked to him long and gently. It was easy to bring the boy to tears, but it was a harder thing to stiffen a will that was of putty and to hearten a soul in mortal fear. But he set himself with all the power in him to combat the influence of his cousin over this boy; and before the camp stirred to life again he knew that he had measurably succeeded.

They ate breakfast in the gray dawn under the stars, and after they had finished their coffee and bacon horses were saddled and the trail taken up again. It led in and out among the foot-hills, sloping upward gradually toward the first long blue line of the Shoshones that stretched before them in the distance. Their nooning was at a running stream called Smith's Creek, and by nightfall the party was well up in the higher foothills.

In the course of the day and the second night both the sheepman and his friend made attempts to establish a more cordial relationship with Chalkeye, but so far as any apparent results went their efforts were vain. He refused grimly to meet their overtures half way, even though it was plain from his manner that a break between him and his chief could not long be avoided.

All day by crooked trails they pushed forward, and as the party advanced into the mountains the gloom of the mournful pines and frowning peaks invaded its spirits. Suspicion and distrust went with it, camped at night by the rushing mountain stream, lay down to sleep in the shadows at every man's shoulder. For each man looked with an ominous eye on his neighbor, watchful of every sudden move, of every careless word that might convey a sudden meaning.

Along a narrow rock-rim trail far above a steep cañon, whose walls shot precipitously down, they were riding in single file, when the outlaw chief pushed his horse forward between the road wall and his cousin's bronco. The sheepman immediately fell back.

"I reckon this trail isn't wide enough for two—unless y'u take the outside," he explained quietly.

The outlaw, who had been drinking steadily ever since leaving the Lazy D, laughed his low, sinister cackle. "Afraid of me, are y'u? Afraid I'll push y'u off?"

"Not when I'm inside and you don't have the chance."

" 'Twas a place about like this I drove four thousand of your sheep over last week. With sheep worth what they are I'm afraid it must have cost y'u quite a bit. Not that y'u'll miss it where you are going," he hastened to add.

"It was very like you to revenge yourself on dumb animals."

"Think so?" The "King's" black gaze rested on him. "Y'u'll sing a different song soon, Mr. Bannister. It's humans I'll drive next time, and don't y'u forget it."

"If you get the chance," amended his cousin gently.

"I'll get the chance. I'm not worrying about that. And about those sheep—any man that hasn't got more sense than to run sheep in a cow country ought to lose them for his pig-headedness."

"Those sheep were on the right side of the dead-line. You had to cross it to reach them." Their owner's steady eyes challenged a denial.

"Is that so? Now how do y'u know that? We didn't leave the herder alive to explain that to y'u, did we?"

"You admit murdering him?"

"To y'u, dear cousin. Y'u see, I have a hunch that maybe y'u'll go join your herder right soon. Y'u'll not do much talking."

The sheepman fell back. "I think I'll ride alone."

Rage flared in the other's eye. "Too good for me, are y'u, my mealy-mouthed cousin? Y'u always thought yourself better than me. When y'u were a boy you used to go sneaking to that old hypocrite, your grandfather—"

"You have said enough," interrupted the other sternly. "I'll not hear another word. Keep your foul tongue off him."

Their eyes silently measured strength.

"Y'u'll not hear a word!" sneered the chief of the rustlers. "What will y'u do, dear cousin?"

"Stand up and fight like a man and settle this thing once for all."

Still their steely eyes crossed as with the thrust of rapiers. The challenged man crouched tensely with a mighty longing for the test, but he had planned a more elaborate revenge and a surer one than this. Reluctantly he shook his head.

268

"Why should I? Y'u're mine. We're four to two, and soon we'll be a dozen to two. I'd like a heap to oblige y'u, but I reckon I can't afford to just now. Y'u will have to wait a little for that bumping off that's coming to y'u."

"In that event I'll trouble you not to inflict your society on me any more than is necessary."

"That's all right, too. If y'u think I enjoy your conversation y'u have got another guess coming."

So by mutual consent the sheepman fell in behind the blatant youth who had wearied McWilliams so, and rode in silence.

It was again getting close to nightfall. The slant sun was throwing its rays on less and less of the trail. They could see the shadows grow and the coolness of night sift into the air. They were pushing on to pass the rim of a great valley basin that lay like a saucer in the mountains in order that they might camp in the valley by a stream all of them knew. Dusk was beginning to fall when they at last reached the saucer edge, and only the opposite peaks were still tipped with the sun rays. This, too, disappeared before they had descended far, and the gloom of the great mountains that girt the valley was on all their spirits, even McWilliams being affected by it.

They were tired with travel, and the long night watches did not improve tempers already overstrained with the expectation of a crisis too long dragged out. Rain fell during the night, and continued gently in a misty drizzle after day broke. It was a situation and an atmosphere ripe for tragedy, and it fell on them like a clap of thunder out of a sodden sky.

Hughie was cook for the day, and he came chill and stiff-fingered to his task. Summer as it was, there lay a thin coating of ice round the edges of the stream, for they had camped in an altitude of about nine thousand feet. The "King" had wakened in a vile humor. He had a splitting headache, as was natural under the circumstances and he had not left in his bottle a single drink to tide him over it. He came cursing to the struggling fire, which was making only fitful headway against the rain which beat down upon it.

"Why didn't y'u build your fire on the other side of the tree?" he growled at Hughie.

Now, Hughie was a tenderfoot, and in his knowledge of outdoor life he was still an infant. "I didn't know—" he was beginning, when his master cut him short with a furious tongue lashing out of all proportion to the offense.

The lad's face blanched with fear, and his terror was so manifest that the bully, who was threatening him with all manner of evils, began to enjoy himself. Chalkeye, returning from watering the horses, got back in time to hear the intemperate fag-end of the scolding. He glanced at Hughie, whose hands were trembling in spite of him, and then darkly at the brute who was attacking him. But he said not a word.

The meal proceeded in silence except for the jeers and taunts of the "King." For nobody cared to venture conversation which might prove as a match to a powder

270

magazine. Whatever his thoughts might be each man kept them to himself.

"Coffee," snapped the single talker, toward the end of breakfast.

Hughie jumped up, filled the cup that was handed him and set the coffee pot back on the fire. As he handed the tin cup with the coffee to the outlaw the lad's foot slipped on a piece of wet wood, and the hot liquid splashed over his chief's leg. The man jumped to his feet in a rage and struck the boy across the face with his whip once, and then again.

"By God, that'll do for you!" cried Chalkeye from the other side of the fire, springing up, revolver in hand. "Draw, you coyote! I come a-shooting."

The "King" wheeled, finding his weapon as he turned. Two shots rang out almost simultaneously, and Chalkeye pitched forward. The outlaw chief sank to his knees, and, with one hand resting on the ground to steady himself, fired two more shots into the twitching body on the other side of the fire. Then he, too, lurched forward and rolled over.

It had come to climax so swiftly that not one of them had moved except the combatants. Bannister rose and walked over to the place where the body of his cousin lay. He knelt down and examined him. When he rose it was with a very grave face.

"He is dead," he said quietly.

McWilliams, who had been bending over Chalkeye, looked up. "Here, too. Any one of the shots would have finished him."

271

Bannister nodded. "Yes. That first exchange killed them both." He looked down at the limp body of his cousin, but a minute before so full of supple, virile life. "But his hate had to reach out and make sure, even though he was as good as dead himself. He was game." Then sharply to the young braggart, who had risen and was edging away with a face of chalk: "Sit down, y'u! What do y'u take us for? Think this is to be a massacre?"

The man came back with palpable hesitancy. "I was aiming to go and get the boys to bury them. My God, did you ever see anything so quick? They drilled through each other like lightning."

Mac looked him over with dry contempt. "My friend, y'u're too tender for a genuwine A1 bad man. If I was handing y'u a bunch of advice it would be to get back to the prosaic paths of peace right prompt. And while we're on the subject I'll borrow your guns. Y'u're scared stiff, and it might get into your fool cocoanut to plug one of us and light out. I'd hate to see y'u commit suicide right before us, so I'll just natcherally unload y'u."

He was talking to lift the strain, and it was for the same purpose that Bannister moved over to Hughie, who sat with his face in his hands, trying to shut out the horror of what he had seen.

The sheepman dropped a hand on his shoulder gently. "Brace up, boy! Don't you see that the very best thing that could have happened is this? It's best for y'u, best for the rest of the gang and best for the whole cattle country. We'll have peace here at last. Now he's gone, honest men are going to breathe easy. I'll take y'u in hand and set y'u at work on one of my stations, if y'u like. Anyhow, you'll have a chance to begin life again in a better way."

"That's right," agreed the blatant youth. "I'm sick of rustling the mails and other folks' calves. I'm glad he got what was coming to him," he concluded vindictively, with a glance at his dead chief and a sudden raucous oath.

McWilliams's cold blue eye transfixed him. "Hadn't you better be a little careful how your mouth goes off? For one thing, he's daid now; and for another, he happens to be Mr. Bannister's cousin."

"But—weren't they enemies?"

"That's how I understand it. But this man's passed over the range. A *man* doesn't unload his hatred on dead folks—and I expect if y'u'll study him, even y'u will be able to figure out that my friend measures up to the size of a real man."

"I don't see why if—"

"No, I don't suppose y'u do," interrupted the foreman, turning on his heel. Then to Bannister, who was looking down at his cousin with a stony face: "I reckon, Bann, we better make arrangements to have the bodies buried right here in the valley," he said gently.

Bannister was thinking of early days, of the time when this miscreant, whose light had just been put out so instantaneously, had played with him day in and day out. They had attended their first school together, had played marbles and prisoners' base a hundred times against each other. He could remember how they used to get up early in the morning to go fishing with each other. And later, when each began, unconsciously, to choose the path he would follow in life, they had been captains of opposing teams at school. For the rivalry between them was already beginning to settle into an established fact. He could see now, by looking back on trifles of their childhood, that his cousin had been badly handicapped in his fight with himself against the evil in him. He had inherited depraved instincts and tastes, and with them somewhere in him a strand of weakness that prevented him from slaying the giants he had to oppose in the making of a good character. From bad to worse he had gone—and here he lay with the drizzling rain on his white face, a warning and a lesson to wayward youths just setting their feet in the wrong direction. Surely it was kismet.

Ned Bannister untied the handkerchief from his neck and laid it across the face of his kinsman. A moment longer he looked down, then passed his hands across his eyes and seemed to brush away the memories that thronged him. He stepped forward to the fire and warmed his hands.

"We'll go on, Mac, to the rendezvous he had appointed with his outfit. We ought to reach there by noon, and the boys can send a wagon back to get the bodies."

CHAPTER XXIII

JOURNEYS END IN LOVERS' MEETING

It had been six days since the two Ned Bannisters had ridden away together into the mountains, and every waking hour since that time had been for Helen one of harassing anxiety. No word had yet reached her of the issue of that dubious undertaking, and she both longed and dreaded to hear. He had promised to send a messenger as soon as he had anything definite to tell, but she knew it would be like his cousin, too, to send her some triumphant word should he prove the victor in the struggle between them. So that every stranger she glimpsed brought to her a sudden beating of the heart.

But it was not the nature of Helen Messiter to sit down and give herself up a prey to foreboding. Her active nature cried out for work to occupy her and distract her attention. Fortunately this was to be had in abundance just now. For the autumn round-up was on, and since her foreman was away the mistress of the Lazy D found plenty of work ready to her hand.

The meeting place for the round-up riders was at Boom Creek, five miles from the ranch, and Helen rode out there to take charge of her own interests in person. With her were six riders, and for the use of each of them in addition to his present mount three extra ponies were brought in the remuda. For the riding is so hard during the round-up that a horse can stand only one day in four of it. At the appointed rendezvous a score of other cow-boys and owners met them. Without any delay they pro-ceeded to business. Mr. Bob Austin, better known as "Texas," was elected boss of the round-up, and he immediately assigned the men to their places and announced that they would work Squaw Creek. They moved camp at once, Helen returning to the ranch.

It was three o'clock in the morning when the men were roused by the cook's triangle calling them to the "chuck wagon" for breakfast. It was still cold and dark as the boys crawled from under their blankets and squatted round the fire to eat jerky, biscuits and gravy, and to drink cupfuls of hot, black coffee. Before sun rose every man was at his post far up on the Squaw Creek ridges ready to begin the drive.

Later in the day Helen rode to the *parada* grounds, toward which a stream of cattle was pouring down the cañon of the creek. Every gulch tributary to the creek contributed its quota of wild cows and calves. These came romping down to the cañon mouth, where four picked men, with a bunch of tame cows in front of them, stopped the rush of flying cattle. Lunch was omitted, and branding began at once. Every calf belonging to a Lazy D cow, after being roped and tied, was flanked with the great ⌂ which indicated its ownership by Miss Messiter, and on account of the recumbent position of which letter the ranch had its name.

It was during the branding that a boyish young fellow rode up and handed Helen a note. Her heart pumped rapidly with relief, for one glance told her that it was in the handwriting of the Ned Bannister she loved. She tore it open and glanced swiftly through it.

DEAR FRIEND: Two hours ago my cousin was killed by one of his own men. I am sending back to you a boy who had been led astray by him, and it would be a great service to me if you would give him something to do till I return. His name is Hugh Rogers. I think if you trust him he will prove worthy of it.

Jim and I are going to stay here a few days longer to finish the work that is begun. We hope to meet and talk with as many of the men implicated in my cousin's lawlessness as is possible. What the result will be I cannot say. We do not consider ourselves in any danger whatever, though we are not taking chances. If all goes well we shall be back within a few days.

I hope you are not missing Jim too much at the round-up. Sincerely,

NED BANNISTER.

She liked the letter because there was not a hint of the relationship between them to be read in it. He had guarded her against the chance of its falling into the wrong hands and creating talk about them.

She turned to Hughie. "Can you ride?"

"In a way, ma'am. I can't ride like these men." His

glance indicated a cow-puncher pounding past after a wild steer that had broken through the cordon of riders and was trying to get away.

"Do you want to learn?"

"I'd like to if I had a chance," he answered wistfully.

"All right. You have your chance. I'll see that Mr. Austin finds something for you to do. From today you are in my employ."

She rode back to the ranch in the late afternoon, while the sun was setting in a great splash of crimson. The round-up boss had hinted that if she were nervous about riding alone he could find it convenient to accompany her. But the girl wanted to be alone with her own thoughts, and she had slipped away while he was busy cutting out calves from the herd. It had been a wonderful relief to her to find that *her* Ned Bannister was the one that had survived in the conflict, and her heart sang a pæan of joy as she rode into the golden glow of the westering sun. He was alive—to love and be loved. The unlived years of her future seemed to unroll before her as a vision. She glowed with a resurgent happiness that was almost an ecstasy. The words of a bit of verse she had once seen—a mere scrap from a magazine that had stuck in an obscure corner of her memory—sang again and again in her heart:

Life and love,
And a bright sky o'er us,
And—God take care
Of the way before us!

Ah, the way before them, before her and her romance-radiating hero! It might he rough and hilly, but if they trod it together—Her tangled thoughts were off again in another glad leap of imagination.

The days passed somehow. She busied herself with the affairs of the ranch, rode out often to the scenes of the cattle drives and watched the round-up, and every twenty-four hours brought her one day nearer to his return, she told herself. Nora, too, was on the lookout under her long-lashed, roguish eyelids; and the two young women discussed the subject of their lovers' return in that elusive, elliptical way common to their sex.

No doubt each of these young women had conjectured as to the manner of that homecoming and the meeting that would accompany it; but it is safe to say that neither of them guessed in her day-dreams how it actually was to occur.

Nora had been eager to see something of the round-up, and as she was no horsewoman her mistress took her out one day in her motor. The drive had been that day on Bronco Mesa, and had finished in the natural corral made by Bear Cañon, fenced with a cordon of riders at the end opening to the plains below. After watching for two hours the busy scenes of cutting out, roping and branding, Helen wheeled her car and started down the cañon on their return.

Now, a herd of wild cattle is uncertain as an April day's behavior. Under the influence of the tame valley cattle among which they are driven, after a little milling around, the whole bunch may gentle almost immediately, or, on the other hand it may break through and go crashing away on a wild stampede at a moment's notice. Every experienced cowman knows enough to expect the unexpected.

At Bronco Mesa the round-up had proceeded with unusual facility. Scores of wiry, long-legged steers had drifted down the ridges or gulches that led to the cañon; and many a cow, followed by its calf, had stumbled forward to the herd and apparently accepted the inevitable. But before Helen Messiter had well started out of the cañon's mouth the situation changed absolutely.

A big hill steer, which had not seen a man for a year, broke through the human corral with a bellow near a point where Reddy kept guard. The puncher wheeled and gave chase. Before the other men could close the opening a couple of two-year-olds seized the opportunity and followed its lead. A second rider gave chase, and at once, as if some imp of mischief had stirred them, fifty tails went up in wild flight. Another minute and the whole herd was in stampede.

Down the gulch the five hundred cattle thundered toward the motor car, which lay directly in their path. Helen turned, appreciated the danger, and put the machine at its full speed. The road branched for a space of about fifty yards, and in her excitement she made the mistake of choosing the lower, more level, one. Into a deep sand bed they plowed, the wheels sinking at every turn. Slower and slower went the car; finally came to a full stop.

Nora glanced back in affright at the two hundred and fifty tons of beef that was charging wildly toward them. "What shall we do?" she gasped, and clambered to the ground.

"Run!" cried Helen, following her example and scudding for the sides of the cañon, which here sloped down less precipitately than at other points. But before they had run a dozen steps each of them was aware that they could not reach safety in time to escape the hoofs rushing toward them so heavily that the ground quaked.

"Look out!" A resonant cry rang out above the dull thud of the stampeding cattle that were almost upon them. Down the steep sides of the gorge two riders were galloping recklessly. It was a race for life between them and the first of the herd, and they won by scarce more than a length. Across the sand the horses plowed, and as they swept past the two trembling young women each rider bent from the saddle without slackening speed, and snatched one almost from under the very hoofs of the leaders.

The danger was not past. As the horses swerved and went forward with the rush Helen knew that a stumble would fling not only her and the man who had saved her, but also the horse down to death. They must contrive to hold their own in that deadly rush until a way could be found of escaping from the path of the living cyclone that trod at their heels, galloped beside them, in front, behind.

For it came to her that the horse was tiring in that rush through the sand with double weight upon its back.

"Courage!" cried the man behind her as her fearful eyes met his.

As he spoke they reached the end of the cañon and firm ground simultaneously. Helen saw that her rescuer had now a revolver in his hand, and that he was firing in such a way as to deflect the leaders to the left. At first the change in course was hardly perceptible, but presently she noticed that they were getting closer to the outskirts of the herd, working gradually to the extreme right, edging inch by inch, ever so warily, toward safety. Going parallel to their course, running neck and neck with the cow pony, lumbered a great dun steer. Unconsciously it blocked every effort of the horseman to escape. He had one shot left in his revolver, and this time he did not fire into the air. It was a mighty risk, for the animal in falling might stagger against the horse and hurl them all down to death. But the man took it without apparent hesitation. Into the ear of the bullock he sent the lead crashing. The brute stumbled and went down head over heels. Its flying hoofs struck the flanks of the pony, but the bronco stuck to its feet, and next moment staggered out from among the herd stragglers and came to halt.

The man slid from its back and lifted down the half-fainting girl. She clung to him, white and trembling. "Oh, it was horrible, Ned!" She could still look down in imagination upon that sea of dun backs that swayed and surged about them like storm-tossed waves.

"It was a near thing, but we made it, girl. So did Jim. He got out before we did. It's all past now. You can remember it as the most exciting experience of your life."

She shuddered. "I don't want to remember it at all." And so shaken was she that she did not realize that his arm was about her the while she sobbed on his shoulder.

"A cattle stampede is a nasty thing to get in front of. Never mind. It's done with now and everybody's safe."

She drew a long breath. "Yes, everybody's safe and you are back home. Why didn't you come after your cousin was killed?"

"I had to finish my work."

"And *did* you finish it?"

"I think we did. There will be no more Shoshone gang. It's members have scattered in directions."

"I'm glad you stayed, then. We can live at peace now." And presently she added: "I knew you would not come back until you had done what you set out to do. You're very obstinate, sir. Do you know that?"

"Perseverance, I call it," he smiled, glad to see that she was recovering her lightness of tone.

"You don't always insist on putting your actions in the most favorable light. Do you remember the first day I ever saw you?"

"Am I likely ever to forget it?" he smiled fondly.

"I didn't mean *that*. What I was getting at was that you let me go away from you thinking you were 'the king.' I haven't forgiven you entirely for that."

"I expect y'u'll always have to be forgiving me things."

"If you valued my good opinion I don't see how you could let me go without telling me. Was it fair or kind?"

"If y'u come to that, was it so fair and kind to convict me so promptly on suspicion?" he retaliated with a smile.

"No, it wasn't. But—" She flushed with a divine shyness. "But I loved you all the time, even when they said you were a villain."

"Even while y'u believed me one?"

"I didn't. I never would believe you one—not deep in my heart. I wouldn't let myself. I made excuses for you—explained everything to myself."

"Yet your reason told y'u I was guilty."

"Yes, I think my mind hated you and my heart loved you."

He adored her for the frank simplicity of her confession, that out of the greatness of her love she dared to make no secret of it to him. Direct as a boy, she was yet as wholly sweet as the most retiring girl could be.

"Y'u always swamp my vocabulary, sweetheart. I can't ever tell y'u—life wouldn't be long enough—how much I care for you."

"I'm glad," she said simply.

They stood looking at each other, palms pressed to palms in meeting hands, supremely happy in this miracle of love that had befallen them. They were alone—for Nora and Jim had gone into temporary eclipse behind a hill and seemed in no hurry to emerge—alone in the sunshine with this wonder that flowed from one to another by shining eyes, by finger touch, and then by meeting lips. He held her close, knew the sweet delight of contact with the supple, surrendered figure, then released her as she drew away in maidenly reserve.

"When shall we be married, Helen? Is the early part of next week too late?" he asked.

Still blushing, she straightened her hat. "That's ridiculous, sir. I haven't got used to the thought of you yet."

"Plenty of time for that afterward. Then we'll say next week if that suits y'u."

"But it doesn't. Don't you know that it is the lady's privilege to name the day? Besides, I want time to change my mind if I should decide to."

"That's what I'm afraid of," he laughed joyfully. "So I have to insist on an early marriage."

"Insist?" she demurred.

"I've been told on the best of authority that I'm very obstinate," he gayly answered.

"I have a mind of my own myself. If I ever marry you be sure I shall name the day, sir."

"Will y'u marry me the day Nora does Jim?"

"We'll see." The eyes slanted at him under the curved lashes, teased him delightfully. "Did Nora tell you she was going to marry Jim?"

Bannister looked mildly hurt. "My common sense has been telling it to me a month."

"How long has your common sense been telling you about us?"

"I didn't use it when I fell in love with y'u," he boldly laughed.

285

"Of all things to say!"

"Because it would have told me y'u couldn't possibly care for me."

"Oh, that's different!"

"Not being able to help myself, I just went ahead."

"Isn't it good? Isn't it too good to be true—Ned?"

Tears brimmed in her happy eyes, and unconsciously she leaned toward him. In an instant she was in his arms again, both of them compelled by the imperative impulse of true lovers.

Out of the hollow presently appeared Nora and McWilliams, very much oblivious of the outside world. Presently they condescended to recognize the existence of Bannister and Helen.

"We're allowin' to be married in September," said Mac sheepishly, by way of explanation.

The two girls flew into each other's arms. Over Nora's shoulder Ned caught his sweetheart's eye and read there a blushing consent to a public announcement.

"That's ce'tainly a strange coincidence, Jim. So are we," he answered immediately.

The two friends shook hands.

NOTES

(pg. 117) A Wind River Bible in the Northwest ranch country is a catalogue of one of the big Chicago department-stores that does a large shipping business in the West.

Center Point Publishing
600 Brooks Road • PO Box 1
Thorndike ME 04986-0001 USA

(207) 568-3717

US & Canada:
1 800 929-9108